The Adventures of Guy
written by a guy
(probably)

*To Kurt!
Enjoy!*

*To my absolute best friend
Alex!*

The Adventures of Guy
written by a guy (probably)

Norm Cowie

Draumr Publishing, LLC
Maryland

The Adventures of Guy

Copyright © 2006 by Norm Cowie.
All rights reserved. No part of this book may be reproduced, stored in a retrieval system, or transmitted in any form or by any means without the prior written permission of the publishers, except by a reviewer who may quote brief passages in a review to be printed in a newspaper, magazine, or journal.

Any resemblance to actual people and events is purely coincidental. This is a work of fiction.

Cover art by Patricia Storms.

ISBN: 1-933157-08-9
PUBLISHED BY DRAUMR PUBLISHING, LLC
www.draumrpublishing.com
Columbia, Maryland

Printed in the United States of America

Dedication

Dedicated to Boo
(now you have to read it, huh?)

Acknowledgements

"I wish I was like you...easily amused." - Kurt Cobain, Nirvana.

Thank you to Rida and Robert, for taking a chance on this guy, and for your witty comments during the editing stage.

I also owe a debt of gratitude to attorneys and telemarketers, whose antics and reputations gave such excellent fodder for this work. If you're an attorney, and take offense at anything in here, please don't sue me.

Thank you, too, to those who read and enjoy my business/humor articles. Your support and encouragement helped give me the impetus to write this.

Prologue

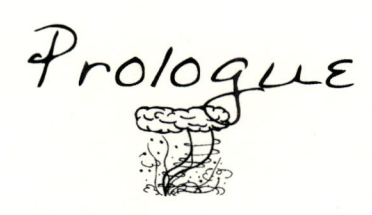

In 2003, the Federal Trade Commission issued an amendment to the Telemarketing Sales Rule (TSR) mandating a Federal "Do Not Call" registry. Millions enthusiastically signed up, happy that they might recapture the sanctity and serenity of their dinner times, and the freedom to answer their phones without having to worry about fending off some jerk, whose thinly veiled purpose is to convince you to take your money and put it in his pocket.

Unfortunately, though, not everybody paid attention to what their government had done for them (quite likely because most people are not used to this kind of help by our elected officials).

"Ring..."
"Ring…"
"Ring…?"
"Ring!"
"Ring…ring…ring…"
The answering machine didn't kick in.
"Ring…ring…ring…"
Mostly because we don't have an answering machine.
"Ring…ring…ring…"
Which doesn't matter, because we won't answer the phone anyway…

"Ring…ring…ring…"
…because of telemarketers.
"Ring…ring…ring…"
Telemarketers don't seem to mind that we don't answer the phone.
"Ring…ring…ring…"
They keep calling.
"Ring…ring…ring…"
Over and over.
"Ring…ring…ring…"
Patience and stamina…telemarketer virtues.
"Ring…ring…ring…"
That is, well, if you feel like you can put 'telemarketer' and 'virtues' in the same sentence.
"Ring…ring…ring…"
We didn't know that the attorneys had waged successful war against the telemarketers, giving us certain rights against their invasion of our privacy.
"Ring…ring…ring…"
As a result of the litigation, the telemarketing firms had to cut back on employees.
"Ring…ring…ring…"
 Nearly wiping out their whole industry almost overnight.
"Ring…ring…ring…"
But not everybody knows about the Opt-out laws.
"Ring…ring…ring…"
There are still some clueless people out there.
"Ring…ring…ring…"
Like us.
"Ring…ring…ring…"
For all I know, there's only one telemarketer left in the world.
"Ring…ring…ring…"
And he has our number.

Chapter One

*I*t all started when the phone rang at the house one day...
"Ring...ring...ring..."
The phone kept ringing.
And I kept ignoring it.
Actually, it wasn't that I ignored it. Since it's always ringing, we just tune it out, so now it's part of the background noise of our apartment, like Dave Matthews, Monday Night Football and DVD's that usually have a woman's name in the title. Nobody important ever calls us anyway. They know better. Even Mom gave up trying to call, and when she wants to reach me, she simply sends a messenger-kid to me, like my little brother Seth.

Seth's over right now, in fact, playing Donkey-Kong on the PlayStation. After his message from Mom was delivered, he was released from further responsibility, regardless of my response, or lack of response.

"Ring...ring...ring..."
Outside, I could hear one of my roommates, Tim, shooting hoops on the neighbor's driveway. The neighbor doesn't know Tim plays on his driveway while he's at work. Tim figures that what he doesn't know, won't hurt him. After all, why let a perfectly good hoop go to waste all day? He's got similar thoughts about their

refrigerator.

"Ring...ring...ring..."

Tim works nights at a lab, and...

Wait. I can't keep calling him Tim, because that's not what we call him. We call him Knob. I couldn't tell you why, though. We were pretty drunk when we came up with the nickname, and later we couldn't figure out where it came from. Still, the nickname stuck.

Me? My name's Guy.

And...get this...I'm a guy.

"Ring...ring...ring..."

That's when it happened.

At first, I didn't notice it, because all of a sudden it was silent in the house. Even Dave Matthews was between songs.

Then a great echoey feeling took shape in my head as a thought successfully passed completely through without bonking into ringing and music.

The thought was, *What is that?*

The 'that' I was trying to identify was something we had not heard in the three years of rooming together.

Silence.

Not only silence, but a huge silence. One of those silences so huge that it had its own echo. I was hearing silence, and then its echo. Silence squared.

A shiver went down my back.

Then it came back up my back.

It took a turn or two around my chest, and my nipples hardened from fear, anxiety, surprise, and some unexplained emotion I'd rather not explore.

The ringing had stopped.

All of a sudden, Dave Matthews started in on his next song, splintering the silence into little shards of chords and notes and coolness.

But I was frozen because of the strange sound I didn't hear.

It was like the time a tornado had hit our neighborhood, wiping out Madame Nirvana's little house down the road. It hadn't destroyed anything else, except for her house and a little sign advertising that Madame Nirvana would read your palm and tell you whether your future would include huge clumps of ear hair.

So wouldn't you think Madame Nirvana would have noticed something like a tornado in her own future?

Her little house had been found a mile away, wrapped around a telephone pole. It knocked out our phone lines for thirty-seven minutes, wiping out pizza delivery profits on a crucial Friday evening.

That's what I was reminded of now.

"Seth?"

My words sounded freakishly loud.

"Knob?"

The silence overwhelmed me with its silence.

Silence, quiet, stillness, calm, and other words that evoke the image of absence of noise. Not even the twitter of a bird.

Well, there was a Dave Matthews song going on, but that doesn't count. Because other than that, there was nothing.

"What?" a voice said quietly behind me.

"Shit!" I screamed, whirling around.

It was Knob, his mouth stuffed with a Cardiac Arrest, a monster sandwich stuffed with whatever's in the kitchen at the time of creation. Ingredients can vary from french fries, SourPatch Kids, hot peppers, jalapeno peppers, entire slices of cold pizza, green beans, conch fritters, cow tongue, ice cream, and whatever else one can find.

Dagwood would swoon with envy.

The caloric count alone could support the entire world's population of people on the Atkins diet for a week. And I won't even get into the overabundance of bad carbohydrates, which shouldn't be confused with good carbohydrates, which I guess do their chores and wash their hands after going to the bathroom.

Somehow though, Knob's metabolism takes it all in and everything runs pretty smoothly. Well, except maybe for his brain. There's definitely something not getting through there. Still though, he's lanky and friendly, and a good friend to hang around with.

A fly buzzed through the room.

Our eyes followed it as it zigged through the room.

We followed it as it zagged through the room.

Something registered on its sensors, and it veered for the sandwich in Knob's hand.

Knob, who while he has nothing against mosquitoes, at least female ones (we'll get into that later), hates flies, so he tried to whap it, swinging the Cardiac Arrest like a racquetball racquet.

The sandwich missed the fly by about a foot, but, strangely, the fly stopped in mid-air, and fluttered to the ground.

We watched until it fell out of sight. Yeah, out of sight. We aren't very good at housecleaning. The fly disappeared somewhere into the clutter that makes up our floor. Bits of paper with music notes scribbled on it, cardboard pizza containers, puzzles and games, stuff like that. Essential stuff. The stuff that makes our home, ah…well, uh…a mess. Hey, I admit it. It's a mess. I told you we aren't very good at housecleaning.

Something nibbled at my brain, reminding me that there had actually been an earlier thought that hadn't been brought to satisfactory conclusion.

Oh, yeah.

The silence.

Dave Matthews was taking another break, so the quiet was even more oppressive.

"What's that?" Knob asked, looking around. He crammed more sandwich into his mouth in hopes it would reduce inertia in his brain.

"I don't know."

"It's weird, like maybe church or something." Bits of sandwich flew through the air like errant meteors.

"Yeah."

"Remember that time with the tornado?"

"Yeah."

"Yeah, it's like that," he mumbled, cramming more into his mouth. Something that looked like an albino worm dangled from the corner of his mouth, before his tongue snaked out and swiped it away. Spaghetti, whew.

"Weird."

"Yeah."

Then it registered.

"What?" Knob asked.
"Do you hear that?"
"No, what?"
"Donkey Kong," I said.
"No, I don't hear any Donkey Kong," he asserted.
"That's just it, we should hear Donkey Kong."

I ran out into the living room, my eyes searching out my little brother.

"Seth?" I skidded to a stop.

He wasn't at the computer.

"Maybe he answered the phone," Knob said.

"Why would he do something like that?"

He shrugged. "I dunno."

"Okay, so where's the phone?"

We looked at each other. We had no idea where it was. We never use the phone, not even for the pizza delivery guy. We didn't need to, because our other roommate Thurman brings home free pizzas often enough to keep our marinara sauce levels from getting too low.

"I'll check the bedrooms," Knob volunteered.

I split off to go check out the basement.

Our house is located in what's known as the college slums; a hundred year-old part of town that went to seed when all the old people died off. All the houses were thin and deep, with steep driveways and old brick. People in this neighborhood were born and lived here until they died. Then they watched their sons and daughters move away and never come back. After the old people died, college kids moved in, renting entire houses, four to eight or more per house.

So we had an entire house to ourselves, for just two hundred bucks a month per person. Pretty slick, especially with the graveyard in the backyard. How can you get any cooler than that?

But the basement. That's another story. Dark, damp, scary, and home to our other roommate. In fact, that's what Thurman likes about it. He's into Goth. Secretly, I think it's just so he can wear black. The girls dig him in black, and he knows it.

He's working the early shift, delivering pizzas between

college classes, so I have to go down into the pit to see if maybe the phone's down there.

Whap! Whap! Whap!

"Bastard!"

Something upstairs. I bolted back up, and ran into the front bedroom.

"What's the matter?"

Knob was at the window, his shoe off, a disgusted look on his face.

"Ah, man, put that shoe back on."

"I was after a mosquito," he apologized.

"Well, don't do that," I told him angrily. My brother's missing, and Knob's out squishing mosquitoes and fostering foot odor.

"C'mon, we have to find Seth."

I promised I'd tell you about Knob and mosquitoes. He once read that only female mosquitoes bite, because they need the blood for egg-laying. And when he learned that a male mosquito is about a bazillion times bigger than the female, Knob, with a heart as soft as his head, concluded that the big hairy male jumps on the female and has his way with her. Afterwards, he merrily buzzes off to play miniature golf with his buddies, leaving the female stuck with whole egg process. Knob didn't think this was fair at all. So ever since, he eradicates any male mosquitoes that he can find, and wouldn't harm a female if she was sucking corpuscles out of his nose.

"It was a *Culex Pipiens*," he said defensively.

"Huh?"

"A *Culex*," he said, slanting a look at me like I was a nit.

"C'mon, you weirdo," I said angrily.

As part of his campaign to help the female mosquito, he'd done considerable research. This research is conducted with liberal amounts of beer, so his facts sometimes got a little scattered.

We headed back to the basement after having concluded the upstairs was Seth-free.

"Did you know that the *Culex* doesn't usually prefer humans?" he asked as we strode through the kitchen towards the basement stairs.

I ignored him.

"And it's known as the common house mosquito?"
I ignored him harder, and started down the stairs.
"In fact, what they actually prefer are birds."
"Shhh!" I hissed. There was something in the dark.

He lowered his voice. "And, did you know that mosquitoes actually don't eat blood? They eat stuff like nectar and…" his voice trailed off as he saw what I was looking at.

"What's he doing?" he asked.

"Shhh!"

It was Seth.

Then again, it wasn't.

Chapter Two

My brother was sitting at Thurman's desk, the phone receiver at his ear. But he wasn't listening to it. He wasn't listening to anything. He had a blank look on his face, his mouth open, eyes glassy.

"Seth?" I stage-whispered at him. "Are you alright?"

He didn't respond. He just sat, like a zombie or a typical geometry student when given a surprise quiz.

"What's wrong with him?" Knob asked, mosquitoes momentarily forgotten.

"I don't know," I managed over my pounding heart.

This was my brother, a fourteen year-old kid with borderline Attention-Deficit Disorder. It was eerie to see him when he wasn't a blur. The hair on my neck was raised, and I could feel goose pimples.

I picked up a weird sound, coming from the phone receiver in Seth's stone hands.

Now I had ostrich pimples, and my stomach felt like a frozen grape popsicle.

"Call an ambulance," I whispered to Knob.

"With what?" he asked.

"The, er..."

The phone that was in Seth's hands? The same phone that may have been some kind of instrument of horror?

"Uh, go to a neighbor's or something," I said, walking warily towards Seth. He ignored me. This was a bad sign, because it was usually the other way around.

"Which one?"

"Huh?"

"Which neighbor?" Knob asked maddeningly.

I gritted my teeth. "Either one."

"Okay, I'll go see the chicks across the street."

"Fine! Get out of here!"

"You don't have to get rude, dude."

The stairs shook as he thumped upstairs.

"Seth? You okay?"

He showed no signs of comprehension, no recognition, nothing.

Up close, I recognized the sound coming from the phone receiver. It was the sound that you get when the call is terminated, but you don't hang up. A nasty, rude, beeping sound.

I pried the phone receiver out of his hands. They were cold and lifeless. The hands, not the phone. The phone had more like a plasticky kind of feel. You're probably familiar with it. Not me, though. I told you that I don't use phones.

I gently shook his shoulders, marveling at how thin his frame felt under the shirt. It occurred to me that we don't usually make any kind of physical exchanges anymore. A feeling of sadness washed through me. The last time I gave him a big hug, he still had that toddler softness to him. Now, he was more of an angular teen. I was so busy ignoring him, I hadn't even noticed.

A clatter on the steps jolted me out of my reverie.

"They're coming," Knob whisper-shouted in my ear.

I gently slapped Seth's face. "Wake up, buddy. C'mon, wake up."

It was like slapping a rubber statue.

Knob stared wonderingly at Seth. "I know what this is, dude."

"Huh?"

"They got him."

"They? What are you talking about?"

"Those guys who've been stalking us all this time. That's why you're never supposed to answer the phone."

"*What?* We don't answer because of telemarketers."

"That's who I'm talking about. They got him."

"Who? Telemarketers? You're crazy!" I shouted.

Seth ignored the whole exchange.

"Yeah, telemarketers. They call and suck your brains out right through the receiver. That's why you have to hang up on them. They call during dinner, while you're mentally at your weakest."

"You're nuts! Telemarketers are just people, like you and me."

"Oh, yeah? Then how come they can keep arguing with you, even when you tell them no way?"

"They're persistent. That doesn't make them monsters."

"Then why do they keep calling, even after you slam the phone on them?"

"I don't know. Maybe it doesn't bug them so much."

"Who doesn't get bugged when someone hangs up the phone on them? If someone hung up on you, wouldn't you want to call them back and tell them what for?"

"Well…"

"And you know they don't eat dinner, because they're always on the phone then."

"Um…"

"That's because they don't eat regular food. They hibernate all day, and come out at dusk and dinnertime, and suck people's brains out through the phone."

"Uh…"

"They're like, you know, big brain-sucking mosquitoes or something."

"Mosquitoes?"

"Look at him!" He pointed at Seth, who was still ignoring the whole exchange. "Tell me they don't have his brain! It's gone. His head is empty."

The black pot pointing at the kettle.

A second person galumphed down the stairs, shaking the foundations of the old house.

"What's up, guys?"

Thurman had a pizza box in his arms, the aroma of pineapple and pepperoni wafting towards me. My stomach was still in clench mode, but relaxed a bit to grumble out a greeting to its Italian friend.

Thurman stopped when he noticed Seth. "Whoa, I've felt like that before."

"The telemarketers got him," Knob said knowingly.

"Telemarketers aren't monsters," I said, a little angry that Knob had almost sucked me into his conspiracy theory.

"That's why you can't answer the phone," Knob added.

"Telemarketers. Yeah, I've heard stuff about them," Thurman said thoughtfully.

"We have to get him back ourselves," Knob said. "So I didn't really call an ambulance."

"You mean, go into the telemarketer's Lair of Evil?" Thurman's eyes were big.

"What are you guys talking about? We have to get him to the hospital!"

"No way, a hospital can't help him."

"He's right," Thurman agreed. "A hospital can't help him. They'll just send him to a nuthouse."

"Yeah, that's what happens. Pills and stuff don't help all those people in nuthouses. Their brains have been sucked up by telemarketers. The medical profession doesn't understand the truth."

"We have to go and get his brain back ourselves!" Thurman exclaimed.

"A Quest!" Knob said, his eyes shining with excitement.

"Yes, a Quest!" Thurman agreed.

"Are you guys crazy? We're not going on any Quest!" I shouted.

"We have to," Knob said.

"Yeah, don't you want your brother back?"

Before I could answer, a buzzing sound cut through the discussion, and we all stopped as a big, fat, black fly flew between us, low and slow like a Warthog fighter plane.

We watched, mesmerized, as it swooped down low and cut a

pattern around the room, then buzzed back upstairs before Knob could recover and try to kill it.

Thurman had a narrowed look in his eyes. "I've got a theory about flies, you know."

"Of course you do, Knob and his mosquitoes, you and flies."

"We gotta hurry and pack," Knob exclaimed.

"Yeah, this could take a while."

"Going to the gates of Hell."

"This is going to be awesome!"

"Yeah, Dungeons and Dragons stuff."

"Forget it," I interjected. "We're not going on any nutso Quest."

"Look, man," Knob said, "would it hurt to try it our way? For a while, at least?"

"Yeah," Thurman added, "he's not going anywhere." He gestured at the statue of my brother.

"And if we don't get anywhere, we'll take him in like you want," Knob said.

"Where they'll shut him up in a cage, and pump him full of noxious chemicals and stuff."

"And he'll rot away."

"Because the doctors have no clue as to what's really going on."

"Enough!" I shouted. "Okay, okay, we'll do it your way. Anything it takes to shut you up."

"All right! The Quest is on!" Knob gushed.

"Hey, we'll need a warrior," Thurman said knowingly.

"Yeah, a warrior is essential."

"Let's get our stuff."

"My dice, I need my dice."

They clattered upstairs, leaving me with the husk of my brother. I could hear excited thumps upstairs.

I looked at my little brother, my only sibling. Except for my older sister. But she didn't count. Because sisters never count, especially older sisters. Except when they have their friends over. Then you notice them. The friends, not your sister. Especially at pajama parties.

But with a brother, there's a special bond, no matter that he's a little pain in the butt who always gets in my way, and eats up all the cookies and good munchie stuff before I get to have my share, which is more than half, because I'm the big brother, and I should get more than half, because I'm bigger and because I was born first, and he should know this and stop telling Mom and Dad on me.

Mom! What am I going to tell Mom?

I pictured her face, and what she would say when she saw her little Zombie-son.

"Guy, you know you're supposed to protect your little brother," she would accuse me.

"But, Mom. I couldn't do anything. The telemarketers got his brain!"

"That doesn't matter. You're his big brother."

"But, Mom—"

"I said," she interrupted, *"you're his big brother, and you have to watch out for him."*

I decided not to tell Mom…for now, at least.

Thurman thumped back down the stairs. "I forgot, all my stuff's down here."

He dove into his closet and started rummaging around, his black-jean clad butt sticking out.

I took my brother by the hand, and he followed me blankly upstairs.

Chapter Three

Later on, we were sitting at the dining room table. I chewed mechanically at a slice of pizza as Knob and Thurman discussed travel plans. Seth sat across from me, oblivious to their excited chatter. A fly kept bumping up against the kitchen screen, trying frantically to get in.

"Where are we going to start?" Knob wondered.

"Well, they use the phone to get around, so I think we have to start with the phone company," Thurman offered.

"Yeah, that makes sense," Knob agreed.

"We could go to the place where we make payments," Thurman said.

Since we're almost always running on a very tight budget, we usually pay in person at a local office just before the deadline where our phone gets turned off. Sometimes I wonder that we even bother, since we never use the phone anyway. Maybe some harbinger of responsibility to come, from when we mature and take on responsibilities like kids and mortgages and 401k plans and stuff like that.

"Who do we get as a warrior?" Thurman asked.

"I know just the person," Knob said.

I wasn't participating in the conversation.

Neither was Seth.

"So, first we pick up the warrior, and then we go to the phone company?"

The fly stopped bouncing against the screen, and settled down to listen.

"Okay, that sounds like a plan. How do we get there?"

"The Hog's gassed up, and ready to rumble," Knob said, referring to the old Dodge Caravan he'd picked up for five hundred bucks, payable at thirty percent interest so that by the time he was done paying for it, he will have paid three times the price of the van.

With a parting buzz, the fly flew off. That's what they do, after all. Sometimes I wonder who named them 'flies.' And why didn't the same person call a centipede a 'walk'? Worm's should have been called 'squirm,' by the same logic.

A stupid joke went through my mind, *What do you call a microwave wok?*

A run, another part of my brain answered.

Jokes at a time like this. I'm starting to lose it. I no it. No, I know it.

My roommates were still making plans.

"Okay, every Quest has to have a warrior, and a sorcerer."

"Yeah, and a dwarf and an elf."

"Yeah, you have to have those," Knob said, bobbing his head in agreement.

"What are you guys talking about?"

Knob looked at me pityingly. "Every Quest has to have the right people. You need to have a warrior, an elf, a wizard…"

"…and a dwarf and a magic sword…" Thurman added.

"…and an evil presence…" Knob continued.

"…and the possibility of sequels…"

"…and movie rights…"

"…special effects…"

"Shut up," I screamed, holding my head. A painful thudding had begun, keeping time with my heart.

THWUMP!

A sound wave rattled the cabinets, and the ground shook underneath us.

"What the…!" Thurman yelled.
"Whoa!" Knob yelled.
"Aaaahhhh!" I yelled.
"……………" Seth yelled.

Okay, Seth didn't really add anything to the dialogue, but I'm sure he would have if he hadn't been a zombie. The entire house had been shaken like a rattle in the hands of a hyperactive baby.

We rushed to the front door, and threw it open.

It was winter…

…in Alaska.

Not here, though. Here it was summer, and a blast of heat blasted by us, blasting us with its passing blast. Beyond it, the sky was blue, the grass was green, and traffic was uncongested. Everything looked peaceful. White clouds floated gracefully in the sky. Birds twittered and pooped on cars.

There was no sign of what had caused the great sound we had heard.

Except, where Knob's Caravan was, or rather, wasn't.

There was a shadow where the van had stood in the driveway, but the van was gone. Or, as we saw as we carefully approached the spot where the van should be, there was something where the van had been, five minutes before. It was in the shape of the van. Kind of. On the driveway, where there had once been a five and a half-foot high pride of Lee Iaccoca Chrysler family of family automobiles, was a one-inch high version of the same vehicle.

Knob's van had been squashed completely flat.

"Wha…?"
"Hunh…?"
"Uh…?"

We looked at each other, stunned.

I looked around. No one was around who could explain what had happened to the two thousand-pound vehicle.

Knob squatted down and sort of patted the van, as if to reassure himself that it wasn't an illusion. Then he looked up at us. "They're on to us."

His words woke me out of my shock. "What are you talking about?"

"The telemarketers. Somehow they learned that we know

about them."

The look on Thurman's face shifted from shock to fear.

"Let's go, there's no time to lose." Knob wheeled, and sprinted back into the house.

Thurman and I looked at each other. Then we looked at what used to be a mini-van. Then we followed Knob back into the house.

Inside, Knob was quickly stuffing his knapsack. We got there just as he was cramming a stack of moist towelettes into the sack.

"What are those for?" I asked.

"You gotta have towelettes," he said.

"What? To keep your hands clean?"

Knob sighed. Sometimes he had trouble explaining things to lesser intellects, like myself. Or me. Or I. Or, whatever it is that signifies me...or I...or myself.

"Didn't you read the Hitchhiker?" he asked, a pained look of put-upon patience plastered to his puss.

"Huh?"

"Doug Adams."

"Huh?"

"I know what he's talking about," Thurman said excitedly, "The Hitchhiker's Guide to the Galaxy."

Knob beamed at him, the bright pupil. Then he turned severe eyes back on me, the dunce. "Yeah, the Hitchhiker's Guide to the Galaxy. The bible for world travelers."

"That's fiction," I fired at him.

He ignored that. "Anybody knows if you're going to travel, you have to bring a towel."

"Yeah," Thurman agreed. "It's got nutrients, and you can wrap it around your head to keep from burning yourself." He was growing a bald spot, and was very concerned about burning his head.

"Those are towelettes, you goof," I said.

"Right, they are the only things available that have both the cleaning ability and nutritional requirements."

"Nutritional requirements?"

"Yeah, they're like concentrated water, hermetically sealed. If you're out in a desert—"

"We're in Chicago!"

He ignored that, too. "—and you lose your canteen, you can suck on one of these towelettes."

"We're not bringing canteens!"

"And these," he held one out to me, "are the best, because they're lemon-flavored."

"There are drinking fountains all over the city!"

"Who's the head of our Quest?" Thurman changed the topic.

"I am," Knob announced.

"*You?*" I said, an amazed look on my face.

I didn't know for a fact that I had an amazed look on my face, since I couldn't see it. But I'm pretty sure there was, because I was amazed.

"You chew your own toenails! How can you be a leader?"

"Yeah, me," he said, narrowing his eyes. "Why, you want the job?"

"He can't be," said Thurman, "he's the Unbeliever, like Thomas Covenant."

"But the Unbeliever was the leader, in a way," Knob mused.

"Hmm...maybe," Thurman agreed thoughtfully.

"Look, we have to get out of here before whatever crunched the Hog comes back for us," Knob said, taking his role of maybe-leader by the horns. Even though his horn, fan belt, and everything else, was squashed to a half-inch little pile.

"How do we get there?"

"Where?"

"To pick up our warrior, of course," Thurman said.

"Warrior?" I said.

"Yeah, I told you I know where we can get one," Knob reassured me. "Let's get Seth and go."

"We're not bringing Seth."

He gave me a serious look. "We're bringing Seth. We don't have a choice." Then he gestured to the van that looked like it could fit in one of Thurman's delivery boxes. "And we can't leave him here. It's not safe."

I couldn't argue with that logic, because, after all, something strange was going on.

"Besides, we need something to put his brain in when we get it back."

"We're also bringing Weezel," Thurman declared, shooting eye darts at us.

"No way!" Knob groaned.

"I said, we're bringing him." Thurman's posture was ramrod straight.

"Oh, shit, don't worry about him," I said. "It's not like he takes up much room."

Weezel is Thurman's dog, vintage maybe twenty years ago, maybe fifty. A ghost dog, if you can believe it. Thurman discovered him one night when we were messing around with an Ouiji Board. He'd asked the board whether his childhood dog was in dog heaven, and the board surprised him by revealing that another dog was presently in the room with them, and wanted Thurman for a master. Another of our normal freaky nights.

Ever since, Thurman swore he could sense the dog, which somehow shifted breeds, manifesting itself as a dachshund, sometimes a collie, once in a while an Irish wolfhound. He'd take it for walks, and ignore when we suggested he could maybe take his imaginary dog on imaginary walks instead, and just hang with us. Once in a while when the jokes got too barbed, he'd snap back, "He's not imaginary, he's invisible!"

He'd also get up in the middle of a television show to let Weezel out. Why Weezel didn't simply go through the door like any other ghost, Thurman wouldn't say.

WHOMPH!

Another explosion shook the room.

"It's back!" Knob shouted.

"We have to get out of here!" Thurman screamed.

WHOMPH! SMACK! CRASH!

"Oh, man, I think that was my car," Thurman moaned.

We jumped up, and Thurman and Knob grabbed their knapsacks. I snatched Seth by the wrist, and we bolted away from the sound. Problem was, there was nothing but a window on that side of the house. We scrambled through the window, Seth allowing himself to be led.

We ran around the side of the house, and Thurman glanced

around the corner. He pulled his head back. "It got my car, too," he said, his face pasty.

"Did you see what did it?" Knob breathed breathlessly.

"No, whatever it was, I didn't see anything. But my car is flat as a pizza," said the pizza delivery boy, who would be in the position to know if something was as flat as a pizza.

"Let's run for it," Knob said.

"Where?" I asked him.

"To get our warrior," he said, with a look that told me what he thought of my stupid questions.

"How do we get there?" I said.

"Wow, he really is the Unbeliever," Thurman said, looking at me with wondering eyes.

"We run!" Knob said. "She's only a few doors down."

"She?"

"A lady warrior?" An excited look flitted across Thurman's face. Then it flitted the other way before settling in to stay for a while, as he most likely considered the idea of half-naked, big-breasted Amazonian warriors. "All right, let's go!"

Knob ran towards the garage, keeping low to the ground. Thurman ran crouched after. I followed, dragging my little brother, who ran upright like Frankenstein in pursuit of a sewing kit.

We flattened against the garage, and sneaked a peek towards our demolished vehicles.

"Let's go." Knob ran around the garage, and sprinted up the hill towards the graveyard.

"Is this a smart idea?" Thurman managed, looking at the tombstones with some trepidation.

"Yeah, I don't think these have anything to do with the telemarketers," Knob assured him, leading a winding path around the graves.

There was another thumping sound behind us.

"Faster!" I yelled.

"C'mon, Weezel," Thurman urged his ghost dog, who no doubt was stopping to check out some ghost pee on one of the gravestones.

We sprinted through the older part of the graveyard, heading for a house about fifty yards away. There was another thumping sound behind us, accompanied by the sound of splintering wood and shattering CDs.

"It got the house," Thurman moaned.

"Faster!" I yelled, again.

"C'mon!" Knob prodded us. He was the fastest of us, and he pulled ahead, knees flying.

I risked a glance behind us. The house was gone. Just an empty space, sitting between our neighbors' houses, the garage still standing with a fateful look, as if somehow knowing that its turn was next.

I couldn't see what was causing all the devastation. It was a beautiful, sunny day, with big fluffy, non-threatening cumulous clouds floating in a sea of blue sky.

"Maybe it's invisible," Thurman said shakily, puffing from the run.

"Don't worry about it," Knob yelled. "Quick, get in."

He was at the back door of the house, gesturing frantically at us.

We shot inside, finding ourselves in the kitchen. Thurman leaned on a counter, panting heavily. Dressed all in black, with heavy jeans, he'd been pounded mercilessly by the sun's rays all the way across the field.

The rest of us were wearing garb more suited for a midnineties day.

"Where are we?" I gasped.

"The Warrior, man," Knob said heavily.

"We...shouldn't...just...have...busted...in," Thurman said, still puffing.

"It was an emergency, I don't think she'd mind."

"What are you doing here?" a voice asked.

We all jumped, except for Seth. Seth was standing placidly, not perspiring or even breathing hard.

In front of us was a brown-haired urchin.

"Who are you?"

We wheeled about to see another little kid, exactly like the first.

"Huh?" Thurman grunted.

"Twins," Knob said, giving them a welcoming smile.

"Where's your Mommy?" he asked, folding down to look one of them in the eyes.

"I'll get her." The kid bolted down the hallway.

I looked at the other one. It was six or seven years old, sex indeterminate. Don't misunderstand, I'm sure there was a sex. And I'm sure it was not androgynous, because it wouldn't matter if it was a little boy or a little girl. Either way, he/she was as cute as hell. Big, lively brown eyes, nut brown skin, longish brown hair sun-streaked from day-long expeditions in the outdoors.

"What's your name?" I asked, leaning to eye level.

"Shawn."

There you go, a girl's name.

"You're a pretty little girl," I exclaimed.

"Uh, dude…" Knob began.

"I'm not a girl, I'm a boy," the child proclaimed hotly.

"S – E – A – N," Knob observed, too late.

"Oh, I'm so sorry," I said, my face turning hot.

I was rescued as the other kid came running in. "She'll be here in a minute."

"Thanks, Chris," Knob said.

"Hi, Chris," I offered, trying to save face, at least once. "How are you, little man?"

"Uh, dude…" Knob began, once again too late to save me.

"I'm not a boy," that child yelled at me.

"K – R – I – S," Knob added helpfully.

I shut up, my face burning.

"Hi, Knob," a new voice said, entering the room. "What's up?"

I slid my gaze sideways, trying to avoid another face-coloring event, to behold the Warrior.

And, I did that.

Yes, I did.

I beheld the Warrior.

Chapter Four

Five and a half foot of Warrior, probably weighing a good one hundred twenty pounds. Almost half of that was on her chest. Yep, her boobs were big, aggressively big. Big in the way the Big Gulp is big. Too big for the cup holder. They stood out straight, defying gravity, defying you to walk by them, defying you to not look at them. They contrasted with the look on her face, which defied you to look at her boobs.

Guiltily, my eyes, which had wandered on out for a good look, sucked back into the sockets. Retreating from her penetrating eyes, mine slid over to go see what Thurman's eyes were up to. His were focused on her chest, and he appeared to have forgotten how to breathe.

If you'd have asked me her hair color, or what she was wearing, I could not have told you. But give me a pen and I'll bet I could have drawn every single detail of her chest, which somehow my imagination had supplied to my mind with newfound X-Ray vision so as to assist me in my mental unveiling.

From the looks of it, this same superpower was infusing Thurman.

"Uh, dudes, bad idea," Knob said, from the corner of his mouth, which was twitching nervously. He alone seemed to be immune from the Power of the Beast, er, Breast.

I blinked, and the spell was gone.

Thurman blinked, and his spell vanished, too.

Seth didn't blink.

I don't know if Weezel blinked, or if he had been under the same thrall. He might have been unimpressed given that there were only two breasts, and he was used to considerably more.

"Come on in," the Warrior said. "Let's take a load off."

She led us out of the kitchen, through the hallway, past Grandmother's house, and into a comfortable sitting room. She sat in the sitting room, inviting us to do the same.

So we did. Sit, that is.

I perched uncomfortably on a comfortable overstuffed loveseat. Thurman and Knob settled easily into easy chairs. Seth just stood.

Now I noticed the Warrior's face. Cute, maybe even more than cute. I could see the resemblance to the twins, who could be heard prattling around in the kitchen.

This was a warrior?

In the background, I could still hear the thumping noise. Whatever had gotten the cars and house was still out there, lurking about. But it seemed that our escape had been unnoticed.

The Warrior smiled pleasantly, and asked Knob, "What can I do for you boys?"

Knob looked uncomfortable.

"We have a problem," Thurman interjected.

"Yeah, we're on a Quest," Knob's tongue loosened enough to say.

Narrowed eyes. "A Quest?"

"Hear that whomping sound?" Thurman continued.

The Warrior cocked her face prettily, her eyes narrowing further. "What is it?" she asked.

"We don't know," Knob said, "but it's after us. We think it's telemarketers."

"Telemarketers. Huh. I've heard about them."

Thurman jumped back in, "Yeah, see what they did to Guy's little brother?" He pointed at Seth.

"That guy?" she asked, pointing to me.

"No, I mean, yeah, but I'm Guy," I interjected.
"Gay?"
"No, Guy."
"Goy?"
"Guy."
"A guy?"
"Guy."
"I said that."
"I know, but…I mean, a guy, not Guy."
"Huh?"
"Um…"
"A…guy…" she said slowly, so that I could better understand.
"Uh…Guy…" I elaborated, just as slowly and for the same reason.
"He's Guy," Knob said helpfully.
"I said that."
"My name is Guy."
"Oh, you're GUY," she said.
"And, not coincidentally, I am a guy."
"But not gay?"
"I'm usually fairly happy, but not gay."
"I think I get it." She crossed her legs, drawing our involuntary attention. She had nice legs. "How come you guys don't just opt out?"
"Opt out?" Knob asked.
"Yes. Laws were passed that would allow you to get off telemarketers' lists."
"Really? You mean, like, we could have our phone back and everything?"
"Yep. The law finally took on the telemarketers for us. Like the cigarette executives, and hopefully soon, spammers, too."
"Wow! Spammers, too?" This sounded truly wonderful, even though we didn't have Internet access.

Just then a news announcement came on the television, cutting into the rerun of *Friends*. An attorney, with a sonorous look on his face to match his sonorous voice, was giving a sonorous speech on a courtroom steps, before dozens of cameras, mikes, and johns, who were disguised as regular newspeople since it was still light outside, and their wives could account for their whereabouts. The strong odor of No-Doz could not be smelled through the television screen, but was doubtless in evidence, because the reporters were alert and conscious.

The attorney was forced to use an interpreter, because he was speaking in an archaic, self-contradictory language known as Attorney-Speak, which was developed solely for the purpose of confounding English teachers and confusing laypersons (defined as a person who passes out when confronting legal issues).

Ancient scrolls have been found that date this language to the Jurassic period, when the first attorney-mammals crawled out of the seas, and traded worthless trinkets and shells to the reptiles in exchange for the continent of Asia, selling it back to them in timeshares with disclaimers written so small the dinosaurs couldn't read them. There are still bad feelings about this massive land swindle, and dinosaurs still eat attorneys at every opportunity.

Sonorously, pompously, the attorney pontificated through his interpreter, a lesser attorney, who, being a recent law school graduate, still retained some ability to speak in common language.

"We are sad to—" relayed the interpreter.

The attorney interrupted him, and spoke in his ear, like Dean's attorney during the Watergate trials.

"We are happy to—" the interpreter began again.

The attorney whispered in his ear again.

Or maybe he was just eating earwax. There was no real way to tell, but, as far as National Geographic can tell, attorneys do not feed on earwax, preferring instead thirty-percent contingency fees.

"Um, we are announcing that we are filing a class-action suit today, on behalf of Sadie Winfrey, and others like her..." and here both the attorney and interpreter gestured towards a forlorn looking old lady standing beside them, almost lost in the shadow of the attorney's ego, "...for one billion dollars..."

There was a gasp in the room as we all watched, transfixed by the melodrama unfolding before us.

"...against McDonald's restaurants..."

We gasped again.

"...for gross negligence and, dare I say it, criminal conduct."

The press erupted in excitement, screaming out their questions, and Knob's Cardiac Arrest sandwich, which he had somehow clung onto during our packing and escape, dropped to the floor with a wet splat.

"Mr. Tort, Mr. Tort, can you tell us why you're suing McDonald's?" one voice penetrated through the mob noise.

The attorney swung his beak, uh, snout, uh, nose toward the questioner.

"Money," the interpreter said.

The attorney turned to his interpreter angrily, and briefly whispered a brief briefly, shielding their faces with his brief.

"Oh, uh..." the interpreter said, "I, mean, uh..."

The attorney addressed the crowd, "Whereas, the party of the first party, hereinafter referred to as the antecedent, prior to the injurious infraction..."

All the donuts in Chicago contained less than the amount of glaze that slid over the eyes of the assembled crowd of reporters and on-lookers.

Fortunately, everybody was saved by the interpreter, who shouted over the attorney's droning voice, "Not money! This suit has nothing to do with money!"

The attorney stopped droning on, saddening some on-looking bees, and the interpreter continued, at a lower level, "Our suit is being filed on behalf of all of the citizens who have suffered the consequences of eating Big Macs."

"What, raised cholesterol levels?" one reporter quipped.

"Getting fat?"

"Allergies to sesame seeds?" another yelled.

"I know," another said, "hatred of the song." He started singing, "'Two all beef paddies, special sauce...'"

The entire crowd started singing along, including those who were too young to have been around when the song was driving the entire nation batty, "'...lettuce, cheese, pickles, onions...'"

Coming together into a rousing finale "'...on a sesame seed buuunnnnnn!'"

The interpreter simply looked at them, eyes glinting behind

spectacles that were worn just for looks, since he'd had laser surgery the year before, paid from a bonus he'd gotten for creative over-billing. He waited until the hubbub died down.

Then he waited some more, since a few cameras were panning the crowd instead of focusing on him.

When he judged that he was once again the center of attention, he continued, "As you know, McDonald's named their cocoa, 'Hot Chocolate.' This implies they are aware of the risks that an inattentive consumer might injure something by incidental contact with intemperate conditions."

"ZZZZZZZZZZZZ," the reporters chorused.

The interpreter looked sheepish, and bleated, "Uh, sorry. I meant, since they named it 'hot,' then it shows they are aware of their duty to warn their consumers of possible hazards of using their products."

"Like the lady who spilled coffee on herself and sued McDonald's, claiming that the coffee was hot," one reporter suggested.

"Exactly." The interpreter beamed. "Definitely a high point in the history of the law profession. Why the fees alone—"

"Don't you think she should have known that coffee is hot?" another reporter interrupted.

"Wha...?" the interpreter started.

"There's cold coffee, nowadays," another reporter said to the first reporter.

"Oh, yeah, I guess so."

The interpreter raised his voice, to draw attention back to him, "Exactly. And now there's a warning label on McDonald's coffee, warning the consumer that coffee is hot."

"Yeah, we feel all comfy, cozy and warm with relief," one reporter said sarcastically. Or maybe he really was all comfy, cozy and warm with relief.

"So what's the problem with Big Macs?" another reporter shouted out.

"We believe," said the interpreter, "that Big Macs should be called 'Sloppy, Warm Big Macs,' so people are warned that you could get stuff all over yourselves, causing great emotional distress and dry-cleaning bills."

There was a snuffle from the shadow caused by the attorney's ego. "Like Ms. Sadie Winfrey, here," the interpreter said, as the attorney put his arm around her and gazed warmly at her like a vampire picking out his next victim.

Knob looked up from the screen. "Yeah, Big Macs are pretty messy."

"I've gotten that orange stuff all over my clothes," Thurman agreed.

"Good thing we have the legal profession to look out after our interests," Knob observed sagely.

"Are we going to get anything out of the multi-billions they won against the cigarette companies?" Thurman asked.

"Hey, yeah! We should get something."

"You don't smoke," I accused him.

"Second-hand, man, just as bad for you."

"Good grief."

Did I say that? 'Good Grief'?

Good grief, I sound like Charlie Brown. Oh, no, I said it again!

"Shut up, you idiots. We've got work to do," I said. I turned back to the Warrior and looked at her breasts.

I had to. I'm a guy.

"U-hem," she cleared her throat, and my head snapped away with an audible click.

"Uh, sorry," I mumbled, my face burning. Defensively, I looked at Knob and Thurman. They were also staring at her breasts, since they are guys, too.

Not the boobs.

They aren't guys.

Knob and Thurman.

Though they are boobs, too.

Not the boobs. Knob and Thurman.

Knob and Thurman are boobs, too, I mean.

Never mind.

"Don't worry about it, I get that all the time," she said not unkindly.

My face turned redder anyway.

Meanwhile, a thought was tumbling through my mind. How

can this diminutive woman be a feared warrior? Cute, a mom to two cute kids, generously endowed. My eyes took a quick moment to verify this fact, even though my mind was still holding the memory clear and dear.

Yep, still big.

I wondered how I could ask the question.

"You don't look like a warrior," Thurman blurted, eyes still focused a foot below her eyes.

"Uh, oh," Knob muttered. "Ix-nay on the arriorway."

The room got ominously silent.

Thump! Thump!

Whatever it was that had chased us could still be heard thumping around outside, but, to my relief, it sounded pretty far away.

Or was it my heart?

The Warrior looked evenly at us, no expression on her face or breasts.

Thump! Thump! said the outside noise, or my heart.

"I think maybe I can tell you something about her abilities in that field," Knob ventured.

"No, that's okay," she said, a pleasant look on her pert face.

The room took a collective breath.

"I'm not a full-time warrior," she said.

"Yeah, but she is one of the most—"

"That's okay, Knob, I can tell this."

She took a deep breath, and we all watched a certain…well, two parts…swell deliciously. When she let her breath back out, we found that we could breathe again, too.

"I get PMS pretty bad," she said, a mixed look of guilt and pride on her face.

"Really bad," Knob chimed in.

"Knob!"

Fearfully, he jerked away, raising his hand defensively.

"Don't worry, Knob. But please let me tell it my way," she said.

"Look, I have a, uh, physical condition…" she began.

We all looked at her, eager to examine both of her physical conditions.

"Not those," she said.
"Um, sorry," I apologized.
"Pardon," Thurman said.
"Damned nice," Knob observed.
"Thank you," she said graciously. "Anyway, I have a physical condition, and once a month, when the moon comes out, it has an effect on me that I simply can't control."
"PMS." Knob nodded again.
"Yes, PMS. But not regular PMS. You see, I have..." And here she turned a pretty pink, and looked away.

We three guys, being guys, took the opportunity to sneak another peek at her twin peaks, Mount Left and Mount Right. Being guys, we sucked in the view, storing it away for later memories. And didn't feel guilty about it, since being guys, we're bred for this kind of surveillance.

"...double PMS."
"Huh?"
"What?"
"Hnnngh?"
We aren't very good at verbal expression though.
"I have double PMS."
"What are you talking about?" Knob asked.
I was surprised that he was surprised, since he knew her. But I guess that kind of thing doesn't come up in normal conversation.
"Double PMS. I have two uteri."
"Uteri?"
"Uteri. The plural of uterus."
"Oooohhhhh," we three guys said in chorus, shrinking away. Woman organ stuff.
"That's why I have twins."
I frowned. "Other women have twins, but don't have two uteruses."
"Uteri."
"Uteri," I repeated.
"I know. Usually twins come from different placenta. But it's different with me. I have two totally separate uteri all together."
"Ooohhhh," we said, still not really taking this in, but hoping we could stop her from continuing this talk about woman organs.

"So, anyway, once a month, I get PMS...pretty bad, too," she said sadly.

"Oooohhhhh," we said, in sympathy.

"I get pretty irritable."

"Ooohhhhh."

Maybe if we keep agreeing, she won't get irritable.

"So, um, this is unusual?" I asked nervously.

"Very! Almost unprecedented, even in the animal world. In fact, the only other creature that my doctor could think of with two uteri is the sand tiger shark."

"Oooohhhh."

Sand tiger shark.

Big teeth.

Man-eater.

"In fact," she laughed nervously, "that's probably what shark attacks are. Women sharks with double PMS."

"Ha, ha," the guys laughed nervously.

"Well, anyway, I'm pretty safe to be around right now. At least for a few more days, ha, ha."

"Ha, ha," the guys laughed nervously in agreement.

"So-o-o-o, what are you guys looking for?"

Silence.

Knob and I looked at each other, silently rehashing the whole leader question. Thurman just sat back, a smug look on his face.

I chew my toenails, remember? Knob thought at me.

Yeah, but I'm the Unbeliever, I thought back furiously.

That was kind of the extent of it, but we repeated it back and forth for a few more eyeblinks.

Oh, okay, I gave up.

"We need a warrior, for our Quest," I said, finally.

"Hmmm, you said that," she reminded me.

"Telemarketers took my brother's brain."

"I gathered."

"We're going to go get it back."

"I see."

"Uh..."

"So, what do I get out of this?" she asked.

Uh, oh.

"Well, we don't really have any money," I started.
"You get out of the house," Knob offered.
"Out of the house?"
"Yeah," Knob said.
"Yeah?" she asked.
"Yeah," he confirmed.
"No kids?"
"No kids."
"Does Jim agree to this?" she asked, interested now.
"It was his idea," Knob said, a hint of nervousness peeking out at this revelation.
"Hmmm, interesting."
"He said he'd take them to his mother's if you had to leave."
There was a silence.
"So how long will this Quest last?"

Chapter Five

*L*ater, we guys were sitting around the table while our warrior was packing in her room. Seth stood quietly in the corner, probably trying to attract cobwebs.

"So, Knob," I said, "she's a warrior?"

"You wouldn't believe," he said.

"But, she's so…"

We all silently reflected on her two considerable 'so's.

"Yeah, man, but I've seen her in action."

"You have?" Thurman asked, eyes wide.

Knob shuddered. "It wasn't pretty."

"Tell us," Thurman urged, flicking eyes nervously towards the back where she'd disappeared. A pleasant humming sound came from that direction.

Vrrrrooommm!

Two kids blasted through the room.

Vrrrrooommmm!

Two more flashed through, screaming at the top of their lungs, flicking wet towels at each other.

Knob's mouth was moving, but we heard nothing over the sound of kids rocketing through the house, knocking over all of the carefully arranged knickknacks and bric-a-brac that had made the house so homey and comfortable a few minutes before.

Vrrroooommmmm!

Two more kids shot through, smacking each other with styrofoam noodles, yelling and laughing crazily.

"What the…" I yelled, startled.

"Hers," Knob yelled back, a satisfied look on his face.

"These are all hers?" Thurman hollered, astonished by the little forms streaking through and around us.

"Yeah, that's why…"

"Ooohhhhh," Thurman and I said in unison. I think that's what we said. Our lips were pursed in the 'Oh' position, but we couldn't hear ourselves over the cacophony around us.

The three sets of twins went screaming out the back door like miniature fighter planes, and the sound of six splashes marked their arrival at some form of liquid.

The humming in the back room sounded carefree.

"So tell us," Thurman whispered, "what have you seen her do?"

Knob shot a look at the back room, and turned back to us. "Remember when the mall had that special sale a few years ago?"

"The fifty-percent off thing?"

"Yeah. Well, she…" and he gestured where the diminutive woman was humming along, "…she got in first."

"Wow! Weren't a lot of people injured at that thing?" I asked.

"Yep, the bloodiest battle this town's ever seen."

"The hospitals were full. I read that some lady went nuts and put almost twenty people in the hospital."

"Yep," Knob said.

"Her?" Thurman said, astonished.

"Yep, she took out twenty experienced women shoppers."

"Wow!"

"By herself."

"Wow!"

"And not a scratch on her," Knob whispered.

"Wow!"

"Fair fight, too."

"Wow!"

We were silent, thinking about this. We all have mothers, and were quite aware of the ferocity and strength a woman in shopping-mode can exhibit. For one person to thrash twenty of these ferocious...

Wow.

"I think, gentlemen, that we have our warrior," Knob said, a satisfied gleam in his eyes.

"I'm ready," from behind us.

We jumped in unison, tumbling our chairs to the floor.

"Whoa..."

"Don't do tha..."

"Whoops..."

"Sorry, fellas, didn't mean to startle you," she said. "Now what?" she asked, sitting at the dining room table.

We grabbed the chairs and sat down with her.

"Well," Knob began, "we have to find out where the telemarketers are."

"Do they have homes?" Thurman wondered.

"They have to live somewhere," I fretted.

"Well, aren't they involved somehow with the phone company?" she wondered.

"Yeah, we were thinking that, too," Knob said.

"Hey, that makes sense," Knob said.

"You know," I said, my brain racing, "didn't telemarketing pretty much start when the phone company broke up?"

"Heyyy. I think I know where you're going," Knob said.

"Maybe there's some kind of connection," I wondered.

When Bell splintered, hundreds of baby phone companies had risen from the monopoly ashes, offering all kinds of plans and rates, undercutting each other, outdoing each other with teeny, tiny print written by attorneys, who...

Attorneys?

Hmmm. Something nibbled at my memory.

"So we go to the phone company?" Knob put in.

"Sounds like a plan," the Warrior agreed.

"Gotta start somewhere," Thurman declared.

They all looked at me.

The Unbeliever. The leader.

"Okay—" I began.

"Wait!" Knob interjected. "We have to make sure we have all of the personnel that a Quest has to have."

"Personnel...?"

"Remember, warrior, elf, dwarf, stuff like that," Knob said, his eyes shining.

"We're not going—"

"I got dibs on sorcerer," Thurman said excitedly.

"You're not a sor—"

"Y'know," Knob interrupted me, "since I can't be a leader, I always wanted to be an elf." He started rummaging in his sack, stacking lemon-scented moist towelettes.

"You can't be an el—"

"I'm definitely the warrior, but since I'm so short, maybe I could be a warrior-dwarf?" the Warrior interjected.

"A dwar—"

"What do you have in that knapsack?" Thurman asked Knob.

"Stuff."

"What kind of stuff?"

"I don't know. I haven't looked yet," Knob said, pawing through the contents.

"How could you not know what you packed?" I shot at him, before someone else could interrupt me.

"I don't know, man. I just filled it with stuff."

"You just put anything in there?" I said, amazed.

"Yeah. How else can you do it? It's not like you know everything you're going to need when you go off on a Quest," he said, pulling out a guitar pick and a vacuum cleaner bag.

"What the heck are you doing with a vacuum cleaner bag?"

"You never know," he said, putting a pepper mill on the table.

"Never know what?"

"When your vacuum cleaner's going to get full," he said logically. "Oh, here it is."

He pulled a green and red object out of the knapsack, and shook out the wrinkles.

It was his elf hat. One of those stupid hats for Christmas with felt pointy ears sewn onto a green and red fake Santa Claus elf hat. Knob wore it every Christmas.

He jammed it on his head, and grinned at us triumphantly. "The Elven-lord!"

Thurman and the Warrior clapped enthusiastically.

I groaned. "People are going to think you're nuts."

"So what do we call you?" Thurman asked the Warrior.

She wrinkled her nose prettily. "I usually pick out a different name every time I go on a Quest."

"You've been on Quests, before?" I asked.

"Oh, yes, my services are required quite often. Let's see," she said, deep in thought.

"We get to pick out new names?" Knob shouted.

"Socrates, I want to be Socrates the Sorcerer," Thurman exclaimed.

"You don't get new names, you nimrods," I growled at them.

The Warrior looked over at me, arching a perfectly plucked eyebrow dangerously.

"Uh, except for the Warrior," I amended quickly.

"Why can't I be Socrates?" Thurman whined.

"And you're definitely not a nimrod," I continued saying to the Warrior. Then I glowered at the elf and sorcerer, known until recently as my roommates. "But you are."

"How about Wanda?" Knob said to the Warrior.

"Wanda the Warrior?" Thurman said skeptically.

"Xena?"

"Taken."

"Conan?" Knob offered.

"Man's name," she said. "If you didn't notice…" She gestured at herself.

We accepted this as an offer, and focused for an intense moment on the dual mounds of pleasure.

"Bertha?" Thurman suggested.

"Wilma?" Knob threw out.

"Dana?"

"Bob?"

"Bob?"

"Yeah, Bob."

"What about Bob?"
"Stop with the Bob, okay?"
She sighed heavily
We looked again.
Because we're guys.
But it's normal.
So it's okay.

"Oh, just call me Warrior for now," she said, resigned. "Maybe we can come up with something better on the road."

Slurp, slurp.

We all looked for the offending noise. Well, not all of us. Knob wasn't, because he was making it.

"What?" he said, when he noticed us glowering at him.

"What are you doing?" I demanded.

"I'm thirsty."

"Put that damned thing away, and get a glass," I snapped.

With a put-upon look, he stuffed the lemon moist towellette back into his sack, and went into the kitchen, pouting.

Ten minutes later, we were stuffed in the Warrior's two-year old SUV. Not stuffed because there were so many of us, but stuffed because there were so many kid toys. After kissing her brood goodbye, she had mounted the SUV with a grimly satisfied look that said she was going to enjoy her time away, no matter what.

"Where to, Kemosabe?" she said cheerfully.

"Where else? The phone company," I replied.

"Which one? Ameritech, Sprint, Verizon, AT&T, MCI, SBC, Bell…"

"Uh, how about just going to the one out on Plank Road?" Knob suggested.

She pulled out of the drive.

"What's that?" I asked, looking at a line of circular smudges on the windshield on the passenger side.

The Warrior blushed prettily. "Oh, those are mine."

"Huh?"

"Toe prints. I put my feet up there when Jim's driving."

"Oh."

"I've been wondering something," Thurman said.

"What?"

"Well, if the telemarketers are the only ones ever using our phones, don't you think it would be in their own interests to pay our phone bill?"

"Huh?"

"How do you know they wouldn't?" Knob said from the back. We couldn't see him, because he was buried under a mound of youth hockey equipment.

"What do you mean?" Thurman asked.

"I mean, how do we know that our phone would get cut off? They always threaten to, but what if we didn't pay? Would they turn us off?"

"Interesting."

"And if they did cut us off, how would the telemarketers respond? Maybe they would pay for it to be reconnected. Otherwise, they would lose the ability to contact us at all."

"Yeah," Thurman said. "How do we know that the phone companies and telemarketers don't have some kind of deal going?"

I was getting scared. Not of the telemarketers, but because Knob and Thurman were making sense, which doesn't happen very often.

Chapter Six

The phone company was on the other side of town, so we took the entrance ramp for the highway. At the merge, the Warrior checked her rear view mirror, and slowed uncertainly. A solid wall of semi-trucks and cars was hurtling down the highway at better than eighty miles per hour. There was no way to merge or squeeze on. Turn signal on, we were stalled on the entrance ramp, cars idling impatiently behind us.

Finally, an oncoming semi slowed, blinked its turn signals, and pushed its way into the next lane, opening a spot for us.

The Warrior jammed her foot on the accelerator, and swung into the spot created by the semi. As we sped up, the semi passed us. There was an 800 number on back, with a message saying to call it with any comments.

The Warrior pulled out her car phone, and quickly dialed.

"I love doing this." She grinned.

"Hello," a gruff voice answered, probably expecting yet another complaint. His voice carried, and I could hear him from my seat.

"Hi," she said cheerfully. "I'm calling about truck number thirty-four."

"Yeah?" the voice said warily. I'm sure her cheerfulness was throwing him. He was probably trying to recognize the unfamiliar tone, which usually only comes at him when he's ordering a Big Mac.

"I just want to tell you that truck number thirty-four is very polite and considerate," she said.

"Huh?"

"Yes. He let me merge into traffic, and was very helpful. I thought you guys should know this, and maybe give him a certificate of appreciation or something."

"Um, okay, we'll make a note of it," he said, his gruff voice croaking awkwardly into pleasant mode.

"Okay, have a great day," she chirped, and punched off.

I sat in my seat, wondering about our warrior.

"When does it kick in?" I asked, after a few moments of silence.

She frowned. "When does what kick in?"

"Your power. The, eh, PMS thingy."

She turned her head, and gazed at me levelly. "Do you want it to kick in?"

I heard a dual intake of breath behind me.

"No, no, no! Don't misunderstand. But if we're going to need your powers I think we should have an idea of when you can use them," I said hastily.

"Yeah, you're right." She sighed. "Sorry, I'm kind of sensitive about it because there's a price that I have to pay for that power."

"A price?"

"Yeah, I feel like shit all the time. I feel good right now, and frankly, I'm not really looking forward to feeling like shit again."

"Yeah, I guess I can understand that."

"You can? How can you possibly relate to how I feel for almost half the month?"

"Uh…"

"Did you ever spit an entire baby out of an opening the size of a fifty-cent piece?" her voice rose.

"Uh…"

"Do you ever get bloaty and have your ankles swell up so bad you can't even put on your shoes?" It rose higher still.

"Uh…"

"Does *your* stomach ever pooch out like you're three months pregnant, because you're retaining five pounds worth of water?"

"Do *you* have to carry around and use mini sponges to staunch heavy bleeding for more than a quarter of *your* life?"

"Do *you* get headaches and body aches, and no matter how crappy *you* feel still have to wait hand and foot on a lazy husband and a bunch of kids who treat dropped socks like they're poisonous snakes?"

"AAAAHHH! Make her stop!" Knob screamed, holding his head with both hands.

She stopped her tirade, breathing heavily.

There were a few moments of saturated silence, punctuated by the sounds of her breathing, and the rest of us holding our breath.

Our exit came up, and silently she pulled off the highway, then turned onto Eightieth Avenue.

Finally she broke the silence, "Damn." Then she fell silent again.

We guys were hurriedly conjuring Harry Potter invisibility spells.

She sighed. "Well, I guess you can tell it's on its way."

She pulled into the parking lot of the phone company and rolled to a stop, where we sat quietly, collecting our thoughts and bracing ourselves for whatever would come next.

The building was low and squat, bereft of soul. Likewise, the reception area was dismal, gloomy, as heartless and lifeless as a driver's education facility, an unemployment office, or the heart of a cop trying to make his ticket quota. I actually felt the happiness and joy get sucked out of me as soon as I entered. An oppressive weight bearing down on my back made me slouch to where the air level was stale and barely life-sustaining. Dampened silence loomed heavily over the room, clamping my head with invisible tendrils.

"Can I help you?" the toad-faced woman said at the counter, in a tone that made it clear that it would give her no pleasure at all to assist you in anything.

A fly went buzzing by the open door, saw us, and invited itself in.

The toad-faced woman saw it, and her wide mouth parted in a hungry smile.

The fly hastily U-turned, and buzzed back out before the door could close.

The receptionist, her face lined with disappointment, sighed and turned bulbous eyes back to our little group.

"Can we see the Manager?" I asked.

"If you came to get your phone turned back on, see Ms. Waite in the far corner," the toad said, pointing with stubby fingers behind us.

I looked back, and saw a harpy-like creature sitting behind an ugly green utility desk. A sign on the desk said, "Our Credit Manager is Helen Waite. If you are here to have your phone turned back on, go to Helen Waite."

Shuddering, I turned back.

"We need to see the Manager," I said stoutly.

"Why?"

"Never you mind," Knob said aggressively.

"In that case, the manager is out," the toad said, her voice dripping disdain.

"Look, let us see him, and I'll feed you a nice juicy worm," I said.

Well, I would have said it if I had any guts. And I think it would have worked.

But before I could say anything else, there was a low voiced growl below and behind me.

I turned around, and saw the Warrior. Her face was almost unrecognizable. Gone was the sweet, pretty cherubic face that had been such pleasant company. Her complexion had gone scarlet, and veins pulsated on her swollen neck. Her arms and breasts had swelled to mammoth proportions, and she looked as dangerous as a huge pimple about to burst at the dinner table.

"YOU WILL LET US IN," she said. Her voice was gravelly and dangerous, but was borne by a force not seen since the second episode of Star Wars.

The toad visibly wilted under the pressure of the Warrior's force of will. "In t-t-th-there-r," she said, shaking violently, pointing to a door in the back of the room.

The Warrior stomped towards the door, menace radiating from her like physical wave.

We were swept into her wake as she opened the door without knocking and stepped in.

She stopped abruptly, and I plowed into her from behind.

Then I plowed into her again because Knob plowed into me.

Then I plowed into her again when Thurman plowed into Knob, who plowed Knob back into me again.

Then there was a fourth generation plowing, so subtle that I immediately forgot it.

But then I saw why the Warrior had stopped.

The room was huge, with an enormous mahogany desk and magnificent furnishings. A plate glass window took up almost the entire wall behind it, and the sun was streaming into the room, illuminating a figure who stood motionless. Rays of light filtered through filmy clothes that swirled like in a bad Celine Dion music video.

"Whoa..." Knob said, slowly.

"Whoa..." I said, just as slowly, but, in my opinion, much more manly.

There was a woman standing in front of the window with her back to us.

And what a back it was, too. Delicious curves that portrayed the female body in a way that made mere cartoons of normal women.

I didn't even notice the heavy klonk behind us as we shuffled slowly towards the lovely vision.

The swirling clothes furled seductively from some hidden wind that was not in evidence, casting shadows and flickering glimpses of a magnificent nude body that could dimly be imagined through the sun-filtered clothes.

I would have said "whoa" again, but was rendered speechless, mostly because my jaw had fallen to somewhere around chest level.

Next to me, Knob whimpered, mute testimony to his inability to speak.

The figure began to turn, full bosoms like ripe buds ready to bear fruit.

Auburn tresses gleamed in the sun, having stolen flame from envious Sun Gods themselves.

She finished her slow revolution, turning her full visage at my gaping face.

KLONG!

The metallic clanging sound was that of my expectations thudding to the ground.

From behind, the woman had been a vision of loveliness, of unsurpassable beauty and grace.

But when she turned around, it was as if excrement had taken human form.

She, if it was indeed a she, had the most ghastly visage known to man. Or dog. Or to any other known animal, beast or monster. Frankenstein would have turned up his nose to this thing and maybe lost his dinner. Saggy breasts drooped towards the floor, which quailed in fear that they might actually descend to it. Wattles started somewhere under the chin, climbing like a leprous growth towards a grotesque protrusion that was either a caricature of a smashed potato or a hideous nose. Knobby, wrinkled knees were barely defined from horrid thighs, where muscle had given up the fight to cellulite and ropey veins.

I shuddered, and bile rose in my throat in what surely was an effort to flee my body because my eyesight would not spare me.

Beside me, I could hear Knob gagging down vomit.

We were frozen to the spot, and the horrible creature started approaching.

We knew we faced death, or something else as bad as foot odor.

Then Thurman, who had fainted, or, um, passed out—guys don't faint—feebly raised his head, and rasped though dry cracking lips, "Quick…" he paused to pant, "…raise…" another pant, "…yrrr…youuu…your…sssshhieldss!"

Of course! Our Shields of Stupidity! A guy's best defense against anything female!

Forcing myself to relax, I let my brain wander, and focused on thinking about sports. Any kind of sports.

Aahhhh…S P O R T S…aaaahhh!

Major League Baseball…The Final Four…munchies…Super

Bowl Sunday...

My eyes began to glaze over as my brain began to slip into the wondrous vacuum that belonged only to guys and sports.

The creature balked at the power of our shields, and faltered, eyes blazing frustrated hot demon fire at us.

I hardly noticed as a parade of NFL quarterbacks, past and present flashed tantalizingly through my mind: Bret Favre, Peyton Manning, Michael Vick, John Elway...

"It's working!" Knob shouted.

"Keep doing it!" Thurman exulted.

Then the creature lashed back by beginning a slow pirouette.

As she swirled, my mind peeked around the Shield, because it saw something that I did not yet see. Flabby breasts beginning to firm, to fill and jiggle in fullness and wonderfulness. White neck, blending into wide shoulders that tapered to a slim, athletic waist, before flaring outward in womanly curves. High, firm buttocks, over toned legs and shapely calves. The sunlight caressed her beautiful figure with...

"Whoa..." I said, my jaw loose with lust.

"Whoa..." Knob said, his tone that of awe and wonder.

"Whoa..." Thurman breathed, his voice raspy with desire.

"......." Seth said, his mind still not yet returned.

But the creature kept spinning, and we saw her front.

"Aaahhhh!"

"Aaahhhh!"

"Aaahhhh!"

"........."

Then she spun again, and we saw her delectable backside.

"Whoa..."

"Whoa..."

"Whoa..."

"......."

And again the front.

"Aaahhhh!"

"Aaahhhh!"

"Aaahhhh!"

"........."

The back.

"Whoa…"
"Whoa…"
"Whoa…"
"………"
The front.
"Aaahhhh!"
"Aaahhhh!"
"Aaahhhh!"
"..ᴧ……"

"What the hell!" another voice said angrily.

Strong fingers grabbed my arm, and jerked me backwards, hurtling me completely through the doorway.

As I stumbled into the lobby, Knob and Thurman skidded to a halt next to me, dazed looks on their faces. They had also been catapulted from the room of horror. Thurman fell to his knees, and sobbed.

The toad-faced woman-thing lay face down on the floor. A crowd of heretofore listless customers were silently applauding at her demise, still unsure whether she might regain consciousness and spitefully stick some long distance charges on their bills.

Behind us, in the room, there was the sound of furniture crashing and splintering, and the splatting sound of a body being hurled through a plate glass window.

Then the Warrior reappeared, grasping Seth's unresisting hand.

Her eyes quickly scanned the room, searching for other adversaries. Then she ordered, "All right, let's go. There's nothing here for us. This was a trap."

I hauled Thurman back to his feet, and we staggered for the door, the Warrior taking up rear guard.

A fly batted up against my face, and I shooed it away.

We stumbled out to the SUV, and clambered in. The engine roared, and the wheels spun in the granite as we shot out of the parking lot.

As the ugly beige building fell behind, the Warrior asked, "Okay, guys, where next?"

"McDonald's," Knob suggested. "I really have to have a Big Mac."

"Yeah," Thurman said, "I gotta recharge."

A chocolate shake was calling to me, so I nodded my head vigorously. Nothing like a good scare to work up an appetite.

"Sounds good to me," the Warrior said grimly. "I get the munchies really bad when I'm menstruating."

"Ohh. Maybe I'm not really hungry," Knob groaned.

Thurman turned ashen.

She ignored them, and headed for the golden arches.

Chapter Seven

Later, as we sat at a table surrounded by french fries, Kids Meal toys, and paper napkins, I asked the Warrior, "So, what do you mean about it being a trap?"

She looked up from her fish sandwich, tartar sauce on her cheek. She didn't look like a warrior now. Though what she had turned into in the phone company had been conclusive about her abilities.

"They knew we were coming," she said, with no hesitancy.

"So what, is there a spy amongst us?" Knob asked, glaring suspiciously at Thurman and me.

"Shut up," I said to him.

"Here ya go," said Thurman, carefully putting a french fry on the floor.

"Dude, you don't have a dog!" Knob remonstrated.

"Shut up," Thurman shot at him. "Or I'll tell him to bite you on the ass."

Knob gave a look of mock concern. "Oh, no, what am I going to do?"

"Shut up, both of you," I growled.

"Hey, what's this?" Knob said, the argument forgotten. He was poking at his Big Mac wrapper.

"What is it?" Thurman asked.

"Check it out!" Knob held the wrapper up for us to see.

On the side of the wrapper was a warning label that read "Caution, sandwich is warm and sloppy. Spillage may cause you to get stuff all over yourself, causing great emotional distress and dry-cleaning bills."

"Wow! Those attorneys really work fast," Thurman said, flipping another french fry onto the floor.

I looked at the floor, and sure enough, the first fry was gone.

I gave it a double take. Nah, couldn't be.

Shrugging, I turned back to the Warrior. "So, how do you think they knew we were coming?"

"Don't know," she said, shrugging back at me. She swallowed the last of her sandwich, and slurped some Coke. Or Pepsi, or whatever caffeinated cola that McDonald's chains use.

"But," she continued, "they are aware of us, and at least slightly worried."

"What was that creature?" Knob asked, worriedly.

"Something from the depths of Hell," Thurman breathed.

"That could be," the Warrior said, unconcerned. "It certainly wasn't anything from around here."

"Maybe it came from New York," Knob wondered.

"Yeah, there are some pretty strange things out there," she said.

We Chicago natives nodded our heads in agreement. After all, we're normal. Thurman flipped another french fry at his invisible ghost dog.

"So, what next?" Knob asked.

The Warrior looked meaningfully at me. Obviously, it was up to me, as the Unbeliever and semi-elected leader, to plan out our next course of action.

"We have to go to their Regional Headquarters, I guess," I said, my brain working quickly.

"What kind of monsters do you think they have there?" Thurman said, a stricken look on his face.

"Doesn't matter," I said grimly, "they have my brother's brain."

A few minutes later, we were done and headed back to the

SUV. As we were pulling out, the smoked driver's and passenger's side windows came down on a silver Grand Pricks, er, Prix, that had been parked next to us.

Then, a McDonald's bag of trash and cup were flipped out of both windows simultaneously.

There was a garbage can just ten feet from its front bumper.

Assholes, I thought to myself.

"Assholes," Knob muttered.

"Assholes," Thurman agreed.

"ASSHOLES!"

The SUV shook, and I gasped as I saw the Warrior leap towards the Grand Prix. Startled, I looked over to see who was driving.

Nobody!

The door was wide open, and the SUV was still in gear and rolling slowly towards the drive-through window. I could hear a tinny voice saying, "Hello, can I take your order?" as we rolled on past.

Quickly, I grabbed the wheel, and pulled us back towards the middle of the lot. A fly buzzed up against my face, then darted out the window.

"Wow! Look what she's doing!" Knob exclaimed behind me.

"Cool. I've always wanted to do that," Thurman exulted.

"......" Seth added.

I heard a bunch of angry yelling behind me. It sounded a little like the Warrior, but I didn't know she knew those words.

I worked my foot over, and managed to push the brake. Then I turned off the ignition, and looked behind me.

The Grand Pricks was closed tightly, windows up, sunroof and doors closed and locked. Exhaust fumes testified that the car was still idling. But they weren't going anywhere, because blocking their exit stood the Warrior, a menacing glower darkening her face.

"What happened?" I asked, frustrated that I'd missed whatever my roommates had witnessed.

"It was cool," Knob said.

"Yeah, you should have seen it," Thurman added.

"Okay, it was cool," I said, exasperated, "but what happened?"

"Well, she jumped out," Knob said.

"Yeah, I noticed," I said glumly.

"...then she ran over to them, and picked up all the garbage they dumped out of their car," Thurman picked up.

"...and then she unwrapped the garbage, so that all the ketchup and stuff was exposed," Knob exclaimed.

"And she dumped the whole thing on top of them through the sunroof," they chorused.

"And now they won't come out," Knob finished.

"I'm glad she's on our side," Thurman said.

The door opened, and the Warrior hopped back in, calm and composed again. "Okay, boys, let's go."

As we pulled out, I heard a noise that made me freeze.

A huge THUMP!

Chapter Eight

"What was that?" the Warrior exclaimed, fighting the wheel. The noise was so loud that the shock wave rattled the SUV.

"I don't know," Knob screamed.

THUMP!

"It's that whatever-it-was that smashed our cars!" Thurman shouted.

The engine roared as the Warrior jammed down the accelerator.

I looked through the back window, and the Grand Prix was gone, flattened. Frantically, I looked all over, trying to see what had done it. A small crowd gathered to applaud its demise.

THUMP!

The McDonald's green dumpster smashed behind us.

"What the hell?" the Warrior said, her eyes darting back and forth.

"It's after us!" Knob yelled.

"What is?" I yelled back.

"I don't know!" he yelled in answer.

"So how do you know that it's an It?" I yelled again.

"I don't know, but something's happening!" he yelled again.

We yelled a few more things at each other, but the bottom line was that we knew something was attacking us, but not how, not why, and not identified. But yelling made us feel better.

THUMP!

The pavement buckled, the force of the blow rocking the SUV wildly.

The Warrior fought for control.

Something black and huge slammed to the ground again, taking another giant chunk out of the road behind us. All six cylinders were screaming as the Warrior coaxed what RPM's she might out of the family vehicle. We were only up to forty or fifty miles per hour.

THUMP!

That one was a little further behind us.

THUMP!

As we speeded up, the thumping fell further and further behind.

"Wow, didja see that?" Knob said over the thumping, which was starting to sound more frustrated than angry as it receded into the distance.

"What is it?" Thurman yelled, his face pushed against the rear window.

"I don't know," Knob answered in wonder. "It looked like a big round tornado or something."

"What are you guys talking about?" I said, trying to peer past them through all the toys behind me.

"I see it," the Warrior said, looking through her side view mirror.

"What is it?" I said.

"I dunno. Looks like a big round tornado or something," she said.

"That's what I said," Knob said.

They weren't making any sense. "How about it, Thurman? What do you see?" I asked him.

"I'm not sure. It looks like, I don't know…maybe, like a big round tornado or something."

"That's what I said," Knob said again.

"Me, too," the Warrior confirmed.

Straining, I couldn't quite see what was going on behind us. I could see people milling around the dumpster and the big holes in the ground, but I couldn't see anything like a big round tornado or something.

"Well, whatever it is, I think we lost it," the Warrior said, a grim look of satisfaction on her face.

"Man, that was cool," Knob enthused.

"Yeah, looked like a science fiction show or something," Thurman said.

"George Lucas-like."

"Fantastic special effects."

"Reminded me of Jurassic Park."

"Yeah, kind of dark, like the third one."

I interrupted their little chat, "Would one of you guys tell me what you think you saw?"

They both started at once, "Yeah, it…"

"It was the…"

"Stop it! Just one of you! Knob?"

Knob shot a triumphant look at Thurman. "Like I was trying to say, before I was interrupted—"

"Hey!" Thurman protested.

"It was like a tornado or something."

"You said that," I gritted.

"Well, what I mean, is, uh—"

Thurman interrupted, "It was swirling, black and gray. But it was round—"

Knob interrupted back in, "It was like somebody grabbed a tornado, squished it into a ball—"

Thurman jumped back in, "And it came down straight from the sky—"

"And whammed into the ground," Knob shot, glaring at Thurman.

"That's what I saw, too," the Warrior said calmly into the silence of Knob and Thurman shooting eye darts at each other.

"So, what…" I said thoughtfully, "there's some kind of killer,…cloud, or…something, chasing after us?"

"Yep, that's about it," Knob chimed in.

"Why would a cloud be after us?" I wondered.

"Maybe it's mad because we, uh, use umbrellas and stuff…" Knob said, his voice trailing off in confusion.

"Maybe the telemarketers have something to do with it?" Thurman suggested hopefully.

"What would telemarketers and clouds have in common?" Knob said, eager to shoot Thurman down.

"What would you know?" Thurman sneered. "You can't even see ghost dogs. Maybe you didn't even really see the cloud."

"Was it a cloud? Or something else?" the Warrior asked.

"Yeah, the more I think about it, the more I think it was a cloud. More compact though, and way blacker."

"I've seen black clouds before," Thurman said, his anger already ebbed. He usually doesn't stay angry long.

"How come clouds don't fall to the ground anyway?" Knob wondered out loud.

"Yeah, don't they weigh, like a trillion tons or something?" Thurman said.

"I've always wondered about that," the Warrior mused, "how clouds float up there, filled with millions of gallons of water, but they never fall to the ground."

"Maybe they don't want to," I said quietly.

We were all quiet for a moment, considering the implications of my statement.

"Clouds can think?" Knob said, an incredulous look on his face.

"Hey, maybe clouds can come down. Maybe that's what fog is!" Thurman said.

"So you think maybe one of those clouds just got it into his head—"

"Or her head," the Warrior interjected.

"Oh, okay, 'his' or 'her' head." Knob looked to the Warrior for approval, then continued, "To come down and wipe out all of our cars and house and lunch, and chase us down the road?"

"I guess it does sound kind of silly when you put it like that," I said.

"But what other explanation is there? Are these things landing all over the place?" Thurman wondered.

"Maybe it's an alien cloud, from another planet."

"Alien cloud?" The Warrior frowned.

"Yeah, it floated through space searching for the right planet with the right atmosphere or something."

"So it came here and decided to crunch cars for fun?" I shot at him.

Thurman looked defensive. "Well, maybe it was all mad when it found out how polluted it is here, so it's going to wipe out all the cars on the planet."

"So what's it got against our house, then?" I asked.

"It did seem like it was concentrating just on us," Knob said, his forehead creased with thought.

"We pissed it off somehow, that's for sure," Thurman agreed after a moment.

"How does it keep finding us?" I wondered aloud.

"I don't know, and I don't care," the Warrior said, "as long as we can keep ahead of it."

"Where are we headed?" Knob asked.

"We're going to their downtown headquarters," the Warrior answered, swinging us onto the entrance ramp for I-55.

"How do you know where it is?" I asked her.

She shot me an amused look. "I did a little digging before I trashed the office back there."

"Oh."

We drove mostly in silence for the next half-hour. The fates were kind to us, and there wasn't any construction to contend with. Not that there weren't construction zones, with orange and black signs, and other signs with childish writing saying, "Please don't speed, my daddy works here." But traffic was light, and there weren't actually any crews, so we were able to move along at the speed limit of twenty miles an hour over the speed limit. We stayed in the slow lanes. We were in Chicago, after all. Actually going the speed limit could get you killed, especially if the person who rams into you from behind is going thirty over the speed limit.

As we got closer to downtown, we could already see the Sears Tower with its twin white antenna, though it was still ten miles away. It towered over the other buildings like a teenager amongst toddlers. Still though, when compared with the vast blue sky above, I realized just how insignificant our monuments are when compared with nature. This, even though the top of the tower actually poked into a low-flying cloud. I wondered again about the cloud that had been pursuing us. What might it do if it caught up to us while we were in one of the skyscrapers?

We took the Washington Street exit, and went east towards the lake and downtown. I watched the pedestrians avidly. People are weird, I decided, but definitely fun to watch.

The Warrior pulled into a parking garage off Wells, and we rode the spiral drive to the higher floors. After parking, we got into an elevator to go to the ground floor, first noticing that we parked on the Greece level. Greek music floated about us. There were also floors dedicated to the Chinese, French, German, each with piped in music from that country.

"Dude! I gotta check out Spain," Knob said, jabbing the button for that floor.

"Hey, the United States is here, too. Let's go there," Thurman enthused, pushing that button.

"Stop it," I said. "We aren't here to sightsee a parking garage."

Of course, I was too late. Since they'd pushed all the buttons, we got to visit each of the floors before we finally got back to the bottom.

I really like my roommates, but sometimes they aren't the sharpest tools in the bathroom.

We finally got to the bottom. Oh, and I know you'd want to know. The United States floor plays Bruce Springsteen's "Born in the USA." Somehow, I had a feeling that song would be stuck in my mind for the rest of the day.

"We have to go to Madison," the Warrior said, consulting her paper. With her powers subsided she looked like any other pretty Chicago pedestrian.

We strolled south on Wells, gawking at the bustle of people and merchandise. As always, I regretted not finding reasons to come downtown more often. At the same time, I knew I was unlikely to come more often. Still, though, a very nice place to visit.

A homeless man stood on the corner, handing out literature. Knob took one, and started reading avidly. I handed the guy a dollar.

"I wouldn't do that," Thurman said.
"Why not?"
"Some of those guys aren't homeless at all. They make more money than I do by pretending."
"You don't make any money!"
"I do too. What do you call the pizza delivery stuff?"
"Slavery. You don't get paid squat."
"Tips, man, that's where you get the real money."
"You don't get tips. You always get lost, and end up delivering cold pizzas. Who's going to tip you for that?"
Thurman looked wounded. "I'm getting better."
"Hey," Knob interrupted, "this says that eighty-five cents of every dollar donated goes to the people that are supposed to benefit."
"Is that good?" Thurman asked.
"Yeah," Knob said. "I heard the United Way is only around fifty cents, or so. The rest goes into administrative stuff, and salaries or something."
"Wow. So Guy just gave eighty-five cents to the people who need it." Thurman gave me an approving look.
"Here it is," the Warrior said, totally unimpressed with our conversation. I guess fighters have to have focus.
The building had two flags on both sides of the entrance. We stood before the revolving doors, and looked up.
"Man, that's got to be sixty floors," Knob said, his head tipped back so far it was almost horizontal. I hoped it might give his brain a little extra oxygen.
We pushed our way through the revolving doors into the lobby.
Knob and Thurman took a couple extra revolutions before staggering out, laughing crazily.
Guess the oxygen didn't help.
The Warrior crossed over to a directory on the wall, which listed the businesses and their floors.
I stood behind her, humming.
"Stop it," she said, not turning around.
I stopped humming "Born in the USA", and stood uncomfortably, trying to think about anything except "Born in the

USA", but I couldn't, because all I could think about was "Born in the USA", and I couldn't get any other song in my mind, because it was all cluttered with Springstein singing "Born in the USA", over and over again.

Slurp!

"Stop it," the Warrior said again, still intent on the directory.

I looked back at Knob. He had a lemon-flavored moist towelette in his mouth.

He took it out, and looked apologetic. "Sorry, I got thirsty."

I was born in the USA.

"Okay, let's go," the Warrior said, and started towards the elevators.

"Where we going?" Thurman asked, pulling at an imaginary leash. I guess it's okay to bring a dog if the security people couldn't see it.

"Does he poop?" I asked him, struck by the thought.

"Huh?"

"Weezel. Does he poop out ghost poop?"

"Don't mock me!"

"I'm not mocking you," I assured him. "I'm curious."

He stared at me, gauging my sincerity.

"Yes, of course he poops. He eats, so why wouldn't he poop?"

"Oh. So we wouldn't, like, step in it, would we?" I asked, fixing a concerned expression on my face.

He studied me again.

"Yes. You step in it all the time," he said. "But since it's from the Other Side, your corporeal matter doesn't come in contact with the matter that makes up his excrement."

"Oh."

We stopped at the elevators and stepped into the first empty one.

The building was so high, that there are two sets of elevators. The first goes from the first floor to the twenty-ninth, then you have to get out, and walk down a corridor to another bank of elevators that will take you to any floor higher than the twenty-ninth.

We rode up in silence. The elevator was plush, with deep burgundy carpet, and lots of mirrors, gold trim and exquisitely carved cherry wood panels.

Born in the USA. I was...born in the USA. I was...born in the USA...

At the twenty-ninth floor, we shuffled out of the elevator and followed signs that directed us to the other set of elevators

"What floor are we looking for," Knob asked the Warrior.

"The thirtieth," she said, walking up and punching the 'up' button. Immediately one of the gilded doors slid open. We filed in and assumed elevator riding positions.

The door slid closed, but the Warrior didn't push a button. She stood, looking at the buttons, a puzzled frown on her face.

"Waddup?" Knob asked her when she didn't move.

"That's strange," she said thoughtfully. "There is no button for the thirtieth floor."

"Huh?" I asked.

"The thirtieth floor, there's no button."

"No button?"

"No button."

I leaned past her considerable bosom, and peered. At her bosom, that is. I couldn't help it. I'm a guy. So it's normal.

She cleared her throat.

Hastily, I redirected my gaze, and looked at the buttons. She was right. The next floor was the thirty-first, then the thirty-second, et cetera.

"Maybe it's a misprint," Thurman suggested.

"Maybe they don't have a thirtieth floor," Knob put in. "You know, like some buildings don't have a thirteenth floor."

"Yeah, maybe the workers got thirteen and thirty mixed up," Thurman offered.

"Then why would they have listed it downstairs?" the Warrior asked.

"And how would anybody else get there?" Knob added.

"Maybe they don't want visitors," Thurman said.

"Okay, let's check it out," I said.

"What do you want to do?" the Warrior asked me.

"Let's, uh, go on up to the next floor, and see for sure if it's the thirtieth, or the thirty-first."

"Sounds like a plan to me," she said approvingly.

I met her eyes for a second, then did a double take. They were still blue. Still pretty. But, for a moment, I thought I'd caught a flash of a reddish glow.

She looked back at me evenly. No sign of the glow now. I averted my eyes, and made like I had to rub something out of them.

The elevator lurched, and we were lifted up to the next floor.

The doors swished open with a swishy sound, and our little group all moved out into the hallway. Thurman had assigned himself to Seth, and they were holding hands like kindergartners. I hoped no one would misinterpret this. I swept my eyes towards the Warrior. Then again, after that McDonald's thing, I knew it would hurt them more than it would hurt us if anyone decided to make an issue of it.

We followed the Warrior down the corridor towards the first suite of offices. The first one was an accounting office, numbered 3101. Without entering, we walked to the next. The attorney firm of Stein, Weinstein, and Rubenstein, Esq. A sense of foreboding seemed to pulsate from the door.

We all backed away several steps.

"What's 'Esq.' mean?" Knob asked, peering nervously through the opaque glass windows.

"Esquire," the Warrior said absently, searching intently down the darkened hallway. Once again, I thought I caught a red glow in her eyes, but when she looked back, it was gone.

"Esquire? What's that?" Thurman asked.

"I don't know." She shrugged, her attention still on the corridor. She was in fighting mode. That relaxed tenseness that came with being readied for action at any moment.

"Hang on," Knob said. Then he pulled out his knapsack, and rifled through it. "Ah, here it is."

"You brought a dictionary?" I said.

"Yeah, you never know when you're going to need one."

"You don't need a dictionary."

"Oh, yeah, do you know what an esquire is?" he shot back, flipping through the e's.

"What's it matter?"

He paused in his flipping, and looked at me with a serious

gaze. "Look, can I help it if I don't want to go through life not knowing stuff, simply because I refuse to put a little effort into looking it up?"

I didn't really have an answer for that.

"Here ya' go," he said. "An esquire is a candidate for knighthood, acting as attendant and shield-bearer for a knight."

"That's not it," I said, grabbing the book from him. "Here," I jabbed at the book, "it's this other definition, a ceremonial title of courtesy used for lawyers."

There was a sound behind us, and Thurman yelped something incoherent.

Chapter Nine

The elevator door had opened again, and two men and a woman, dressed crisply in business suits, briskly disembarked, and headed our way, speaking some foreign language on separate cell phones. We backed away, clearing a path to the door of the attorney office.

"All previous encumbrances are preferred to the extent of the value at the time of the making of the contract…"

"But the rules of committee on malfeasance are clearly stipulated…"

"We all know that the Defendant may make any defense by way of counter claim that he could in any civil action, and have the same right on proof of such in excess of the claim…"

Without sparing us a single glance, they swept by, intent on their phone conversations, and through the glass doors. The sounds of torts faded away as the door closed.

"Wow! What were those?" Thurman breathed.

"I think they are Esquires," Knob said, his eyes wide with awe.

"What were they saying?" Thurman asked.

"I don't know," I said. "I think they were speaking Attorney-Speak."

"Oh. Attorney-Speak," Knob said, nodding his noggin.

"I thought I recognized some of the words," Thurman said, a puzzled look on his face.

"We studied it back in school," I said. "It was developed solely for the purpose of confusing laypersons."

"What's a layperson?" Thurman wondered.

"Me. I'm a layperson," Knob said, a pleased look on his face.

"I like to lay around, sounds right to me," Thurman agreed.

"What's up with her?" Knob said, pointing at the Warrior.

I turned around. The Warrior had backed herself into a defensible position, in a ready fighting crouch. She was like a coiled spring, teeth bared, pink fingernail polish glinting threateningly. Now I could see for sure that her eyes definitely had a red tint to them. They were glowing with their own light in the dim corridor.

"You okay?" I asked worriedly, not daring to get any closer.

There was a moment, then she shook herself, like a lioness after keeping a hunting position too long.

"I'm okay," she said fourteen heartbeats later. I counted. Mostly because the thumping was so loud.

"Sorry," she added.

"What happened?" Thurman asked with concern.

"I don't know. It was weird." Her eyes looked a little glazed, but they were clearing rapidly. "When they came towards me, something came over me."

She had a faraway look on her face, like she was trying to remember something.

Her eyes were fading, but the red cast didn't go away entirely this time.

Knob approached her diffidently. "Um, Warrior, can I ask you something?"

"Yes, Knob."

"Well, I, um…"

"Go ahead," she urged.

"I…was kinda…wondering…"

"Knob, it's okay. Ask me whatever you want," she said.

He took a deep breath, steeled himself. "I just want to know if

I can be your esquire."

"Huh?"

"Esquire," I told her. "We just looked it up."

"Esquire?"

"Yeah," Knob enthused, "I want to be your esquire. You know, your attendant and shield-bearer."

"I don't have a shield—"

"That's okay! I'll do other stuff. Polish your armor, and—"

"I don't have armor—"

"No problem! I'll, like, open doors and stuff," he said, refusing to be distracted from his goal.

"Well, I guess that's okay—"

"That settles it, then! I'm your Esquire!" he said, puffing out his chest.

"Knob…" I said reprovingly.

"That's Knob, Esq. to you," he said looking at me disdainfully down his nose.

"Uh, Knob, I'm still the leader…"

"Oh, yeah, I forgot. You may call me, Knob," he said graciously. "But you," he shot at Thurman, "must call me Esquire."

"No problemo, Esquire," Thurman said, far more agreeably than I could have managed.

I sighed. "Okay, guys…and lady, uh, Warrior…let's get right back to it. We have to find the thirtieth floor."

With that, we reformed back into a group, and made our way down the hall.

When we got to the end of the hall, it branched to the right only, so we followed that way. Two more turns, and we were back at the elevators. All of the suites were in the thirty-one hundreds. Also, all of the suites were accounting firms, attorneys or financial investment companies.

"Now what?" Esquire Knob inquired.

"We knock," the Warrior said, advancing on the attorney office.

But as she approached it, some force seemed to prevent her from getting all the way to the door. Her eyes were glowing hotly again, and the struggle of trying to walk caused muscles and veins to erupt from her arms, neck and legs.

"What the…?" she gritted, trying to push her way through.

Knob walked around her easily. "Weird, man. It, like, keeps you away, but not me."

Thurman also found it easy to approach the attorney's office, even hauling Seth behind him. I didn't have any problem, either.

"Magic," Thurman enthused.

"It's not magic!" I shot at him.

"Is so," he said, sagely. "I'm our sorcerer, remember, and I have a sense for magic."

"You do not—"

"I don't know, he might be right." The Warrior had given up trying to fight her way through whatever it was that barred her path.

"There's no such thing as magic," I said hotly.

"Sure there is," Knob said.

"There is not," I argued.

"Why don't you believe in magic?" Thurman asked innocently.

"Because, uh…"

"Because you can't see it?" he asked.

"Uh, yeah, I've never—"

"Can you see wind?" he shot at me.

"Wind? Well, no, it's invisi—"

"But do you believe in wind?"

"Of course I believe—"

"So you believe in wind even though you can't see it, but you don't believe in magic because it's invisible?" he said, triumph on his face.

"Well, I…"

"He's got you there, champ," Knob said.

"Okay, okay, you win," I snapped.

"One of you guys is going to have to go in," the Warrior interrupted.

"I'll do it," I said, happy to find a way out of losing an argument. This was a totally new experience for me, losing an argument to Thurman.

I went to the door.

"Wait!" Knob shouted.

"What?"

He caught up to me, and studied the door carefully. "How do we know this isn't a trap?"

"A trap? How could it be a trap?"

"Well look at the facts. Something is physically keeping the Warrior out. Our best fighter. And whatever is doing it, is willing to let the rest of us in. Why?"

"I don't know," I admitted.

"Maybe it's...nah, I'm sure that's not it," the Warrior said, frowning with thought. I noticed that her eyes still were tinged with red.

"What?"

"I've had a few bad experiences with attorneys..." she began.

"Who could have a good experience with an attorney?" I laughed.

"No, seriously," she said seriously. "Look, see, Jim isn't my first husband."

"No?"

"I've had a couple, uh, bad experiences, and gotten divorced a couple times."

"A couple?"

"Okay, three times."

"You've been divorced twice?"

"Uh, no. Three times."

"You've been divorced *three times*?" This didn't compute. Sure, she got a little angry at times, but I couldn't see anything that would make her hard to live with. My eyes swept across her bosom. And I could think of a couple things that would make it easy to live with.

"Well, not really divorces," she amended, shooting an eye dart at my wandering eye.

Ouch. "Huh? What do you mean?"

"I'm Catholic."

Knob interrupted excitedly, "That's right! Catholics don't get divorced, right?"

"Our marriages get annulled," she agreed.

"Annulled?" Thurman asked.

"Yeah, like it didn't happen," Knob said, having consulted his dictionary again. "It means to do away with, put an end to, make no longer binding under the law."

"I don't get it," Thurman wondered, "why not simply get divorced?"

"Catholics aren't allowed to divorce," I said.

"Why not?" he asked, puzzled.

"It's a sin," Knob put in.

Thurman looked really confused. "Wait, I'm lost. Are Catholics allowed to live together without being married?"

"No, that's a sin," the Warrior answered.

"If someone is married for a while, and they decide to break it up, then they have the marriage…what is it?…annulled?"

"Right," Knob said.

"And if their marriage is annulled, it's like it never happened?"

"Essentially," the Warrior agreed.

"So, if the marriage is cancelled, like it had never happened, does that mean that they were living together instead of being married?"

"Uh…maybe, I guess…yeah," the Warrior said slowly, a troubled look on her face.

"And isn't that a sin?" he followed.

"Um…"

"And if they have children, does that mean—"

"I don't know," she shouted angrily. Muscles started shuffling and bunching, as the unmistakable signs of her Hulk-like transformation began to threaten.

Hastily, I interrupted, "Look, the Catholic faith has one of the most formative histories of all religions, arduously built by centuries of Popes, who create doctrine only after—"

"Isn't the Pope God's representative on Earth?" Thurman wondered.

"Uh, yeah," I agreed.

"Hey! Weren't there two Popes once?" Knob interjected.

"Well, uh…"

"That's right!" Thurman said excitedly. "I remember reading about the Great Chasm."

"Great Schism," I said, resigning myself to the turn the conversation had taken. I cast a covert glance at the Warrior. She was following the conversation, but seemed to have backed off going through transformation.

"Didn't the Hundred Year War resolve all that?" Knob asked.

"Hundred Year War?" Thurman wondered.

"Where are you getting this information?" I shot at Knob.

"Books, man."

"No." I sighed. "It was—"

"So who was in the Hundred Year War?" Thurman asked Knob, interested.

"The English and French," Knob told him. "It was about the same time when the French elected their own Pope."

"Ahh...the French," Thurman said, an enlightened look on his face.

"Yeah, the French," Knob agreed knowingly.

"Look," I said angrily, "the Great Schism had nothing to do with the Hundred Year War!"

"Oh, yeah?" Knob retorted. "Didn't both of them take place in the 1300's?"

"That was a coincidence."

"Wasn't the War of the Roses around then, too?" Thurman asked.

"No, I mean, yes...how do you...?"

"That didn't have anything to do with the French," Knob put in.

"No?"

"No, it was a civil war in England."

"Where are you getting all this stuff?" I asked Knob.

"England had a civil war?" Thurman asked, his eyes wide with wonder.

"Yes," Knob said, proud of his pupil.

"I thought the Civil War was our thing," Thurman said.

"Sure, we had one, but many countries have had civil wars," Knob told him.

"Wow!"

"Not only that, but revolutions, too."

"Really? Revolutions, too?"

"Yep, let's see," Knob ticked off his fingers, "there was the French Revolution, the Russian—"

"The Diet Revolution, Industrial Revolution and Earth's revolution," I put in.

"You mean we didn't make up these things?" Thurman asked, ignoring me.

"Nope. They were around way before we ever had ours," Knob said.

"This is cool. I didn't know history was so interesting."

"Look guys," I interrupted, "this history lesson is all well and good, but we have work to do."

"That's right, the Quest," Knob said.

"Yeah, the…Quest," I agreed. I turned back to the Warrior, "What were you starting to say about attorneys?"

"Well," she began, "during all of my, um…annulments," she shot a nasty look at Knob, who shrugged in defense, "I had a few, uh, run-ins with my…uh…ex-husbands' attorneys," she concluded.

"Run-ins?" I queried.

"Run-ins," she said, giving me a look that warned not to ask any more about it.

"Oh, okay, then, so what is—"

"I know! I know!" Knob shouted.

"What?"

"Maybe attorneys have some kind of force field, or something."

"Yeah," Thurman agreed. "Maybe it's a shield that keeps enemies out."

"She's not an enem—"

"Actually, yes, I am," she said. "I hate attorneys."

"Everybody hates attorneys," I said, confused.

"No, it's more than that," she disagreed. "I don't just hate attorneys. I *hate* them."

We were all silent for a moment, digesting this.

"Actually, I hate to admit it," I said, "but you guys might have something there." Clouds trying to kill us, double PMS warriors, I was starting to doubt my doubtfulness.

"Hey, is our Unbeliever coming around?" Knob enthused.

"Shut up," I said, without much force. "We still have to find the thirtieth floor."

I started thinking about attorneys, and their place in our world.

Congressmen and Senators are usually attorneys. Judges, by definition, are, as far as I know, attorneys. I know this wasn't always the case, but it certainly is now. The Supreme Court, charged with ruling on interpretation of our laws, are all judges, hence attorneys. Most of our Presidents are, or have been, attorneys. All three branches of the United States government are composed almost entirely of attorneys.

So attorneys run our government.

Why is this so troubling?

Attorneys introduce laws. Attorneys vote on those laws. By extension, attorneys are in charge of the largest and most powerful army in the world. Attorneys also dictate the policies that govern how our economic might is used and governed.

I remembered something that an attorney once said. A lower wattage bulb, but maybe a higher wattage thought.

Former Vice President Dan Quayle, who told the American Bar Association in a speech on August 13, 1991, that the nation had too many lawyers, once said, "We have allowed our legal system to distort and deny the role of faith in American life, and unfortunately it's had a harmful ripple effect."

Then again, the same guy followed this brilliant thought with these gems:

- "Our government, unlike many governments, and particularly the governments of where the people that founded this country came from, is a government that is derived from the people that consent to govern. The freedom that is based in the people that then elect their representative to represent them in a free, representative democracy that we have today."

And, if that wasn't enough:

- "It's a good Supreme Court. They're lawyers…they're judges…they're appointed for life." (August 10, 1992)

Appointed for life, huh?

Of course, as an attorney, he had a wonderful grasp of geography:

- "It's wonderful to be here in the great state of Chicago." (Ap. 30, 1991)
- "We have a firm commitment to Europe. We are part of Europe."
- "I love California. I practically grew up in Phoenix."

And a lawyer's typical take on the Economy:
- "If you listen to the news, read the news, you'd think we were still in a recession. Well, we're not in a recession. We've had growth; people need to know that. They need to be more upbeat, more positive..." (Oct. 91)

And on elections:
- "A low voter turnout is an indication of fewer people going to the polls."

The environment:
- "It isn't pollution that's harming the environment. It's the impurities in our air and water that are doing it."

"Uh, Guy?"

"Wha...?"

"Guy, are you all right?" Knob asked, a concerned look on his face.

"Do you know how many lawyers are in the United States?" I asked him dazedly.

"Huh?"

"Lawyers, in the United States."

"Uh, I don't know," he started shuffling through his backpack, looking for the right book.

"Never mind, I already know. It's three hundred seventy thousand."

"Huh?"

"There are three hundred seventy thousand attorneys in the American Bar Association."

"Three hundred seventy thousand?" he breathed.

"Yeah, as of 1995. There are probably quite a few more now. Plus support personnel, like paralegals, executive secretaries, and whatnot. Not to mention other attorneys that maybe aren't in the Bar anymore, for one reason or another."

"That's almost, like an army," he said, his eyes wide.

"Yes, it is," I said quietly.

He was silent for a moment, stunned by this thought.

"Are you wondering if maybe attorneys and telemarketers are working in cahoots, or something?" he said finally.

"I don't know."

"Look, we have to do something," the Warrior said.

"We have to chance it," I said, finally. "I don't see any choice here."

I took a deep breath, and pushed through the door into the attorney's office.

Chapter Ten

"May I help you?" the receptionist asked, flashing barracuda teeth at me. She was dressed all in black pinstripe and creases, the pallor of her white skin accentuated by slick hair, also black and creased.

"Yeah, uh, I need—"

"We specialize in torts, contract law and litigation, property law, and a wide array of commercial law," the vampire said brightly, white incisors set off by black lipstick.

"Well, I—"

"We don't handle criminal law, though we accept occasional pro bono cases," she continued, after having appraised my overall appearance more carefully.

"No, I don't need—"

"If you're here for the keys to the rest room, I'm sorry, but we only issue them to clients," she said, having mentally slid me further down her priority list.

"I'm just asking for directions!" I finally said forcefully.

"Oh, well, that is…" she said, nonplussed and non-minus'ed. "There was a directory down on the first floor."

"That's just it," I said, "the room I'm looking for, it's on the thirtieth floor."

She started, and one of her hands slid unobtrusively under the desktop like a white snake gliding into its hole. Ringing security? A nervous feeling tickled my gut, like how you feel when you learned that your roommates both just came down with the stomach flu, the same day you stuffed yourself with four cheese and sauerkraut brats.

"The thirtieth floor?" she said slowly.

I could recognize a stall when I saw it. Usually they were located in bathrooms.

"Look, I have to go." I started for the door.

"No, wait!" she called, grabbing futilely for me over her desk.

"ThanksalotIgottagoI'llfinditonmyown," I said, fumbling for the knob.

All of a sudden, she leaped over the desk with the lightning move of a teenager going for a ringing phone.

I yanked at the doorknob, and jammed my fingers as it opened on its own.

"Aahhh," I squeaked...

no, not squeaked...*screamed*...

no, no, not that either...I'm a guy, not a mouse or woman...

I *yelled*...

that's it...

I yelled dammit!

Like a man.

Yeah.

Bornnnn in the U S Aieee...

Suddenly, the Warrior leaped into the room, stopping the receptionist in her pointy heeled tracks. Somehow she had made it through the barrier.

With amazing reflexes, the receptionist spun to a halt, and kicked up with one of her feet. A stiletto-heeled shoe shrieked through the air at the Warrior, who contemptuously swatted it out of the air. It thudded into the wall, and stuck there, vibrating.

The receptionist kicked again, and another deadly spiked heel darted at the Warrior, who this time batted it away with a huge sword that had appeared out of nowhere. The shoe split in two, thudding against the wall on either side.

Where the hell had she gotten that sword? I scuttled backwards until I was against the wall, and hopefully out of weapons range.

The Warrior leaped forward thundering a battle cry, "TWENTY FOUR HOUR SALE!" She swept her mighty sword, blasting the receptionist's desk out of existence, but missed the receptionist, who back-flipped just out of range, landing athletically on a three-drawer filing cabinet.

The Warrior vaulted over the remnants of the desk, scattering pictures of what I thought had been the receptionist's family, but looked more like mini legal documents, and drove her sword, which I now recognized as one of those expandable umbrellas that fit in a purse, straight at the chest of the receptionist.

The receptionist twisted away like a mongoose evading a snake oil salesman, scooped up a legal brief and hurled it at our heroine. As the brief briefly distracted the Warrior, the vampire swiped viciously at her with a plaintiff's affidavit.

The Warrior wasn't affable about the affidavit, and parried the blow. Then, in the same motion, she swung her mighty blade of rain-repel in a rainbow arc, scattering torts and bankruptcy petitions that exploded like shrapnel through the office. I ducked as a Stipulation for Attorney's Fees thudded into the wall next to my face.

"Let's get out of here," the Warrior said, brandishing her sword at the receptionist, who was digging frantically through reclamations and reaffirmations, looking for something more potent, like a judgment or a writ or something.

I scampered through the door, the Warrior hot on my heels. We ran into Knob, Thurman and Seth.

"C'mon," I yelled, grabbing Thurman's sleeve. He was goggling at the receptionist's Goth-like makeup.

I heard a whooshing sound, and ducked as a motion for Contempt of Court whistled through where my head had been. It flew down the corridor ahead of us, searching another way to be served.

We pelted towards the elevators, dodging Orders for Relief and Priority Claims hurled at us by the angry receptionist.

"There they are," Thurman panted, as we neared the elevators.

Suddenly the doors opened, and three pinstriped suits stepped out, brandishing security interests.

We skidded into a course change, and ran down another corridor.

"Where now?" Knob managed.

I looked back at Thurman, and saw that Seth was slowing him down. Quickly, I grabbed Seth's other arm, and together we hauled Seth behind the Warrior and Knob, who were frantically searching the offices for escape or a hiding spot.

Behind us, we could hear the attorneys' creased suits whishing as they chased after us.

"Here," the Warrior said, stopping at the only unmarked door we'd seen.

Her sword sliced through the doorknob, and she kicked it open.

"Get in," she said, stepping past us to guard the doorway behind us.

I ran in after Knob, pulling Thurman and Seth behind me.

Behind me, I heard the attorneys' arrival, and the clash of sword against briefcases.

The only thing behind the door was a small staircase that went down. As we clattered to the next level, we discovered that it ended at another door.

"It's locked," Knob said, yanking at the doorknob.

We could hear the Warrior's battle cries up on the next level, as she fought off the attorneys, "YOU TRY TAKING CARE OF KIDS WHEN YOU'RE ALL CRAMPY!"

"YOU THINK WORKING AT HOME IS EASIER THAN WORKING IN AN OFFICE?"

"Wow, she fights dirty," Thurman exclaimed.

Knob was still pushing and kicking at the door, which wasn't budging.

"YOU EVER SHOPPED WITH A TODDLER?" she yelled, accompanied by the clang of her sword against shield.

"I'VE EARNED THESE SPIDER VEINS!" I heard a thump as an attorney fell to the floor.

"KETCHUP IS A FOOD GROUP!"
WHACK!

Another attorney fell.

There was a clatter of heels coming down the stairs, and Knob leaped out of the way just as the Warrior vaulted the last few stairs and slammed into the door.

The door burst open, and we quickly followed after her.

There was another corridor, this time without any offices. Just a gray door at the other end, fifty yards away, and a drinking fountain, halfway down.

We pelted down the hallway, wondering at the lack of offices.

At least I was wondering.

I don't know if the others were wondering.

But it made sense for them to wonder...

...since I was...

...so I figured they probably were.

Because if I were them, I would have...

...like I was.

If I'd have been them.

But I'm not, so all I could do is wonder...

...if they were wondering...

...like I was...

...about the offices...

...or lack of offices.

The Warrior ran down the hallway in front of us, brandishing her umbrella before her.

Suddenly I slammed into Knob, who stopped abruptly at the drinking fountain. The Warrior ran on ahead.

"What are you *doing*?" I yelled at him.

"You were right," he panted, out of breath.

I quickly looked behind us. The attorneys were not yet in sight.

"What are you talking about!"

"Drinking fountains. There really are a lot of drinking fountains in Chicago." He stooped down, and slurped noisily.

"Knob!" I screamed at him. "We're being chased."

"I know," he said, looking at me, water steaming down his cheeks. "That's why it's important to keep hydrated."

"I think he's right," Thurman agreed.

"Shut up!" I yelled, fear coloring my words.

There was a crash as the Warrior crashed crashingly through the door at the end of the hall. "DOUBLE COUPON DAYS!" she bellowed, before disappearing inside.

"This stuff's pretty good," Knob said.

Thurman leaned down to take a drink.

I looked down the hallway again. The attorneys still weren't in sight. I wondered if the Warrior had disabled them all. I looked the other way. The door was open, but I couldn't see the Warrior. The hallway was silent.

"Yeah, this stuff's pretty good," Thurman agreed. He pushed Seth towards the fountain, and guided his face down to give him a drink.

"I forget. Why'd we bring him?" Knob said, gazing at Seth.

"Huh?"

"Why didn't we just go out and get his brain, then bring it back to him?"

"Duh," Thurman said. "What would you keep the brain in?"

Knob looked surprised. "I didn't think of that."

"Yeah, you did. It was your idea."

"Uh."

"We don't know what the telemarketers are keeping it in, but can you think of a better receptacle to bring it back in?"

"No, I guess not," Knob said. "Plus it's pretty hard."

"Yeah, it's safer than anything I can think of," Knob agreed.

"Guys, we have to get going," I said urgently. The silence up the hallway was unnerving me.

"Okey-doke, I'm ready," Thurman said.

"Yeah, let's do it," Knob agreed.

I led towards the door, which had been mangled by the Warrior's not so subtle entrance.

"…the square root of…"

I slowed, hearing a voice from inside the room.

"…the tangent of the coefficient…"

"Shhh," I told Knob and Thurman. I edged nearer to the door, straining to hear.

"…with bell curves and median lengths…"

I peeked into the door, and beheld a strange sight.

A short and wide man stood facing the Warrior, who was standing seemingly at attention. In the corner, a man who looked like an accountant probably was an accountant. Mostly I could tell because he had a calculator, which he brandished at the Warrior as if it were some kind of weapon.

Which it was, as I began to understand, because he was mumbling words at her, like some kind of incantation. "Using analysis of variance, test the null hypothesis of equal population test scores…"

"Bayes' theorem for discrete random variables…"

Quickly I donned my Shield of Stupidity, and crept into the room. I sensed Knob and Thurman, leading Seth, behind. Blue sparks ricocheted as math variables bounced harmlessly off my shield. I breathed a sigh of relief that its powers worked against forces other than female logic.

"What's wrong with her?" Knob whispered.

The Warrior's eyes were vacant, her mouth slack.

Unfortunately, Knob's whisper got the squat man's attention, who quickly stepped up to us, a wide, beaming smile splitting his face. "How are you doing?" he said, holding his hand out like a car salesman.

With a confused look, Knob straightened, and tentatively took the proffered hand.

The squat man pumped vigorously. "How ya' doing? Glad to meet 'cha."

Then, for some reason, Knob collapsed to his knees.

Dropping Knob's hand, the man came at me. "Good to see ya'. I'm happy you could make it."

He thrust his hand at me, and I grabbed it defensively. His strong hand enveloped just my fingers. With his elbow out wide, he yanked my hand up and down, with a crushing grip on my fingers. A finger crushing grip. I couldn't get any grip, but tried to fend him off. But the grip was unbreakable, vice-like. Unable to extricate myself, I dropped weakly to the floor.

Dazed, I could only watch as the man approached our only remaining Questor.

"Thurman," I struggled to say, "don't."

I couldn't finish my sentence, and with horror, saw the squat man grab Thurman's hand.

"No!"

Then, to my surprise, the man yanked his hand back, staggering backwards with fear and revulsion.

Thurman quickly wheeled, and grabbed the Warrior's hand. "C'mon!" Tugging the dazed warrior, he raced back towards us.

"Let's go! Let's get out of here!" he yelled, herding us towards the door.

Somehow I made it to my feet, stumbling after Knob through the door. Thurman pulling the Warrior, was pushing me from behind.

Meanwhile, the accountant kept firing math darts. "The construction of a frequency distribution from ungrouped data varies as there are many possible frequency distributions that can be formed from one set of data."

"The area of each rectangle is proportional to the class frequency with a constant coefficient of proportionality…"

I could feel my Shield of Stupidity weakening with each salvo.

"Hurry," I gasped.

We ran through the door.

"What was that?" Knob said, ashen faced, as we staggered through the hallway, running into the walls.

"Yeah, how did he weaken us like that?" I asked.

"He had pee on his hand," Thurman managed, breathing heavily.

"Pee?"

"Yeah, he didn't wash his hands after going to the bathroom," Thurman added.

"What did that—"

"Plus he got you guys with an Aggressive Handshake."

"I figured that out," Knob said out of the corner of his mouth. "So how did you escape it?"

"Well, the dissolved pee droplets almost got me, but I used the Limp, Dead Handshake to fight off the Aggressive Handshake. As you saw, he dropped me right away. The pee wasn't enough to incapacitate me in that short of time."

"Oh."

We were almost to the drinking fountain when I noticed that someone was bending next to it.

It was a man wearing a Union card and tool belt.

"Whoa, quick, avert your eyes!" Knob yelled, grabbing his knapsack.

We skidded to a halt, rolling our eyes up towards the ceiling. Behind, I could hear the sounds of pursuit.

"The counting random variable typically is appropriate when the countably infinite correspondence of positive integers..."

"Hurry up, whatever you're doing," I urged Knob.

"Take my hand," he said. I felt his hand and grabbed on.

"Hold hands," he instructed.

I grabbed one of the Warrior's unresisting hands, and Thurman took the other. We formed a human chain, and followed Knob down the corridor.

"What's going on?" I hissed.

"That dude by the drinking fountain. He's a plumber."

"Yeah? So?"

"Plumber's Butt. If he'd have gotten us with it, we'd be stunned for sixty seconds."

"Oh, yeah! I've heard about that," Knob said from behind me.

"It's like cleavage. You just have to look," Thurman explained.

"Cleavage," Knob breathed rapturously.

"Well, it's not exactly like cleavage," I protested.

"Maybe not, but like cleavage, you have no choice but to look."

"Even if you don't want to," Knob added.

"But you have to."

"Man, they fight dirty," Knob said.

Shouting drew my attention, and I glanced back. A horde of people casually dressed in Dockers, plaid shirts and Nikes were sprinting up the aisle. I realized that we wouldn't make it to the end of the hall before we were overwhelmed.

"Knob, we aren't going to have time," I screamed.

"I have an idea," Knob said.

He ran at the plumber, who was kneeling at the water fountain, his butt cleavage in full moon.

Knob whirled the Warrior around, who had been catatonic ever since the accountant mesmerized her in the office.

Knob shoved her head right into the plumber's butt.

"Hey," the plumber yelled.

Somehow this revitalized our warrior, and she shook her head like a lioness waking to find weasels in her bed.

Turning her eyes towards the plumber butt, she suddenly yelled, "AND MY WORTHLESS HUSBAND WON'T FIX ANYTHING AROUND THE HOUSE, SO WE HAVE TO CALL A DAMNED PLUMBER!"

With a huge arching swing of her sword, she smote the plumber, driving him crunchingly against the wall.

Meanwhile, Knob was huddled at the drinking fountain.

"Here, take this," he urged, thrusting something into my hands.

"A water balloon?" I asked, thoroughly confused.

"Throw it!" he said grimly, filling another.

"Huh?"

"Throw it!" he screamed.

I turned around. There were perhaps twenty men and women running at us, closing quickly.

"What the—"

"Throw the damned balloon!"

Hesitantly, I flung the water balloon at the onrushing crowd. It was yellow. The balloon, not the crowd. The crowd was colored Docker.

Out of the corner of my eyes, I saw Thurman make a motion, and a red balloon whistled down the hall, following mine.

"Here," Knob urged, thrusting a green one at me. I turned so I didn't see what had happened with my first throw.

Because of that, when I turned back to throw the next one, I was completely unprepared for the sight. Three bodies were splayed out on the floor, with the others scrambling to get past their prone bodies.

"How'd...?"

"Wow, didja see that?" Thurman exulted. He cocked, and flung another balloon at one man who had somehow gotten past his fallen comrades, and who was rushing at us. The blue balloon smacked him in the chest, driving him backwards into another man.

I stared with disbelief at the water balloon in my hand. It looked normal. Felt normal. Even smelled normal. Rubber.

Suddenly Thurman snatched it out of my hand. "Hurry, there are more coming!" He whipped it, knocking another man and woman backwards.

"But these are just water balloons," I said confusedly.

"Get him!" Knob yelled, shoving a pink water balloon into my hands. I looked where he was pointing. The mathematician was scrabbling over the horde of writhing bodies, still muttering.

"...using statistical hypothesis based on large samples for a significance distribution..."

I whipped the balloon, and the pink blur slammed into his shirt, which I now noticed was a pink button-down. The mathematician fell as if someone had yanked him backwards with a string. He disappeared into the snakelike mass of Dockers and button-down shirts.

With her adversary vanquished, the Warrior leaped back into the fray, expertly whirling the umbrella sword as she ran screaming at the horde.

"TAKE OUT THE GARBAGE!"

Slam!

Bodies flew.

"SCRAPE THE FOOD OFF THE PLATE BEFORE YOU DUMP YOUR DISHES IN THE SINK!"

"ASS IS TOO A CUSSWORD!"

Whack!

More fell, screaming with rage and pain.

"Wow, how can they take that?" Knob asked, his hands clamped over his ears.

"It's got to hurt," I agreed numbly.

"Yeah, and they're getting it face on," Thurman said through gritted teeth.

"Let's get out of here, while we can," I urged.

"But what about the Warrior...?"

"Don't worry, she can take care of herself," I assured Knob.

We ran down the hall, away from the sounds of fighting behind us. From the sound of it, the Warrior was proving my words correct.

"AND RATHER THAN STEPPING OVER IT, TRY PICKING IT UP!"

We ran back up the one flight of stairs to the thirty-first. The attorneys were nowhere in sight. They had probably crept back into their holes to prepare court summons and calculate their hourly rates.

"C'mon," I breathed, "to the elevators."

We sprinted towards the elevators, and I quickly jabbed the 'down' button.

Knob caught up, and saw that the down light was lighted. So naturally, he jabbed it again.

Thurman stumbled to a stop, still pulling my brother along. He saw the lit down light, and jabbed it again.

Seth didn't.

He couldn't.

But if he could have, he would have.

With a whoosh, the doors slid open, and I leaped into combat pose. Meaning I backed up really fast to assume running position if 'Something Evil' was in the elevator.

Fortunately, it was empty, so we leaped inside.

Knob held the 'door open' button, and we craned our necks to watch for the Warrior, whose battle cries could be heard dimly down the hallway.

I took advantage of the moment to ask him, "What the hell was it with the water balloons?"

"Yeah, worked pretty good, huh?"

I sputtered, "They're water balloons! How the hell did they do that?"

"Hard water, man."

"Huh?"

"Hard water. You don't want to get hit with hard water."

"What the...?"

Suddenly the Warrior sprinted around the corner, saw us in the elevator, and hopped in. "Let's go," she ordered.

Knob jabbed the button for the first floor, and we all watched nervously as the numbers showed the elevator descending rapidly.

At the bottom, no reception had been arranged for us, so we quickly escaped from the building.

Chapter Eleven

Outside, we walked rapidly towards the parking garage.

The Sears Tower towered overhead. When I looked up, it appeared to curve over our heads.

"Wow," I enthused.

"Watch where you're going," Knob cautioned me.

Chicago pedestrians hurried around us, yakking on cell phones, dodging cabs, oblivious to homeless men sitting in wheelchairs or rattling cups of coins. They rushed past, parting like a bad comb-over.

I could see the empty sky past the skyscrapers, marking where Illinois' side of Lake Michigan dwelled, a great beast deep and dark. A strong wind, funneled by the skyscrapers, blew briskly from the lake, cooling the city ten degrees cooler than the collar counties, and blowing late summer skirts enticingly.

We walked past clothing stores, banks, eateries. The crowd was oblivious to our strange group, as they were strange themselves, and as such, tolerated strange as a normal part of the town. Chicago has its own personality, quirks and charm, utterly different than its larger coastal brethren. A city of big shoulders, large appetites, inspired diversity.

As we hurried along, casting nervous glances behind us, the

Warrior caught up to me. Her expression was a mixed brew of anxiety, thoughtfulness, exhaustion and other emotional hybrids no guy was equipped to decipher.

"Hey, you okay?" I asked.

"No." Her face tightened.

"What's wrong?"

She gave me a grim look. "I froze back there. I don't know what happened, but I froze."

"Yeah, he had your number," I agreed.

"I hate math!"

"I wouldn't worry about it. You came through when it mattered."

She searched my face, gauging my sincerity.

Hastily, I put on my sincere face.

It must have worked, because her face relaxed.

We continued walking, but the silence was comfortable now. She was the first to break it.

"How'd you do it?" she asked, not looking at me.

"Huh? Do what?"

"Break the trance."

"Oh. Besides Seth, I also have a sister."

"Sister?"

"Yeah, older." I grimaced, remembering a few not so pleasant memories of dress up, where the little brother assumes unwilling model duties. Thankfully, Seth came around.

She frowned. "Okay, so what's that got to do with it?"

We rounded the corner before I responded. "I've seen PMS before," I said hesitantly, "what with her and Mom."

"Okay. So?"

"So I've given it a lot of thought over the years."

"And?"

I took a deep breath. "Look, a human is almost totally made out of water, right?"

"Huh?"

"Our bodies, they're almost all water."

"Er, okay, if you say so."

"Like ninety percent."

"Um. All right."

"And you women get PMS once a month, right?"

"Yeah." She grimaced.

"Okay, so here's what I figure. You get PMS because the moon goes through its phases every month. And the pull of the moon's orbit affects the waters in a woman's body in much the same way it causes tides."

"Uh."

"So, basically, every month you have the equivalent of a tidal wave inside your body."

"Well, why wouldn't we have one every day, like the tides?"

"I dunno. I guess I haven't thought it through all the way. It's not like I'm a scientist who can use test subjects and stuff."

She was quiet, thinking about what I said.

"Okay," she said finally, "if that's true, can't we wipe PMS out by getting rid of the moon?"

"I thought about that," I said, "but I'm not sure that it's a good idea. Sure, if you got rid of the moon, you wouldn't get your period. But what would trigger the whole egg thing?"

"We'd die out."

"Yep, we'd die out as a species. Maybe the animal kingdom would, too, for that matter. In fact," I continued, "sometimes I wondered what would happen if we had two moons. Would you get two periods a month? What happens if Man goes to other worlds? If we went to a world with no moons, would Woman be unable to have a period? Or, what if we went to Jupiter where they have dozens of moons?"

"That could be bad," she agreed. "Multiple PMS's per month."

"Yeah, science fiction shows don't talk about this kind of thing, huh?"

She shuddered.

So did I.

"Okay," she finally said, "so what's this got to do with how you broke the trance?"

"You're going to think this is stupid," I warned her.

"Probably not. Let's hear it."

"Well, you know the power of a plumber's butt, right?"

"Yeah, like cleavage. You have to look." She looked down at

her own ample valley.

To be polite, I looked, too.

Because when there's cleavage you have to. Even if you don't want to. Not that I didn't want to. Because I did want to. Because, after all, I'm a guy.

"Okay, so about the plumber's butt?"

"Well, I figured it had powers, and since something was blocking yours, you needed the power of the moon."

"Ah. So the plumber's butt..." she started.

"...was a moon..." I continued.

"...and it triggered my PMS," she concluded.

"Yep."

"Hmmm. I don't know," she said, speculatively. "Could be, I guess." She shrugged. "Whatever it was, it worked."

She was quiet again, thinking it over.

A Grand Prix drove by, and the driver flipped a cigarette butt out the window.

There was a rush of air to fill the vacuum next to me.

The vacuum was caused when the Warrior took off sprinting towards the car, weaving through taxis and screaming.

"YOU IDIOT! YOU HAVE AN ASHTRAY IN YOUR DAMNED CAR! STUPID SONOFABITCH!"

The driver saw this wild woman coming at him. He was stopped at a red light, and traffic was racing by.

"WAIT 'TIL I CATCH YOU, ASSHOLE! I'M GOING TO SHOVE THAT BUTT UP YOUR BUTT!"

The driver, whoever he was, must have weighed his options, because, wisely, he decided to take his chances in the intersection rather than dealing with this dervish. Tires screaming, he shot into the intersection blowing right through the red.

CRASH! BANG! ...tinkle.

Horns blared, and the sound of crumpling metal filled the intersection.

The Grand Prix was sandwiched between a panel truck advertising adult diapers, and a taxi, whose driver was already unleashing what was likely a torrent of Middle-Eastern swear words.

The Warrior watched, a satisfied look on her face, and strolled casually back to us.

Knob leaned over, and picked up the offending cigarette butt. He put it in his pocket. "Don't worry. I'll throw it away."

"All right," she said finally. Calmly she resumed our discussion, "Let's say I buy what you said. Aren't men ninety percent water, too?"

"Uh. Yes."

"So how come you don't get periods?"

I thought about it.

"I think maybe we do," I said finally. "A woman gets crampy, bloaty, and generally feels lousy, right?"

"Yeah, that's about it," she said sourly.

"Okay, so if she feels this way, but keeps it to herself, how's the guy going to know?"

"If he's any kind of man, he'll be sensitive enough to know," she said through gritted teeth.

I just looked at her. "We're talking about men."

"Oh, yeah, stupid and insensitive."

"Right." I wasn't offended, she was right. "Anyway, I figure that God made it so that a woman has to feel so rotten that she has no choice but to take it out on the guy. That way he notices!"

"And takes care of her," she said.

"Uh. No. More so that he knows he should get out of there, for his own good."

"Yeah, men are pretty cowardly. You know, you might have something here."

"And I believe men are affected by the moon's tidal effect, too. Except it doesn't trigger reproductive activity. It just sort of messes with his mind—"

"Which is already a mess," she interjected.

"And then he just jumps in a car, and takes it out on other drivers."

"That would explain a lot," she said thoughtfully.

We turned into the parking building, and took the elevator up to the the Greece floor. But before I could stop him, Thurman punched the key for the USA floor. As soon as the door opened, the Boss was singing again, "Born, in the USA, I was..."

"Damn," I said, clamping my hands over my ears.

"What?" the Warrior asked.
"I just got that song out of my head."
She laughed.

That night, we all made our plans over clam sauce linguini in a corner booth at an Olive Garden restaurant. A decorative light fixture hung over our table by a chain, casting us in intimate lighting.

"Anyone want to guess who the heck we were fighting back there?" the Warrior said, twirling noodles around her fork. For one so petite, she could pack it away.

"Yeah, who is our enemy?" Knob asked.

Two very troubling questions. I had thought our enemy were the telemarketers, but what had happened in the attorney offices and both telephone company offices had raised serious issues. Plus, who would consider us a threat?

I looked at my brother, his blonde head down as he mechanically shoved ravioli into his mouth.

"I think we have to research," I stated. "I really thought it was the telemarketers, but...hey, take that stupid thing off!"

I glared at Knob.

"What thing, man?"

"The stupid hat."

"Hat, this isn't a hat. These are my ears."

"This is a restaurant, for crying out loud."

"So how am I supposed to hear what people are saying?"

"Knob, it's a hat, not ears."

"That's what you think," he said, a stubborn look on his face. "I'm an Elf-Esquire." He looked at the Warrior for approval. She rewarded him with a slight smile.

"I give up," I said, realizing I wasn't going to win this one.

"I'm wondering if there isn't some kind of war going on here," Thurman interrupted.

"Huh? War? What kind of war?" Knob asked him.

"Well, I've been doing some thinking," he began.

Shocking news.

"Remember when Guy told us about the lawyers, like where there are three hundred seventy thousand of them in the American

Bar Association?"

"Yeah, so?" I asked.

"Well, think about it. Remember the cigarette companies? They got sued for bajillions of dollars because they put chemicals into cigarettes to make them more addictive. It would have put them out of business, except they simply raised the price of cigarettes to pay for the fines and legal costs and stuff."

"So the people who smoke end up financing it," Knob agreed.

"Yeah, ironic, huh? So smokers end up paying not only for cigarettes, but also the additional medical costs the states pay because of smoking," Thurman continued.

"Too bad they couldn't find some way to stick it to the cigarette company executives who made the decisions to hook kids with advertising, and then make it impossible to quit," Knob put in.

"Remember the Congressional hearings?" I asked.

"Oh, yeah, what a joke," Knob said.

"What hearings?" the Warrior mumbled through a mouth stuffed with noodles.

"We were watching the C-Span coverage where a bunch of cigarette corporation CEO's all stood in a line, put up their right hands, and swore oaths to Congress that they don't believe cigarettes are addictive," I said.

The Warrior snorted back a laugh.

"They were just stating their beliefs, after all," Knob said, laughter in his eyes.

"Yeah," Thurman added, "and maybe they think high cholesterol is good for you, because clogged arteries make your heart work harder, so it gets more exercise."

"And they also believe a stroke is good for you, because half your brain gets to rest," Knob said, a grin splitting his face.

The Warrior giggled.

"And comas help you improve yourself through meditation," I put in.

"And," Thurman said, laughing so hard he could barely talk, "cancer is good for stimulating your nerve endings."

The Warrior hurriedly swallowed noodles, and blurted, "And they believe hell is a nice place, because you can light up a cigarette without a match."

We all laughed. Some of the tension from the afternoon's fighting and chases rode with the laughter out of us.

When the hilarity had faded, Knob said darkly, "I think they'll have a chance to find out about that hell thing."

We thought about this for a minute.

Like a Huey, a fly swooped low over the table, then buzzed away urgently on some errand.

"You know, I have a theory about flies," Thurman mumbled.

"Don't you worry about gaining weight?" Knob asked the Warrior. A second, heaping plate had been put in front of her, half shells steaming.

"I don't worry about weight," she said, intent on her food.

"Huh? I thought all women worried about their weight."

"Not me," she mumbled, her mouth full.

"Yeah, I always thought that was kind of weird," Thurman said into the silence as she chewed robustly.

"What's that?" Knob asked him.

"The whole weight thing."

"What do you mean?" Knob asked, interested.

"Think about it," Thurman explained, "weight is just the effect of gravity. If we were on the moon, we'd weigh less. If we were on Mercury, we'd weigh more. It's all relative."

"So if we could lessen gravity, women could lose all that weight they want to lose?" Knob asked.

"It's not only women," the Warrior said through a mouthful of linguini.

"But if we could reduce gravity, and people lost weight, would they be happy?" Knob asked.

"Nope, they'd still look the same," Thurman said.

"So people don't want to lose weight after all," Knob said.

"Right, they want to lose mass."

"So why don't they say mass instead of saying weight?"

"Hey guys, we have to think about our problem, not weight," I interrupted.

"Oh, yeah, I was telling you about the war," Thurman said.

"There's no war," I said.

"The Unbeliever speaks," Knob said.

"I don't know, Guy," Thurman said. "Think about it. The attorneys wage war on the cigarette industry, and crushed it. Have you thought about how powerful the cigarette lobby was?"

"Yeah," I admitted grudgingly.

"The attorneys wiped them out effortlessly. And look what they did to the telephone companies. They broke a huge monopoly up into all kinds of little pieces. Do you realize what kind of power that takes?"

"And look what they did to telemarketers," the Warrior put in.

"I think you're going to have to tell us more about that," Knob said. "We weren't exactly in the loop on that thing."

"They wiped them by passing a law creating a 'Do Not Call' registry, where people could sign up, making it illegal for telemarketers to call."

"So you could have a peaceful dinner without having to go to a restaurant?" Knob asked.

"Yep. You could actually sit down to dinner, in your own house, and enjoy the bickering of your kids without the interruption of the phone," the Warrior said.

"Wow. And maybe we could actually use our phone," Knob said.

"What for?" Thurman asked.

"Uh, to order pizza."

"I bring pizzas home every day," Thurman told him.

"Well, we could use them to see if the library is open," Knob said.

"You buy all your books," Thurman said.

"We could call to, uh, um…make reservations, or something."

"You eat McDonald's almost every day."

"I don't know, then, smart-Alec," Knob said angrily.

"You guys don't use your phone?" the Warrior asked, temporarily between bites.

I wondered where she put all the food. Then I looked at her bosom, and kinda figured it out. Definitely put to good use.

"Nah, we never use it," Thurman said.

"Boy, you guys are really out of it. Almost everybody uses

phones or cell phones, or text messaging, emailing, and everything. Everybody's wired for instant communications with anyone, anywhere," the Warrior said.

"Uh, I guess we never saw the need," Knob said defensively.

"Why don't you finish your thoughts," I suggested to Thurman, trying to steer him back to our predicament.

"Oh, yeah, about the War. So, anyway, the lawyers took on three very influential organizations, and knocked them down to size."

"So you think this is some kind of war we're in the middle of?" I asked.

"Maybe. Maybe we stumbled into the middle of something back at that attorney office. Maybe they're fighting with the telephone company on the thirteenth floor."

"Or watching them," Knob offered.

"Yeah, maybe they're watching them."

"You think maybe attorneys are trying to take over the world?" Knob asked.

"Oh, I think they already own the world," Thurman said. "Think about it. Judges are lawyers, politicians are lawyers. And if you have to go to court for any reason, you have to have a lawyer. Not only that, because in every suit, at least one attorney wins. Either the defense or the prosecutor. Both sides have an attorney."

"And half the time, the attorneys for both sides come out laughing and shaking hands," the Warrior said darkly, with the benefit of some experience.

"Man, it's almost like a casino. They don't care who wins, as long as they get their cut," Knob said.

A small commotion broke out at a nearby booth.

Chapter Twelve

"Gimme!" a small voice pleaded.
"No! They're mine!" another shrieked.
"Daddy! She won't give me the purple one."
A man's low voice could just be heard, "Shhh, be quiet, Kenny."
"I want the purple one!" the first one whined loudly in a voice that raked a painful path through my noggin.

The restaurant hushed uncomfortably. The kids were probably fighting over the crayons that came with the kids' menus. A similar menu sat in front of Knob. He had added drawings of mosquitoes and colored it with crazy and interesting hue and color.

"If you can't be quiet, you're going to have to have a time out," the beleaguered father said, trying in vain to negotiate with a toddler. The mother, who wasn't in evidence, surely would have handled this much better.

"*I want the purple crayon!*" the kid screamed.
"Kenny!" hissed the father remonstratively.
"*Gimme!*"

And now the sounds of scrabbling and fighting for possession of valuable Crayola could be heard over sniveling and shrieking.

Suddenly there was a whoosh next to me as a vacuum set in

temporary residence on the chair next to me.

"Uh oh," Knob muttered, having noticed.

The fly went buzzing by again, and Thurman swatted at it, his hands cupped for catching rather than smashing the bug. He missed, and it wobbled away on disturbed air currents. He jumped up and lunged forward for a last swipe, but hit the light over our dinner. The bulb went out, casting dimness on our table, and the lamp swung crazily over our heads.

Meanwhile, a new sound came from the family nearby.

"YOU KIDS STOP THAT RACKET RIGHT NOW!"

"But he—"

"I SAID *NOW!*" the voice thundered.

"But—" the father started weakly.

"YOU STAY OUT OF THIS," the Warrior warned him.

He didn't heed her warning. Then again, he was from the genus Male, where intelligence is only suspected, but merely in the same general vagueness and with the same lack of proof as been offered for intelligent life on Mars.

"Um, but I—"

"I SAID, YOU KEEP QUIET!" she said, her words displacing air over their table, and reducing the amount of breathable oxygen. The kids and father got quiet, conserving what oxygen they could.

"AND IF I HEAR ANY MORE OF THIS RACKET, I'M COMING BACK." She glared at them, veins popping from her neck. "AND YOU DON'T WANT THAT!"

She stood there, hands on hips, breathing heavily, waiting to see if anyone would dare offer any resistance. Most of us, the guys at least, were distracted by the sight of her heaving bosom, and were thus rendered speechless anyway.

I could see the bus boys and waitresses huddled by the waitress station, with the same shocked look and half-dollar sized eyes saved for disgruntled postal workers.

After another moment of concentrated glare, the Warrior came back down the hallway. She shrank steadily as she approached, and when she slid back into her seat next to me, she was once again the diminutive blonde whom we had met at her house.

We were quiet for a moment, then Knob spoke, "Do you, like,

turn it on and off?"

"Huh?" she said, her breathing still accelerated.

"The, uh, PMS-thing. Do you have any control over it?"

"Why? Do you want me to?" she glared at him.

"No! No! No! Don't misunderstand," he said, waving his hands to indicate his question had been harmless. "It's just that—"

"Look. I don't have any control over it," she snapped.

He didn't say anything.

"I'm not proud of it. But when it takes over, it takes over. And when it does, you don't want to get in the way," she said, giving him a look before picking up her fork again.

"Amen," Thurman said admiringly.

"What I want to know is why the telemarketers would want Seth's brain," Knob said, adroitly changing the subject.

"It's not even a particularly good brain," said Seth's big brother.

"That's not nice, Guy," Thurman admonished.

"Still though. What are they going to do with a brain?" Knob continued.

"I think we need to do some research," I said. "We need to know more about our enemy."

"We need the Internet," the Warrior said, her calm restored. Once again, she looked normal and pretty. No signs of danger. But there was the hint of suppressed violence in the air, in the manner of a cat's sheathed claws.

"Okay, let's get some rest, and we'll go to the library in the morning," I decided.

The waitress stopped by, keeping a wary distance from the Warrior, who wordlessly was finishing up her plate.

"May I have a doggy bag?" Thurman asked.

"Is this for your…um…'dog'?" Knob asked with a hint of sarcasm.

"Yes, it is," Thurman said, shooting him a defiant look that banked off the rim.

"Hey, do you have any moist towelettes?" Knob asked the waitress.

"Let's get out of here," I growled. "I'm tired."

WHOOMP!

Chapter Thirteen

"What the...?"
"Oh, no!"
"It found us!"
We all recognized the noise, which shook the entire building.
As one, we rushed to our feet, and ran towards the south exit, away from the origin of the noise.
WHOMP!
Patrons dove under tables to escape shards of glass, brick and rubble that sprayed through the restaurant from the wrecked entranceway near the front lobby. They were probably thinking terrorists. Wires and conduit swung crazily back and forth from the ceiling.
WHOOMMPP!
As if pulverized by a gigantic fist, a huge section roof suddenly slammed to the ground, billowing out dust and splintering furniture that flew like shrapnel through gloom, smoke and pandemonium.
WHHHOOOMMMPPP!
With a gigantic crash, brick walls disintegrated, and buckled inward, driven by the weight of adjoining rooms. Ragged glimpses of sky could be seen through a huge hole in the ceiling. There was no sign of what was causing the devastation. But we knew, for we

had seen it many times.

"C'mon," the Warrior instructed. She swept through the rubble, clearing a path through confused and milling people. We stayed on her heels. When I looked back I saw others, both employees and customers, following in our wake.

WHHHOOMMMPPP!

The concussion from the blast nearly swept us off our feet. Others did fall. Other people helped them up, and we struggled through the wreckage towards the undamaged back exit. Knickknacks decorating the walls crashed to the ground, adding their small breaking noises to the tumultuous cacophony splitting the air.

We emerged from the back door into darkening evening, and without delay, bolted for the SUV. Another concussion ripped the air behind us, shaking the parking lot and bouncing vehicles like exploding popcorn.

A milling crowd of shell-shocked people flowed out of the building. Knowing that the attack had been aimed at us, I hoped that everyone had escaped harm, and that it would end once we were gone.

We leaped into the SUV, and with screaming tires pealed out of the parking lot. "Make sure it follows us," I yelled.

"What, that thing doesn't like it when we eat?" Thurman said.

"Yeah," Knob agreed, his face ashen. "First McDonald's, and now here."

A windy howl of fury behind us showed that our departure had been noticed.

"Get out of here!" Thurman screamed, his face pressed against the rear glass.

"Look what it's doing now!" Knob yelped.

"*What?*"

I couldn't see it.

Suddenly, a whistling, whooshing blast of wind caught us, rocking the SUV violently. The Warrior cursed as she fought the steering wheel, vainly trying to see the road through black, swirling torrents of air.

"Whoa!"

"What the...?"

"Hey!"

Tires screamed as a fierce wind buffeted the windows mercilessly. My ears popped as the air pressure skipped off merrily in a different direction. I could see Knob and Thurman were yelling and pointing, but couldn't hear them over the roaring blasts.

Abruptly, it was gone. One minute we were getting rocked, the next we were riding unimpeded down the highway. The resultant silence was almost deafening after the storm-like fury. My heart was still pounding, but there was no sign of the wild wind. It had gone as quickly as it had appeared.

I looked out the window. Cars and trucks drove by, having apparently been unaffected by the storm cell that had emptied out its rage on us. The setting sun colored the western sky shades of yellow and orange and red. Grass grew, bugs bugged. Altogether, a pleasant evening.

"What the hell was that?"

"You should have seen it," Knob said, his face animated by fear and excitement.

"It was like a sci-fi movie!" Thurman had the look of someone who had just gotten off the fastest, steepest roller-coaster ever. Exhilarated that he was alive, but wanting to get right back on.

"*What?*" I shouted. I hadn't seen a thing.

"Okay," Knob said, trying to calm down, "imagine a tornado, like, rolled up in a ball."

"Like a snowball," Thurman put in.

They took turns.

"And the ball bounced up and down on top of a building."

"Smashing it around and knocking things around."

"But the tornado-ball is alive and aware, and it's alive and chasing something."

"Bouncing with malice."

"Yeah, it's pretty pissed off."

"So, okay, the ball sees its quarry."

"That's us."

"Getting away, and it's already been outrun once."

"From McDonald's."

"So all of a sudden it kind of, uh, undo's itself."
"Undo's?"
"Undoes?"
"Yeah, that sounds better."
"Or maybe it's more like it unwinds."
"Yeah, like unwinding. Thanks."
"You're welcome."
"So it unwinds, and then it makes itself into a, um…"
"Like a windtunnel."
"Yeah, but without the tunnel."
"But it was tunnel-shaped."
"I dunno, man, it was more snake-shaped."
"Snakes are tunnel-shaped."
"They are not!"
"They are too!"
"They live in tunnels, but they aren't tunnel shaped."
"Both of them are long and skinny, aren't they?"
"So's a cucumber."
"Okay, it was cucumber-shaped."
"It was not!"
"What? You said it, I didn't."
"I did not!"
"You did too! You said, and I quote, 'So's a cucumber.'"
"I know I said that."
"Then why are you arguing?"
"I didn't say that the wind was cucumber-shaped. I said that a cucumber is long and skinny."
"So?"
"So, uh—"
I interrupted, "Are you guys done?"
"Uh, um…"
"Are you guys saying that the tornado ball pulled itself apart, and came after us in a condensed wind?" I asked.
"Yeah! That's what happened," Knob exulted.
"Yeah! That's it," Thurman agreed.
"Hmmm. Why would a wind be chasing us?" I wondered aloud.
Nobody answered.

Scenery flew by the darkening window as nighttime fought to wrestle control from daylight.

"You know, I have a theory about flies," Thurman offered.

"You've been saying that," Knob said. "What's your theory?"

He cleared his throat. "Ahem. I think flies are spies."

"Spies, that's ridiculous!" I said.

He looked hurt, but still defiant. "Yes, that's exactly what I think."

"Why do you think that?" Knob said, shooting me a look that told me to back off.

"You ever look at a fly under a microscope?" Thurman asked him.

"Well, I've been meaning to," Knob answered.

"Well, I have. And they don't look like anything biological. They look like machines."

"They lay eggs in shit," I said meanly.

"Sure, they do certain things that mimic biological functions, but what spy wouldn't do his best to fit into the environment that he is studying?"

Knob looked intrigued. "Studying?"

"Yeah, I think they are studying us. They're like little information-gathering devices. They study what we eat, how we live, they listen to us, and then they report it."

"Report to whom?" I asked.

He gave a helpless shrug. "I don't know. Could be anything. Alien, government, whatever. Think about how flies work so hard to get into our houses. Open a door, and there's one just hiding there, ready to zoom in. Why? There's no proof that there's anything in there that nature would determine they should have to investigate. They aren't coming in for food. I think they are curious, and come in to watch, listen—"

"Watch ESPN," I interjected.

"Sure, you laugh. But maybe they do study our television-watching habits. They might even be reporting to the television networks."

"The television networks," I said skeptically.

"Yeah. Where do they get these ratings, anyway? Did Nielsen

ever call you to find out what you watch?"

"Well, no."

"Have they ever called anyone you know?"

"Um, not that I know of."

"So how do they know that two million people watched this show, or four million people watched that show? And if they didn't have a really good scientific way to establish audience, what advertiser would be willing to pay millions of dollars for a thirty-second commercial?"

Knob interrupted before I could answer. Good thing, too, since I didn't have an answer. "So how come other animals, like birds and stuff, eat them, if they aren't biological?"

"They might actually be biologically-based, but what if they are alien-created, and are studying the internal and external aspects of all Earth creatures? Think about it, look how flies start biting before a storm. This could be some kind of test, to see how Earth creatures respond to changes in environmental climate alterations."

"So you don't know who they're working for?" Knob put in.

"No, but think about this. Every single time that we see that cloud thing, we see a fly first. And we already know that flies are impacted by the weather. Maybe there's some kind of connection or relationship."

"Flies work for clouds?" I said doubtfully.

"What about other insects?" the Warrior asked.

He wrinkled his forehead. "I've been wondering about that. Like how maybe mosquitoes are blood-specimen collectors."

"You know, I actually saw a *quinquefasciatus* the other day," said Knob.

"A kinky what?" the Warrior asked.

"*Quinquefasciatus*. It's the common southern house mosquito."

"So what?" I said.

"It's rare up here," he said, "we usually just see the *pipiens* up here. The *quinquefasciatus* usually can't handle our weather."

"Who cares? They bite us, that's all I care about. Damn bugs."

"They don't actually 'bite.' That's a common misconception.

They 'feed' on us. There's a difference."

"What do you mean, 'feed'?" Thurman asked. "I thought they bite so they can obtain something for laying eggs."

Knob beamed at him. "Almost. Remember what I said the other day? Only the female feeds on us, bites if you prefer. But she does actually consume the blood, and uses protein from animal and human blood to produce the eggs. They don't use the blood to sustain themselves. They actually consume nectar and fruit."

"That kind of knocks your whole blood specimen theory, Thurman," the Warrior said.

"Not really," Thurman disagreed. "It's like with the flies. They still use shit and spoiled meat for laying biological eggs, but it's not impossible that they a dual-role; both collecting statistics and doing what they can to produce more biological insect machines."

"Like the penis, right?"

"Huh?"

"I get it," the Warrior said. "The same instrument serves both as waste eliminator and reproductive organ."

"Right!"

"So, what's the deal with diseases, then?" I asked.

"I don't know. Could be aliens testing to see what kind of biological weapons they could use against us?"

"Or maybe we're just some kind of zoo creatures to them, and they use malaria, West Nile, yellow fever and encephalitis to keep the population of the herd down," Knob surmised.

I didn't like thinking of humans as herd animals for some kind of alien pod creatures. But the comparison of rush hour traffic and cattle drives came uncomfortably to mind.

"Hey, remember that Sci-Fi show? *Farscape*?" Thurman said excitedly.

"What about it?"

"They had a living space ship that carried them all around. It was a creature, yet it would let humans and other small aliens use it for transport."

"Oh, yeah! I remember that," Knob said. "Wasn't there another show, too, where they rode in a huge dragon spaceship?"

"Yeah. But you see what I mean. If man could even think of

stuff like this, who knows what greater or more advanced minds could actually accomplish?"

"We're already doing it," I said, as a thought crossed my mind.

"What do you mean?"

"Nanotechnology. We use atoms and particles to make machines. The small machines we make are biological."

"Nanotechnology?" Knob asked.

"Yeah, I don't know a lot about it, but scientists can create small machines where each part is made up of an electron. Some geeks at IBM actually took a bunch of electrons and lined them up on the head of a pin to spell 'IBM.'"

"Wow!"

"What do we do next?" the Warrior asked.

"Well, like I said earlier, I think we have to know more about our enemy," I said.

"So we hit the library?"

"Yep, and hope nothing hits us."

"Yeah, and I'm getting myself a fly swatter," Thurman said fiercely.

Chapter Fourteen

While we were driving to the hotel, our supply of moist towelettes having been replenished at the restaurant, I asked the Warrior if she minded if I turned on the radio to catch the Sox score.

I turned on the AM all-sports network just in time for a commercial.

"Are you tired of meeting women at the bars, tired of the same old lines? Well, come to the Sports Cabaret, a full nude bar with lap…"

Quickly, I punched off the radio, shooting the Warrior a quick look.

The corner of her mouth twitched.

I felt my face color.

A few minutes later, when I judged the commercial was over, I turned it back on.

"Try the only physician-approved, male enhancement pill…"

I jabbed the radio off again, feeling the color heighten in my cheeks. When I glanced at the Warrior again, a smile was tugging at her lips.

After a few moments, I gave it another attempt.

"…send for our free video, where we will show you our time-tested, no risk method for putting dollars in your pocket, while you sit back and do nothing. For the next thirty days, you can have this free video, that will only cost you Nineteen-Ninety-Nine…"

Hastily, I switched to the other sports station.

"Tired of burning your head every summer? Try our hair replacement…"

I switched back.

"…and you can wipe out your debts with this no hassle bankruptcy, and still retain your credit rating…"

Switch again.

"Log onto our website 'dubya dubya dubya suckers dot com' for the best in on-line betting, where you are guaranteed a winner every…"

The Warrior's face was in full smirk now.

"I think I'll just watch ESPN at the hotel," I said meekly, turning off the radio.

"I don't know," she said. "It seems like they pretty much hit on everything that's important to you guys."

"Well, sure…" I stumbled.

"Don't worry. I'm married. I didn't hear anything I didn't already know," she reassured me.

I wasn't reassured, though, and was in fact slightly disturbed. In the course of sixty seconds we'd heard snippets of five commercials dealing with sex, money, and slacking around.

We pulled into the hotel parking lot.

"That's only a partial list," Knob put in from the back seat.

"What do you mean?" the Warrior asked.

"Well, they didn't get food."

"Or pizza," Thurman said.

"Pizza is food," Knob cut in.

"But it's got its own category, though."

"Yeah, I guess."

"We also like electronics," Thurman put in.

"And literature," Knob added.

"And comics."

"And entertainment," Thurman said.

"And the nurturing of a loving relationship with a compassionate, caring, intelligent woman," I put in.

There was an embarrassing silence that lasted about five seconds or five minutes, depending on whether or not you were me.

Which you aren't.

And I am.

So it was five minutes.

"Hey, Guy, I didn't know you felt that deeply about it," Knob said, his unseen grin linked to the words.

"Whoo-hoo, that's deep, man." Thurman snickered.

"Shut up!" I told them.

I got out of the SUV, and headed towards the door without waiting.

"Hey, don't feel bad, Guy. That was a very nice thing to say," the Warrior said, catching up.

"You know something?" Knob asked from behind.

"Shut up!" I said, letting the door close on him.

"No, I'm not talking about that," he said, pushing his way in.

"Shut up, anyway!"

"Seriously, though. If the lawyers wiped out the cigarette companies, telephone companies and telemarketing, maybe they are trying to wipe out all competition. Then they could run everything."

"What if it's not that? What if they simply go after deep pockets with the purpose of making a big, long, dragged out legal battle that will run up millions or billions in legal fees?" Thurman asked.

I slid my card down the key lock and stepped inside the room that I would be sharing with my roommates and Seth. The Warrior was staying in an adjoining suite with Thurman's invisible dog.

They followed in, and flopped onto the two queen sized beds.

"You knew that the cigarette lobby wouldn't back down without a fight. And they'd have to hire attorneys to fight the government's attorneys. Then, when the fight's over, the attorneys double dip, having collected from both sides," Knob said.

"Hey!" Thurman asked, "Do you think that's what the whole Bill Gates, Microsoft thing was all about? Another taking on the Big Guy to generate legal billings?"

"I dunno, it sounds like it. Man, this sure makes too much sense," Knob said, a worried look on his face. He isn't generally a worrier, so the look didn't suit him very well.

"Who else is out there?" the Warrior put in, drawn into the discussion. She was sitting at the desk, and was doodling on some hotel stationary.

"Spammers," Thurman spit.

"Spammers are pretty bad," the Warrior agreed, a sour look on her face.

"And hackers, too. If the attorneys could find some way to get the people who create worms and bugs, I'd love them," Knob said.

"What kind of person would enjoy creating a worm that destroys computers of people whom he doesn't even know?" Thurman said angrily.

"Good, English, man," Knob said to Thurman.

"Huh?"

"Whom."

"Whom?"

"Yeah, you spoke English good."

"Well."

"Well, what?"

"You spoke English well."

"That's what I said."

"Uh, okay."

"What were we talking about?"

"Germs."

"No, worms."

"Germs by worms?"

"No, bugs by worms."

"Oh, yeah, those slime who create viruses."

"And there's no benefit from it," the Warrior added, who had watched their exchange with a slight smile on her face. "They do it out of spite and hatred."

"And envy, and probably more dark emotions. We have no idea what motivates these creeps," I said.

"You know what it's like?" Thurman asked. "It's like a person who gets a cold and then wipes his snot everywhere, hoping someone else, anyone, will catch the cold."

The Warrior looked fearsome. "Or like people that litter, even when a trash can is five feet away."

"No, it's different than that. That's just laziness and stupidity," I disagreed. "People who create worms crave attention and notoriety, and want to lash out at people, innocent or not. They do it in a weak attempt to breathe legitimacy to a pathetic existence."

Knob nodded in agreement. "Well said. Still, if the attorneys could get their hooks in them."

"I don't know," I said doubtfully, "there might not be enough money there to interest attorneys. Nobody knows who these computer jerks are."

"If they could get them somehow, though, I'd get a lawyer bobble head doll, and put it on my dashboard to honor their existence," Knob said.

"You don't have a dashboard, anymore," I reminded him.

"Oh, yeah. I forgot." He paused, dolefully considering the thin sliver that was all that was left of his treasured van, now a squashed splat of metal and plastic resting next to our squashed flat house. He looked up hopefully. "You think…?"

"No, I'm sure the tennis racquets didn't survive."

"Bummer," he said dejectedly.

The next morning, we ate, checked out, and headed to the local library. It was a slow summer day, and we figured kids would be sleeping in until afternoon, so we could get on the Internet as long as needed.

"We could have gone back to my house for this," the Warrior said, as she punched up a search page.

"Nah, last thing we want is for your house to get flattened, too," Knob said.

"Yeah, we'll have to stay on the move, because we can't dodge every fly in the world," I added.

"Let's see," the Warrior said to herself, keying in numbers. "I'll just punch in 'telemarketers' and see what we come up with."

She hit the return key and waited for the results.

"This is a pretty fast computer. Must have a T-1 cable."

"Whoa, check it out," Knob gushed, looking over her

shoulder.

"Wow, there are tons of sites," Thurman said, looking over her other shoulder. We were all clustered around the screen, sitting behind the Warrior, who, being somewhat diminutive, was easy to see past. Especially since her breasts were well below the level of the screen. We wouldn't have been able to see past them. Not that we would have wanted to. Or would have.

"Yeah, and they're mostly all about how to deal with annoying telemarketers," Knob agreed.

"That's an oxymoron," I said.

"Oxymoron?"

"Yeah, all telemarketers are by definition annoying."

"Yeah, I guess."

"Uh."

"What, Thurman?"

"Um, actually I think you mean redundancy."

"What?"

"Redundancy."

"I heard you! What do you mean, 'redundancy'?"

"Uh, an oxymoron is when you have two incongruent words, like jumbo shrimp."

"What?"

"I mean, er…an oxymoron is, uh…"

"You're an oxymoron!" I snapped.

Knob snickered. "Yeah, a moron that needs oxygen."

"I don't know." The Warrior was still reading. "It looks a like quite a few of the sites are about how to annoy a telemarketer."

"Annoy a telemarketer?'

"Yes, watch." The Warrior clicked into one of these sites.

"Check it out. This one has a bunch of creative suggestions for what to say to a telemarketer who calls."

Knob read, "If a telemarketer calls, ask him to repeat everything he says, over and over."

"I like this one," Thurman said. "Ask them meaningless questions, like where they are located, how to spell it, what game shows they like."

I laughed. "This one would have been fun, too. Tell them that it's dinnertime, and ask them if they would please hold. Then put them on speaker while you eat really loudly, and have a normal dinner conversation as if they aren't there."

"That's good." Knob chuckled. "How about this one, tell them that you're hard of hearing, and they need to speak up...louder... and louder...and louder."

"Ha, ha! Okay, or tell them to talk really slowly because you want to write every word they say," Thurman said, his face flushed with glee.

I guffawed. "Or as soon as you realize that it's a telemarketer, put down the receiver, scream 'Oh, my God!' and hang up."

"Or tell him you work for the same company and that they can't sell to employees."

"When he asks how you're doing, tell him all of your medical problems, in lengthy detail."

We were laughing hard by this point.

The Warrior wiped tears from her eyes, and said, "You know what I used to do?"

"No, what?"

"I'd have them hold on, and get my kids to the phone. Then they'd all sing the theme song to *Josie and the Pussycats*. The kids loved it."

"Cool, I'm starting to think maybe we should have been answering the phone all this time," Knob said.

Thurman suddenly got a serious look on his face. "I don't know guys, there's quite a bit of subtle hostility here."

The smile left Knob's face. "Yeah, and they do have Seth's brain."

"Hey, look," the Warrior said, clicking the cursor for the U. S. Department of Labor website. "Maybe this will give us some idea of who and what we're dealing with."

We waited as the page downloaded. It was an older page.

"It's the 2001 National Occupational Employment and Wage Estimates from the Bureau of Labor Statistics," she said. "Let's see, Standard Occupational Classification code number four one dash nine zero four one is telemarketers. The site says telemarketers 'Solicit orders for goods or services over the telephone.'"

She clicked the next page. "Oh, look, it tells how many telemarketers there are and what they make."

Knob whistled. "There are 437,510 telemarketers!"

"Incredible!" Thurman said. "There are even more telemarketers than attorneys!"

I read further' "And more than a third of them make less than eight bucks an hour."

"You could get that much at McDonald's," Knob said. "Plus a food allowance."

"Kinda makes you feel sorry for them," the Warrior said.

"Not me. Instead it makes me wonder what their real agenda is, since it's obvious they aren't in it for the money."

"Yeah, and remember, they call at dinner time. Maybe food just isn't important to them."

I kept thinking. Between telemarketers and attorneys, there was a force greater in size than the United States Army. Not only that, but they were, in their own ways, as lethal and dangerous as any man with an assault rifle. Attorneys have their writs and subpoenas. Telemarketers have their uncanny ability to catch you at home during dinner, and ward off all of the killing rays that you direct at them through the phone.

What were we in the middle of? Two armies?

The Warrior kept clicking. "Look at this."

Thurman read over her shoulder, "'Telemarketers get the most charity money, New York Attorney General Alleges.'"

"Are you reading this?" the Warrior said to me.

I nodded, hardly believing what I was reading. The New York Attorney General had issued a report saying that non-profit charities actually only receive a fraction of money raised in their name by telemarketers hired to make the calls. In some cases, the charity would receive as little as ten percent of the money, with the other ninety percent going to the telemarketers.

"Wow! Telemarketers raised $188 million in fundraising in 2000 in New York, and kept sixty-eight percent of it!" Knob exclaimed, his face turning red with anger.

"Yeah! And the charities know it," Thurman said. "Look here, it says it's actually cheaper and more efficient for a charity to hire out soliciting than to hire its own employees. Since there's no overhead this way, it still works out for the charity. So both the charity and the telemarketers are happy."

"But that's not fair to the people who give to them hoping to help people," the Warrior said, a dangerous glint in her eyes.

"I don't know, guys," I said, "but I think it's interesting that the Attorney General stirred this up."

"Yeah, that's right. He's an attorney, isn't he?"

"Yep, and I'm betting it's not a coincidence, either," I said.

No matter where we went, we kept coming back to attorneys.

"They brought all that money in, and the people who make calls only get paid a little over minimum wage?" Thurman asked.

"Yeah," I grumbled. "It sure looks like there's a lot more than meets the eye here."

"So if telemarketers make that much off of charities, then how come they get paid so little?" Knob wondered.

"And what do they do with all the money?"

"Building some kind of war chest, maybe?"

"You know one of the weird things?" the Warrior asked, still scrolling through sites.

"No, what?"

"For as many sites as there are *about* telemarketers, there aren't really any sites *by* telemarketers."

"That is weird," I agreed.

"There are a few, but there's really nothing in their sites. Here, look at this one," she said, punching more keys.

It was the site for a company named Scamya & Associates, Telemarketing and Consultants, Inc. The menu on the first page gave contact information, and a link to an informational page about the company.

We looked at the informational page, which included a mission statement that said, "Since 1989, Scamya has assisted organizations with the development, improvement and/or implementation of telemarketing and tele-sales applications, with the ability to market a broad spectrum of industry. The firm's President, Andile Scamya, has extensive background in call center/tele-sales, including a superb track record of guiding organizations through the process of initiating a program or determining strategies to improve an existing program."

"Ouch," Knob said, rubbing his temples.

Thurman's eyes were glazed. "Yeah, it hurts to read all this gobbly-gook."

"I'm interested in whether they belong to any kind of organization of telemarketers," I said. "That's where I think we have to go."

We rapidly went through the rest of the website, which included a section on consulting and training, script writing, hiring, a newsletter with tele-sales tips, outsourcing.

"It's got a contact email, do you want me to email them with that question?"

"No!" I screamed. "I mean, don't do that! We can't alert them."

"Don't they already know about us?" Knob asked.

"I don't know. Maybe. But we can't tip our hand as to what we're doing."

"That shouldn't be a problem," Thurman said, "since we don't know what we're doing anyway."

"Yeah, so what hand is there to tip?"

"And what is hand-tipping, anyway?" Knob asked.

"Yeah, I hate it when we use a phrase all the time, and don't have any clue what it really means," Thurman agreed.

"Well," Knob said, "hand-tipping in normal usage means to disclose a secret prematurely, right?"

"Yep."

"So maybe it had something to do with kids. Like you have some kind of present for them, and you hold it up high where they can't see it. Then, if you tip your hand, it falls out, and they discover what you were hiding from them."

"Hmmm," Thurman said. "Maybe."

"Could it have something to do with waiters or waitresses?" the Warrior asked. "Like if they are walking through a restaurant with a tray over their head, and somehow their hand tips, and the food falls out?"

"That's a good thought, too," Thurman agreed. "Or," he continued, "maybe it has something to do with slipping a tip into a maitre d's hand for a better table. So tipping their hand gets you something you wouldn't have had."

"What would that have to do with giving up a secret prematurely?" the Warrior asked.

"Uh, I don't know," Thurman said, a confused look on his face.

"Where can you look this kind of stuff up, anyway?" Knob wondered.

"Yeah, there should be some kind of book or something," Thurman said.

I interrupted, "C'mon, guys, we have work to do."

"Here, I've got another one," the Warrior said.

We looked at the monitor. It was the web-site for Aiyle, Botheryore-Repast Associates. A big red banner blazed across the site, "Should Teleservices be a Part of Your Marketing and Sales Plans?"

"It's in Oak Brook," the Warrior said. "It wouldn't take long to get there, if you guys want to go check it out."

"Yeah, maybe that's what we need to do," I agreed.

"We going to rough them up?" Knob said, a hopeful look on his face. With the elf hat and his thin face, he really did look like some kind of crazed faerie creature.

"No, we're not going to rough them up," I said.

"I don't know," the Warrior said thoughtfully, "violence might be necessary."

"Yeah, let's torture them 'til they squeal like pigs," said the mad elf.

"There won't be any torturing," I said sternly.

The Warrior shrugged. "Fine with me. He's your brother. All I know, is that if he were my brother, I'd hurt whomever I had to."

She hit a button, and a soft whir came from the printer as it spit out a copy of the web page.

"Let's go," she said, grabbing the paper and her purse.

As we headed out to the SUV, I thought about what she had said. Seth, walking jerkily ahead of me, was hand in hand with Thurman, who had appointed himself Seth's guardian. Guardian of the physical Seth, that is. The mental Seth was off somewhere at the present, until we could find a way to join the two back together.

A computer whiz with borderline Attention-Deficit Disorder, and a secret collector of girlie magazines, he'd also been published three times in Penthouse forum although, in truth, he'd never seen a naked woman in the flesh. He had a wide engaging smile, with the remarkable ability to insinuate himself smoothly in any social group.

I thought about his favorite holidays, Halloween and April Fool's Day. Typical choices, if you knew him. Of course he'd pick the holidays with pranks. Never harmful, occasionally outrageous, almost always well strategized. Altogether, a pretty cool kid. Well liked, and fun to be around. I'd never really realized it before.

"*Down!*" Knob hissed, throwing himself on the ground.

Chapter Fifteen

Like well-trained commandos, we flopped onto our bellies, and looked around like a bunch of golfers after hearing, "Fore!"

"What is it?" I whispered to Knob. His hat was askew, and one of the ears was on the top of his head, looking like a pointy satellite dish.

"Shhhhh," he said, his eyes darting back and forth.

The Warrior dragged herself over to us, her eyes alert and threatening. Her umbrella was out, and she looked prepared to use it. "What's going on?" she said in a low intense voice.

"I saw a fly," the elf said furtively.

"A fly?"

"Yeah, a fly."

I stood, angrily dusting myself off. "You mean we dumped ourselves on the ground, just because you saw a *fly*?"

He yanked me back down. "Get back down here," he hissed.

Thurman crawled over. "Did I hear that you saw a fly?"

"Yeah, it went over there." Knob pointed towards a dumpster.

"Oh sure," I scoffed, "there are all kinds of important human secrets in a dumpster."

"You mock," Knob said seriously, "but there really are."

"Yeah, haven't you ever heard of 'dumpster-diving'?" Thurman added.

"Dumpster-diving?"

"Yeah, there are lots of secrets in peoples' trash cans," Knob said, his eyes still searching out flying critters.

"Things like charge card receipts, AOL CD's," Thurman said.

"Old homework, ketchup packets, junk mail," I countered.

"Junk mail can be scary," Knob said, his elf ears quivering from the passion of his statement.

"Yeah, like someone might get their hands on Ed McMahon's offer of a winning sweepstake, right?" I laughed.

"No, serious stuff. Think about it. All these charge card companies send stuff offering pre-approved credit. If the wrong people get their hands on it, they can take over your identity."

"So the flies are in the dumpster, trying to set up a Visa charge card in my name, so they can charge a bunch of Kibbles and Bits, so they can lure dogs to them for the purpose of collecting dog poop?"

"Hey, laugh if you want. But this stuff happens," Thurman admonished me.

"I think the coast is clear," Knob said.

I looked at the dumpster. It was almost fifty yards away.

"How the heck could you see a fly from here?" I asked him.

He turned and looked at me seriously. "Elf Eyes, man. We see better than you ordinary humans."

"What the—?"

"Let's get going," the Warrior said urgently, pushing us towards the SUV. "We have to get out of here before any more flies show up."

"There weren't any—" I started.

Thurman interrupted, talking to Knob, "Elf Eyes, huh? That's pretty cool."

"He doesn't have Elf—"

"Not only that, but I'm an Esquire, too, remember?"

"He's not an esq—"

"So what kind of powers does an Esquire have?" Thurman

asked, his eyes round.

"They don't have pow—"

"I don't know yet," Knob interjected. "I'm waiting for the powers to manifest themselves in some way."

We swept into the SUV, and the Warrior revved the engine, drowning out my protestations. Then we squealed out of the parking lot.

A couple hours later, we were searching the discarded flotsam and jetsam in what had formerly been the offices of Aiyle, Botheryore-Repast Associates.

"Looks like they left in a hurry," Thurman said, reading through some glossy brochures.

That was an understatement. Papers were strewn about the floor. Drag marks through the carpet showed where something heavy had been hauled out. Desks and file cabinets topped with yellowing plants stood abandoned, drawers open, obviously having been hastily riffled through.

The Warrior stood looking out the window at a nearby mall, deep in thought. The office was on the fifth floor of an eight-story building just off the East-West Tollway.

"What's up, Warrior?" I said joshingly.

"Huh? What? Oh, sorry."

"You okay?"

"Yeah. Did you notice who the other tenants are in this building?" she asked.

"No. Should I have?"

She turned back to the window. "Attorneys. The whole damned building is full of attorneys."

Attorneys? All of a sudden, the walls seemed to close on me.

"We should get out of here!" I exclaimed.

"We keep running into attorneys," she said, gazing pensively at shoppers as they scurried in and out a nearby Von Maur Department store. The parking lot was littered with Lexus and Mercedes.

"Okay, okay, let's go!" I shouted.

Knob looked up from a pile of papers. "What's up?"

"Attorneys!" I yelled. "The building is full of them."

"Maybe they should call Orkin," Thurman observed.

The Warrior turned back. "Guy's right, we should get out of here."

Quickly, we ran back out of the office. The Warrior paused to replace the lock she had busted to gain entrance to the deserted office. If you didn't look very carefully, you'd be fooled.

As we hurried to the elevator, I saw that she had been right. All of the offices were attorney and accounting firms. I felt sick, either by suppressed fear or the after-effects of our Taco Bell lunch.

"Let's go, let's go, let's go," I urged, holding my tortured gut.

The elevator doors slid open, and three attorneys suddenly leaped out, waving briefs. I ducked under their briefs, Jockey and Fruit of the Looms mostly, and bolted for the staircase. I heard the clang of umbrella as the Warrior efficiently dispatched them with deadly force.

We clattered down the stairwell, squealing like panicked pigs.

"Go! Go! Go!" I shouted.

Thirty seconds later we were burning rubber.

A minute later we were on the expressway.

Five minutes later we were still on the expressway.

Ten minutes later we were finally breathing normally again, but were still on the expressway.

Thirty minutes later we were off the highway, pulled into the parking lot of a Wal-Mart. The lot was full, so we were well concealed.

A minute later we were out of the SUV, and walking towards the Wal-Mart, Knob keeping an eye out for spy-flies.

Three minutes later, we were in Wal-Mart, at the food court, ordering stuff that would probably kill us, if the attorneys didn't get to us first.

Four minutes later, we were sitting at a sticky table, eating hotdogs, and nachos and cheese. I was sipping a cola, trying to settle my stomach.

"Can't you at least take the hat off when you're eating?" I said grumpily to Knob. He dipped his finger in nacho cheese, and spread it on a chip.

"Ears, man, I can't hear without them."

"Oh, never mind. What next?" I wondered aloud.

The answer came from a surprising source. "We gotta go to another telemarketing place," Thurman said around a mouthful of hotdog.

"Why?"

"I dunno," he mumbled, "but I wonder if all the telemarketing joints got hit by lawyers."

"Hmmm, good thought," the Warrior said. She was eating chocolate cake. There were two Hershey bars waiting their turn on the table next to her plate.

"Okay, so where do we go?" I asked.

"Mfggh, blufghfg," he answered.

"Swallow, Thurman, swallow."

He swallowed. "Here." And he gave me a brochure he'd picked up in the telemarketer office.

It was the attendance list for a group of marketing seminars, some of which were titled: Interrupting Dinner, a Necessary Duty; What They Don't Eat Isn't Good For Them Anyway; So Why Do They Complain?; Stupid Lemming Tricks and How to Get Them To Say Yes.

On it was a list of the attendees, along with their addresses and phone numbers.

Knob scanned the list. "There must be two or three hundred names here. Are we going to go to all of these?"

The names and addresses were from all over the United States.

"No, I think we can concentrate on the ones in and near Chicago," I answered.

"Here's one in Lombard. That's really close," Thurman said.

"Let's go," I said.

Chapter Sixteen

Six hours later, a disconsolate bunch was standing in a deserted office.

"They're gone."

"This reminds me of when the elves all moved back over the ocean in *The Lord of the Rings*," Knob said knowingly.

"It's not—" I started.

Thurman cut me off, "Oh, yeah! *The Two Towers*, right?"

"Yeah. Maybe the telemarketers did the same thing," Knob observed.

"What, moved over the ocean?" I said cuttingly.

Actually, I was more bothered than I wanted to admit. We couldn't find a single live telemarketer. What if they had all moved away, slithering back to where they had come from? How would I get Seth's brain back?

"This isn't good," the Warrior said, looking at the deserted office, her face a stone.

The last office we had checked, the seventh one overall, was as empty and deserted as all of the others. We hadn't seen a soul.

Not that we expected telemarketers to have souls. We didn't see any soles either. They, and whatever telemarketers they had supported, had abruptly fled.

Though we hadn't seen any attorneys, each telemarketer's office had been located near one, if not multiple, attorney nests. Or maybe the attorneys were located near to the telemarketers. We didn't know who was keeping on eye on whom. Still, we felt the evil presence of attorney-stink permeating the hallways and corridors of each of the buildings. A fetid, rotting stench.

Okay, maybe I'm exaggerating, but my nose squinkled with distaste whenever we had gotten very near any plaques containing "Esq." Unfortunately, this building had a lot of squinkles in it!

I strolled around the empty office, kicking at the occasional styrofoam coffee cup. Knob was looking out the window, smearing nose juice on the glass. Thurman was riffling through loose paper. The Warrior surveyed the room, as if somehow she could see back in time to where its occupants had gone.

That's when they came for us!

Their arrival was marked by a loud explosion that blew the front doors off the office suite. Shards of broken glass whistled through the reception area, thudding into wood and crashing loudly into empty metal filing cabinets.

"What the hell?" Thurman yelled, as we all dropped to the floor.

The Warrior had her sword out, and crawled towards the office door. We were in one of the deepest offices in the warren of offices and cubicles. The ones with the best view, more likely to be those of owner or manager of the marketing firm.

She took a quick peek out the doorway. Then, keeping low, she hooked the door with her sword, and pulled it closed.

Once the heavy oak door was closed, she stood and locked it.

"We don't have much time," she said. We knew this, because we could hear people barking orders outside the door.

"We have to get out of here," Knob said, his face pasty with fear.

I looked out the window. There was an excellent view of a park, complete with fountain. But we were five floors up.

"There's nowhere to go," I said.

There was a thump as something rocked the door.

It was solid oak. It shook, but held.

"We have to get out of here," Knob repeated.

Thurman picked up a phone, and put it to his ear, his eyebrows knotted.

"That's not going to do us any good," I told him.

The oak door shuddered again.

"They're going to get through," Knob screamed.

"Calm down, Knob, I'm working on it," Thurman said. He was fumbling through his pockets.

Frantically, I looked for anything I could use as a weapon. The office was almost totally empty of furnishings. I grabbed a metal trashcan, not at all sure what I would do with it. Maybe just put it on my head and pretend I'm an ostrich.

The Warrior guarded the door as it rocked from a steady pounding. It was taking a beating.

"Why aren't they blowing that door open?" I wondered with a weird sort of calmness.

"Maybe they want us alive," the Warrior said, fingering her weapon restlessly.

"Do you know how they got in? That was a pretty strong explosive."

"Yeah. I think it was an anti-trust suit. Pretty strong stuff."

"So it's the attorneys again, isn't it?"

"Yeah. Nobody else could handle suits like that."

"Except maybe cleaners, right?" I laughed at my own lame joke.

A panel in the door buckled from the force of another blow.

I got my trashcan ready.

"You guys wanna leave?" Thurman asked.

We looked at him. He was holding the phone up to his ear with one hand. In the other hand was an object that I recognized as part of his Harry Potter Halloween costume from last year.

"What the—"

"We're getting out of here," he said, and twirled the object. It was a wizard's wand.

"We're not—"

The door buckled and crashed resoundingly onto the floor.

There was a clanging sound as the Warrior's sword met the briefcase of the attorney who bounded into the office. The force of her blow knocked him into the horde of attorneys behind him, scattering subpoenas. Paper fluttered to the floor like swirling leaves.

Thurman waved his wizard's wand like a band conductor. The tip of the wand had disappeared, like the top of a skyscraper into low flying clouds. The room took on a purple tint, sucking clarity from the air. Everything began to lose focus.

The pressure in the room changed, sucking noise from the air.

Suddenly, a concussive blow shattered the plate glass windows. Shards exploded outwards into the air, shimmering as they plummeted to the courtyard far below. Shock waves buffeted me, and I staggered backwards. Losing my balance, I fell. My flailing arms caught Seth, and together we tumbled to the floor.

The room had darkened with a swirling purplish tint. The combatants were indistinct, vague images in hallucinogenic haze. Dimly I could make out the Warrior, who was still fighting off a horde of attorneys, some of whom had gained entrance into the room.

She was screaming her war cries, "WHO DO YOU EXPECT TO PICK UP THIS MESS! WELL LET ME TELL YOU, IT'S NOT GOING TO BE ME!"

Thurman had gotten on top of a desk, waving his Harry Potter wand. For some reason, he still had the phone receiver tucked under his chin. He kicked at an attorney who was trying to grab his leg. The attorney crashed backwards into a wandering deposition.

The air was swirling, whether by the influx of incoming atmosphere from the devastated windows, or by whatever it was that Thurman was doing, I didn't know.

Several attorneys managed to duck under the Warrior's wide swinging blade, and they rushed at me. I felt powerless to do anything.

There was a buzzing sound in my ears.

Then I realized it was because a fly had come in the window.

"Quick, we have to get out of here," I screamed.

THUMP!

It was back, whatever it was. The round cloud of pound.

Did the attorneys bring it?

WHOOOMMMPPP!

The room shook again, not very happy about the pounding it was getting today.

An attorney rushed to the broken window, and hurled a stack of rubber banded subpoenas at the cloud.

I grabbed Seth, and ducked. This was going to be bad.

Suddenly, the purple tint in the room intensified, swirling and obscuring everything with a purple haze. Loud distorted sounds, like an electric guitar gone haywire, thundered in my tortured earballs, and I lost the room.

Not that I lost it, really. More like it had lost me.

I couldn't feel the floor beneath me. I could see nothing except purple and black swirls. Somehow I had the motion of floating, without the motion of floating. We were moving, but not moving.

I could sense that the others were with me. I wondered if the attorneys had also been sucked into whatever we had been sucked into. Or spit into. Or whatever it was that took us from that room and put us in this indefinable existence.

A long time, or a short time, later, we fell without falling into a place that wasn't a place. Not that it wasn't a place. It was a place. But not like a place in the ordinary sense of, uh, placeness. When I found I still was holding Seth's hand, I didn't let go.

"Whoa," Knob said. His hat was skewed, and one of his elf ears stuck out of the middle of his forehead like the horn of a mutant unicorn. I assumed the other ear was listening from the back of his head.

"Where are we?" the Warrior groaned, weaving on her feet.

At least it looked like she was on her feet. Beneath, below and above us was a purplish black cloud that billowed rhythmically, pulsating as if it were breathing.

Thurman stood between us, his wand still aloft in one hand.

"You really *are* a sorcerer!" Knob gushed.

Thurman gave him a look that somehow blended wise and smug. "Of course I am."

"You're not a sorcerer!" I retorted.

He looked at me.

"Are you?" I added weakly.

"Yep, and I'm really an elf," Knob said, with a mug full of smug.

"Straighten your ears," the Warrior suggested to the elf.

"So, okay, Mr. Sorcerer, where are we?" I asked, disguising my fear as sarcasm.

The confident look fled Thurman's face. "Uh, I'm not really sure."

"*You're not sure?*"

"Well," he looked around at the swirling clouds of purple, "it looks like we're in a kind of…" his voice trailed away.

The purple smoke pulsated helpfully.

"You think this smoke is some kind of relation to the cloud that's been chasing us?" Knob asked.

"Oh, like some kind of 'fallen' cloud, the same way Satan was a fallen angel?" the Warrior wondered.

"That wouldn't make any sense. Why would a fallen cloud chase us and threaten our McDonald's french fries?" I said.

"Maybe it knew that we had a sorcerer who could send it home," Knob suggested.

"I'm thirsty," Thurman complained.

"Yeah, sorcering probably takes it out of you," the Warrior sympathized.

"We don't have any—"

"Here ya' go, man," Knob interrupted, thrusting a handful of lemon-flavored moist towelettes at our sorcerer. "Told you they'd come in handy," he added in full smug.

"Well, that's all fine and dandy," I said, "but what are we going to do about food?" I waved at the whirling purple smoke. The air was breathable, even pleasant. But it was as if we were in some kind of sensory deprivation that only allowed the smoke. Our voices were muffled, and there was no sign of what caused the light source.

I felt what passed for the ground, but my hands were repelled before touching anything. It was as if there were a force field hovering just below us, whose force got stronger as you neared it.

"We won't starve, for a while," Thurman said.

"Why, is this smoke edible?" I spat.

"Well, no," he said, "but I have a bag of dog treats. I'm sure Weezel wouldn't mind sharing."

"Are they invisible, too?" I asked nastily. I was feeling bitchy. No, not bitchy, I'm not a girl. I was feeling bastardy.

He looked hurt. "No, they aren't invisible."

"Yeah, and they taste pretty good," Knob said sagely.

Thurman glared at him. "How would you know that?"

Knob looked sheepish. "Well, you know, sometimes when we're between grocery shopping..."

"You steal Weezel's food!"

"Oh, ah...I'm sorr—"

Something flew at my head. I screamed like a little girl. "AAAAIIIIEEEEEE!" I ducked, waving my hands frantically.

"What was that?" Thurman asked.

"Sounded like some kind of siren," Knob said.

"It was Guy," the Warrior said, pointing at me.

"I didn't say anyth...AAAIIEEEE!" I said calmly.

Okay, not so calmly. But what would you do if a cloud kept tabs on you by sending spy flies at you, and then all of a sudden a bug flies at your face? Yeah, you'd have screamed, too.

"What are they?" Thurman asked, looking wonderingly at the tiny buzzing metallic objects darting around us.

"Coleoptera, man," Knob said, cupping his hands around one of them.

"Cleopatra?"

"No, Coleoptera."

"Huh?"

"Coleoptera, the ladybug, from the family Coccinellidae."

"Oh, no," I groaned.

"What?"

"We're going to hear all about ladybugs," I moaned.

"What's this about ladybugs?" the Warrior asked.

"Actually, the ladybird beetle," Knob said, busy leafing through another book from his knapsack.

"I like ladybugs," Thurman said.

"AAAAAIIIIEEEEEE!" I screamed.

"*What?*"

"It bit me! The damned bug bit me!"

"Oh, that's because this particular beetle is the Asian Lady Beetle. They are far more aggressive than the North American beetle."

"What the hell did it bite me for? I'm not a leaf!"

"Yeah," Knob chuckled, "that's a common misconception. Except for one genus, ladybugs are carnivorous insects."

"They eat humans?" I snarled

"I heard ladybugs were named for the Virgin Mary," the Warrior said.

"Hey, very good," Knob approved. "In fact, back in the Middle Ages they were regarded as benevolent intervention by the Virgin Mary, because they helped farmers by controlling agricultural pests. So that's how they got the common name ladybird."

"I always find them in my house in the winter," the Warrior said.

"Yep. They're mountain insects, and usually spend winters hiding in crevices on cliffs. Since we don't have mountains here, they crawl into houses instead."

"I like doing this," Thurman said.

He had one in his hand, and it looked like he was drawing on it.

"Whatcha doing?" Knob said, interested.

"Check it out." Thurman opened his hand, and we could see a ladybug in his palm.

"It's purple," the Warrior said.

"Yeah, you get really cool colors if you color them with magic markers. I used a green marker, but it colored the beetle purple."

"Cool, man."

The ladybug's shell flipped open, and it buzzed off to go bite someone else.

As we watched it fly away, we saw hundreds more flying around like mini Huey helicopters.

"I don't know why, but somehow I don't feel so scared anymore," Knob said, looking wonderingly at the purple clouds billowing around us.

"Yeah, if the ladybugs are safe, maybe we are, too," Thurman agreed.

"So what now, Mr. Sorcerer?"

"I guess I have to get us out of here," he said resolutely.

"Can you do it?" the Warrior asked.

"I don't know, but I can try."

Thurman took out the Harry Potter wand, and waved it experimentally.

I cringed, waiting for what came next. I guess, in a way, this was a compliment to Thurman, because I wasn't so sure anymore that he couldn't do magic. The Warrior and Knob braced themselves, too. Only Seth seemed unaffected, but, then again, he didn't have a brain anyway.

The wand circled and circled while Thurman recited incantations.

I edged closer to listen.

He was singing under his breath, "Bye, bye, Miss American Pie..."

Nothing was happening.

"...drove my Chevy to the levee..."

A ladybug swooped low for a closer look. Or maybe it just wanted to sing along to that catchy tune.

"...but the levee was dry..."

It circled, deciding whether to bite me again.

"...and good ole boys were drinking whiskey and rye..."

Purple cloud swirled around the end of the wand.

"...singing, 'this will be the day that I die'..."

"Hey!"

I looked up. I didn't know the voice. It was getting darker.

"Hey! Wait!"

"...singing, 'this will be the day, that I die'..."

"Come back!"

But it was too late. We were gone.

Chapter Seventeen

"You know what I always wondered about?" Knob asked.

"Huh?" I said.

"Why humans keep getting bigger, but animals are getting smaller."

"Huh?" My head was spinning.

"Think about it. The average height for a man nowadays is almost six-foot. Two hundred years ago, someone that tall was considered a giant."

"Wha...?" The room was spinning, too.

"That's barely more than average now, though."

"Uh."

Knob continued on, "And two hundred years before that, you'd be tall if you were five and half feet tall. But if you look at animals, they're smaller than they used to be."

My head and the room were spinning in different directions. Maybe this wasn't normal for me, but Knob wouldn't notice the difference.

"Think about it, crocodiles from the dinosaur days could be as long as a hundred feet, or even more."

His head was always spinning anyway, so this was probably pretty typical for him.

"Nowadays, it isn't unusual to be six and a half, or even seven feet tall."

"Knob?"

"Yeah?"

"Shut up."

"Where are we?" Thurman groaned.

"Ohhh," the Warrior moaned.

I smelled something.

"You know," Knob continued, "I think it has a lot to do with the Big Gulp."

"Huh?"

"Do I smell hamburgers?" Thurman asked groggily.

"And bigger sized portions," Knob said. "And what's worse, is that bigger portions are almost forced upon us. Do you want to biggie-size it for forty-nine cents?" he mimicked.

I opened my eyes, and peered blearily towards the sound of his voice. He was sitting at a table, waving a french fry as he made his points.

"Where'd you get that?" I asked, vaguely noticing that I was sitting at the table, too.

"You want some?" he said, standing, and pulling his wallet out of his pocket.

"What are we doing here?" the Warrior asked.

For the first time, I looked around, and was startled when I realized that I recognized where we were. Well, not exactly where we were. But I knew where we were.

In a way.

Kind of.

Well, specifically, if not exactly.

A McDonald's restaurant.

Not that this shed any light, because we could be anywhere in the world, and be pretty darn close to a McDonald's somewhere. Russia, China, whatever. For that matter, we might be anywhere in the universe, and there could be a McDonald's. The power of franchising.

The purple fog was gone, and this place looked like any old American McDonald's. American writing on the menu above the counters, American flag flying outside the building, American (or

English, if you prefer) being spoken by the other people in the half-filled restaurant.

"How'd we get here?" I wondered.

"I think it was the song," Thurman said.

Now I remembered. When Thurman was doing his magic... (what else would you call it, admitted the Unbeliever?)...he was singing, "American Pie." Somehow, it brought us to McDonald's, as American a place as you could come up with. Sure enough, there was a pie on our table in front of Knob. Dutch Apple.

Frankly, after getting sucked into a purple cloud and spit back out into a McDonald's restaurant, a chocolate shake sounded pretty good.

"Well, do you guys want anything?" Knob asked, still on his feet.

"Yeah, I'm starved," I said, getting to my feet, and pulling out my wallet. "Anyone else?"

A few minutes later, digging into our food, I asked the question that had been bugging me, "How come we keep ending up in McDonald's?"

"We like McNuggets?" Thurman offered.

"Maybe."

"Okay, how about the flies?"

"Maybe they like McNuggets, too," Knob suggested.

"I don't know," I said, rubbing my temple. "It seems like there are themes that keep running through this Quest."

"Like the cloud," Thurman said.

"Yeah, the cloud." I looked around nervously. Nothing in sight yet, but it always appeared without warning.

"So what was that place?" the Warrior asked Thurman, watching as he fed a french fry to Seth.

"The purple place? I really don't know. When the attorneys attacked us, I wasn't really aiming anyplace in particular. I was just trying to escape. I didn't know where we would end up."

"How long have you known you were a sorcerer?" Knob asked.

Thurman grinned. "About as long as you've known you're an elf."

Knob nodded, and looked critically down at his lanky frame.

"Yeah, I know I don't look it, but I've always had an affinity for nature and stuff."

"Yeah," Thurman laughed, "and you always get perky around Christmas."

"The most wonderful holiday," Knob intoned.

Thurman flipped a french fry onto the floor. The fry disappeared.

Shrugging, I ignored it, and we ate in silence, the only sound that of Knob sucking a shake.

"OWWWW!" He grabbed his head, his elf hat tumbling onto the floor.

Seasoned warriors now, we all dove for the floor.

"Knob, are you okay?" Thurman said.

"Oh, man!" Knob groaned, squeezing his head at the temples.

"*Knob?*"

"Ice cream brain freeze!" Knob said through gritted teeth.

"Sheesh! Don't do that!" I grumped.

We regained our seats.

"Ohhh, this hurts, man!"

"So what do we do now?" the Warrior asked, ignoring the tortured elf, and gazing speculatively out the window.

"I'm not sure," I admitted.

"Whew, it's going away," Knob said with relief.

Thurman broke in, "I think we were close with the telemarketer thing. That's probably why the attorneys panicked and attacked us."

"You think they panicked?" I asked him.

"Ahhhh," Knob groaned.

"Yeah, it didn't seem like they were very well coordinated," Thurman said to me.

"Who the heck are we fighting, attorneys or telemarketers?" the Warrior said, exasperation breaking through.

"I wish I knew," I said. "I wish I knew."

Slurp, slurp, slurp. "OWWWW!"

"Knob, you idiot!"

"So where's the SUV?" the Warrior wondered.

We were strolling through the parking lot, scanning the sky for round, angry clouds. Our elf, recovered from the attack on his alleged brain, was scouting for flies.

"Hey," Thurman pointed, "isn't that it right there?"

Sure enough, it was in the parking lot adjacent to the McDonald's parking lot.

"Hey, it's the building where we found the advertising agency," Knob exclaimed.

"Yeah, we're back where we started from," Thurman said.

"Hey, man, good job," Knob told him. "You got us right back into the same place we came from."

"Good aim, Thurman," the Warrior said. "Not only that, but you set us down safely away from the building."

Thurman flushed. "Uh, yeah, I guess."

We walked towards the SUV. It was a pretty nice day, and the sun cast long shadows as fall approached.

Someone stepped from the SUV's shadow. "Hello, you've given us quite the run."

Like an alarmed hedgehog, we bristled. Thurman whipped out his wand, Knob dropped into a crouch, the Warrior's muscles sprung out with an audible sound, Seth didn't move really hard, and I, uh, was startled.

"Who are you?" the Warrior demanded.

Another figure stepped out from the other side of the SUV. "We come in peace."

"Don't believe 'em," Knob said. "Didn't you see the movie?"

"Huh?" I asked.

"The movie. You know, the movie where these aliens come to Earth and say, 'We come in peace,' and people lower their defenses, and the alien blows them away," he said, wide-eyed.

"They aren't aliens," I snapped.

In fact, they didn't look like aliens. They looked like attorneys.

"We aren't aliens," the one said.

"Yeah, that's what all aliens say," Knob countered.

"They're attorneys," I told him.

"No, we aren't attorneys," the not-the-alien one disagreed.

"Well, you sure look like attorneys to me," I shot.

"It's true we're in the legal profession," he said. "But we're paralegals, not attorneys."

"Is that like paratroopers?" Knob demanded. "Or paramilitary? Some kind of fighting force?"

"No. Paralegals are normal people who do legal work, but who aren't attorneys. Or in some cases, not yet attorneys."

"So you're still human?" Knob asked.

"Attorneys are hu... Look, we've been instructed to try and talk with you. It was thought we'd be less threatening."

They were, in fact, less threatening. The two of them, paralegal number one and paralegal number two, were dressed in button down shirts, loafers and comfortable sweaters. Still though, the stench of legal action emanated from them.

"What do you want to talk about?" the Warrior asked, her guard still not relaxed.

"We'd like to ask you to come to a pretrial conference," the second paralegal said. He was blonde, short, with a soft body from hours of looking up precedents in dusty old legal books.

"Are we being sued?" I asked.

"A pretrial conference?" the Warrior wondered at the same time.

"No, you aren't being sued," he said.

"Uh, Bob, we don't know that for sure," the other paralegal corrected. He had the same puffiness, but had unruly dark hair.

Bob furrowed his brows in thought. "Oh, yeah, I guess they could be."

"Yeah, we don't know for sure," the first paralegal said.

Bob's face cleared. "Well, it's safe to say that no litigation has yet been initiated."

"Yes, that you can do," the first paralegal agreed.

"Huh?" the Warrior said brightly. Okay, not so brightly.

Bob turned to the other paralegal. "Explain it to them, okay, Tom?"

Tom cleared his throat. "We're here with the covenant."

"What's a 'covenant'?" the Warrior interrupted.

"A promise," Knob interjected.

"How'd you know that?" I demanded. Knob wasn't supposed

to know long words, other than Latin words for bugs.

"Did you forget?" he asked smugly.

"Forget what?"

"I'm an esquire, just like these gentlemen."

"That doesn't make you a lawyer," I retorted.

"I don't know," he said with an air of importance, "whether the estoppel of fact could preclude you from making that statement."

"What are you talking about?" I shot at him.

"Hmmm," paralegal Bob said, "he might be right."

"What are you talking about?" I shot at him.

Paralegal Tom answered, "I think they're trying to say that the law prevents you from denying certain facts because of previous conduct or statements."

"Huh?"

"I don't know if an estoppel would be warranted under situations like this," Tom said to Bob.

"Maybe, maybe not, that's why we need a judge," Bob answered.

"Yes, we need a judge," they chimed in unison, rapt looks on their faces. "A judge would clear up everything."

"Well, there is certainly no condition of *lis pendens* that could create a condition where we might be summoned to any type action," Knob told them.

"How do you know this stuff?" I screamed at him.

"That's true," paralegal Bob answered Knob. "In fact, there is a possibility that the matter with regard to your actions is *res judicata.*"

"That'd be for a judge to rule on," paralegal Tom declared.

"Yes, we need a judge," they chimed in unison, looking prayerfully at the sky. This time Knob joined them.

"Look," paralegal Bob said, "we're just inviting you to a small conference where possibly we could work out our differences."

"A settlement," paralegal Tom added.

"Perhaps," Knob said, "but there would have to exist a temporary condition of clemency, attested to and notarized, by a party with the inchoate power to represent the interests of the law profession, prior to my clients—"

"Your clients!" I screamed.

"—my Clients," he continued deliberately, giving me the 'shut up' look that I usually gave to him, "entering into a negotiation wherein adjudicated action may result in incrimination leading to incarceration."

"Man, you're good," Thurman exclaimed to Knob.

During the discussion, someone else had approached quietly.

"What is it, boy?" Thurman asked the air below him.

"Weezel?" Knob asked.

"Yeah, he's barking his brains out," Thurman said, with a puzzled look on his face.

"I think he's trying to warn you about me," a deep voice said.

"Damn!" I did one of those startled dorky jump things. Then I recovered and tried to look cool.

"Who the hell are you?" the Warrior said, quickly bristling back into fight-mode.

"Judge Wopner," the figure said.

Chapter Eighteen

"Judge Wopner?" I asked.

"The TV judge?" Thurman asked.

"Well, yes and, er, no," he said, with an embarrassed air.

"Is it 'yes' or 'no'?" the Warrior accused. She had backed until she was positioned to see all three of our adversaries with a single glance. I tried to mimic her, but backed up against a Volkswagon Bug.

The judge continued, "I am Judge Wopner, but I'm not *the* Judge Wopner."

"That's got to confuse people," Thurman said.

"Yes, it is my cross to bear," the Judge agreed.

He turned to the two paralegals, including Knob in his glance, "I think we can dispense with the legal jargon for the sake of our little discussion."

The two paralegals looked relieved.

Knob looked disappointed.

The judge turned back to me, somehow having decided that I was the person to talk with. "We're not after you, and I'd like to explain it to you. But not here." He looked around. "It would be safer in my chambers. Would you trust me?"

We all looked at each other, and with unspoken assent, I

nodded.

"Okay, then please follow me."

"Where?" I asked.

He pointed to a nearby building. "Over there."

The county courthouse.

"Ah, man," Knob said, cuffing himself, "no wonder there were so many lawyers in that building."

"Yeah," Thurman said, a shaken look on his face, "we were on their turf."

We entered a private gated parking lot next to the building, and went in through a small side door, manned by an armed security guard. From there, we went down a long corridor lined with glossy mahogany walls, and framed photos of judges. At one point, the judge simply pushed on the wall, which revealed itself to be an extremely high door, going all the way to the ceiling. It swung open slowly and majestically. The paralegals stopped at the door, assuming guard positions on either side.

We had entered a cavernous courtroom. On one side of the room was the jury box, on the opposite side a bas relief seal of the State of Illinois, flanked by the United States flag and flag for the State of Illinois. Long tables for the plaintiff and defendant bisected the room, with a small podium in front of each. Wooden pew-like seats were empty of spectators, forlorn in the dim room. It was a place of shadows and echoes, in that void between confrontation and argument.

"We'll be in the conference room," the judge said, as he led us through another door on the other side of the courtroom.

This led to a smaller room. The only items were a round table and several chairs.

"Have a seat," the judge said kindly.

He waited for us to sit, and then he sat, his back to the door.

The door itself opened again, and a beautiful, young buxom woman entered the room, dressed in a gray pinstriped suit, though with a very short skirt rather than trousers. Her legs were magnificent. She had a white dress shirt, with the first four buttons unbuttoned, exposing about three inches of finely sculpted cleavage. My breath caught. I could hear similar sucking sounds as Knob and Thurman both inhaled in unison.

"Ah, my dear, that won't be necessary. We," and he gestured at us, "are dispensing with the need to record this session."

She nodded professionally, and retreated out the door. As my eyes cleared of cleavage, I noticed her wonderful calves. I mean, that she was pulling a small bag on wheels behind, her Court Reporter's stenotype machine.

As the door slid closed, the quiet was broken by the lungs of three men exhaling with relief.

"Wow!" Thurman breathed.

"Wow!" I breathed.

"Wow!" Knob breathed.

Seth just breathed.

The Warrior snorted, and turned to Judge Wopner. "Okay, what do you want from us?"

"She's quite lovely, isn't she?" he said.

"Huh?" Knob asked.

"Melissa, my Court Reporter. Of course, you," and he gestured towards the Warrior, "are no slouch yourself."

She tried to look offended, but it was obvious she was flattered.

"She's right," I said. "What exactly are you looking for from us?"

"Yeah, and why have you been chasing us all over hell?" Knob demanded. "And, uh, back again?"

"We're in a war," Judge Wopner said, "and you people got yourselves involved."

We all erupted.

"What do you mean, *got ourselves involved?*"

"Somebody stole my brother's brain!" I screamed at him.

"What the hell are you talking about?"

He held his hands out placatingly. "Whoa, calm down, calm down."

He waited until we were quiet. "Okay, perhaps my words were a little unfortunate."

I snorted. "Yeah, just a little unfortunate."

"I didn't mean to imply that you had voluntarily involved yourself in a war that had nothing to do with you. Nor did I mean that you were any bit at fault for having stumbled into our battlefield. What I meant was that in your attempts to investigate telemarketers, you inadvertently entered into our arena."

"Your arena?" the Warrior prompted.

"Well, the arena of battle," the Judge amended.

"What's all of that got to do with Seth?" I demanded.

"Nothing, and that's my point," the Judge answered. "We have no interest in your brother's brain."

"Then why are you chasing us all over?" Knob demanded.

"Yeah!" Thurman shot at him.

The judge didn't answer for a moment, allowing the silence to build.

"We wanted you to be couriers," he said finally.

"Couriers?" I asked.

"Yes, we wanted to get a message through to the Grand Telemarketer. And we thought that you might be the means to achieve this."

"Why?"

"We can't reach him ourselves, and we had some confidence that you, because of your vested interest, might succeed where we failed."

I thought about it. I was certainly motivated. I looked at Seth, his blank face illustrating incomprehension to what was going on around him. It was like he was an unthinking zombie. Images of his face, alight with mischief and life, flitted through my mind, searing with the poignant memories of a happy-go-lucky little brother. A friendly little scamp. I made a pact with myself that when I got his brain back, I was going to show him a lot more appreciation in the future.

That is, if we succeeded.

"You have half a million lawyers," I reminded him, "surely you can find him, yourself."

"You'd think so," he agreed. "But how long did it take that many soldiers to find Saddam Hussein?"

Hmmm, good point.

"Not only that, but we can't devote all of our resources to that front. In fact, I'm not so very certain that it is important at all."

"Why, what kind of message are we supposed to give him?" I asked.

Before he could answer, Knob interrupted, "We've been wondering about you guys."

"What's that?" the Judge asked, nonplussed.

"I don't know," Knob said. "But it seems to me that you guys are on a campaign to, I don't know, take over the world, or something."

"What makes you say that?" the Judge asked him, his face a mask.

"I'm not sure. But it seems to me that whenever anyone gets too big, you guys try to take them down."

"Indeed."

"Yeah, like the cigarette companies. You guys tore them down with suits."

"Cigarettes are bad for you," the Judge said. "Surely you don't have a problem with them paying their fair share of the medical care caused by their product."

"Then how about McDonald's? You sued them because some lady burned herself when she dumped coffee on herself!"

"Well, McDonald's food isn't very healthy, either," the Judge said calmly. "So why would you have a problem with them paying a woman for disfigurement and pain?"

"That's not the point," Knob said, shaking with exasperation. "What about Microsoft? Their stuff isn't bad for you."

"Antitrust. They knowingly stifled competition. It would have hurt the consumer had they continued their conquests unchecked."

"Telemarketing?"

"Shouldn't a family be able to eat a meal in peace?"

"Hey, wait a minute," I said.

They all looked at me.

"You guys represent both sides. You don't lose either way."

"What are you saying?" the Warrior asked.

Ideas were spinning in my mind.

"Think about it. Cigarette companies were money machines. McDonald's rolls in money. Microsoft was loaded. And look at all of the tort actions against drug companies and airlines. Attorneys," and I pointed at the Judge, "simply pick out the fattest cat, come up with some reason to sue them, then they attack like piranha, ripping huge chunks of cash out of their prey."

"You don't say," the Judge said, his face blank.

"Who's next?" I accused him, pointing a shaky finger at him. "The oil companies? The NRA?"

"No, the NRA makes us nervous. Those bastards are crazy," Wopner said nervously.

"You're already after the oil companies, aren't you? Oil spills and stuff. But something happened to slow you down."

"I know," Knob said, "I'll bet those safety warnings about not using cell phones while filling your gas tank screwed them up."

"Lousy meddlers," the Judge muttered.

"You've already taken over the United States," I yelled, on a roll now. "Almost every Senator, Congressman and President is a lawyer. You guys write the laws, judge the laws, and then make money litigating both sides of every issue."

"Not to mention double damages, treble damages, and everything else," Thurman put in.

"Yeah, and every contract, which is written by attorneys, includes provisions for fees and stuff," Knob added.

Another thought occurred to me. "Think about it. In every sale there are a bunch of terms written by the seller, and a bunch of contrary terms written by the buyer, but it's all written in such gobbly-gook that if something goes wrong, there's almost no way to resolve it short of hiring lawyers."

"Yeah, the words are written in a language nobody understands," Knob said, his face ashen.

"Yeah, with words that aren't even in the dictionary," Thurman breathed. "So you need to fight them with other attorneys who understand the same language."

"And divorces," the Warrior gasped. "Even if they start off friendly, everything always ends up in a huge fight, taking too much time, which all ends up being to the advantage of the attorneys, who end up getting everything."

"Yeah," Knob said. "And who's the only person who always receives their money in a bankruptcy?"

"Attorneys," we all breathed together.

"Okay, you found us out," Judge Wopner said dryly. He looked at each of us. "We're not the bad guys, despite what you think."

"Oh, yeah?' Thurman challenged him.

The judge gave him a scathing look. Thurman, rather than backing down, returned the look. I had the feeling he was going to pull his wand out and start laying purple Harry Potter smoke again.

I think the judge had a similar impression, because he backed off, maybe sorry he left his paralegals outside. "Really, boys and lady, we are the arbiters of our society, keeping the playing field level for all citizens."

"'Arbiter.' See, he used one of those words again," Thurman pointed out.

"What are you talking about?" the Warrior asked Judge Wopner.

He looked haughtily at us. "Well, you're right, actually. We attorneys are in a win-win situation, but not for the reasons that you think."

"How's that?" the Warrior spat.

"Think about it," he said. "You're right in that we don't truly care about the outcome for ourselves. We win either way, so what is it that we are truly accomplishing?"

"Double-dipping," I sneered.

"No, that's not it. Because we have no vested interest, we supply every possible argument—"

"At three hundred dollars per hour," I interjected.

The Judge's finger jerked, as if he wanted to bang an imaginary gavel. "—with a non-biased judge—"

"Who can't be voted out of office," I put in snidely. Without the gavel, he was powerless to stop me.

"—ruling fairly on the basis of arguments alone, factoring out the emotionalism of the two sides—"

"Because you don't care."

"—and, in essence," he said, manfully, or judgefully, trying to press his point through my interruptions, "we present the same fairness and evenhandedness to the situation as," and he paused.

"As what?" the Warrior asked.

"As a gambling casino," he said, unexpectedly.

"A gambling casino?" Knob asked.

"More like bookies," I uttered.

"Think about it," the Judge said. "Gambling casinos. The only reason we have gambling is because people want them, right?"

"Let's say we'll grant that point. What's that got to do with suing people?" I asked.

"Yeah, people don't enjoy suing each other," Thurman added.

"Oh?" the Judge said. "You don't think so? If somebody makes you really angry, you don't enjoy threatening to sue their pants off?"

As much as I hated to admit it, he had a point.

"I still don't get the connection to gambling casinos," I said.

"Where does a casino make its money?" he asked.

"They take money off the top."

"And the question who wins isn't important to them at all, right?" he asked. "Isn't that pretty much what lawyers do?"

We were silent, for a moment, digesting this argument.

"They don't pick fights, though," Knob said quietly.

"What do you mean, Knob?" I asked him.

"Ambulance chasing, product liability and tort actions, stuff like that. Things where maybe no one would file a suit, if some attorney weren't whispering in their ear."

"We're protecting people, making sure they are fully advised and properly recompensed for actionable negligence or malfeasance on the parts of corporate evildoers," Wopner said.

"You need half a million lawyers to do that?" the Warrior asked.

"Yeah, you guys make the stakes so much higher than necessary, like suing a homeowner if a door to door salesperson slips on ice on their sidewalk while doing what basically amounts to an invasion of privacy, or trespassing."

"And how about burglars who sue a property owner for shooting them when they're in the act of trying to steal their possessions?"

The Judge didn't answer.

"You know," I said, "I had another thought. How come you guys haven't gone after the casinos yet? Talk about money."

"We're working on it," the Judge muttered.

Then he straightened. "Anyway, it doesn't matter what you

people think. You can't stop what we're doing, and half the time you probably wouldn't want to stop what we're doing. Who cares if we go after cigarette companies, Microsoft and drug companies? We get cheered for doing this. What you hate us for is all the other stuff. But get this. We have thick skins. We don't care! You can't bring us down. What would you do, sue us? Ha, ha, ha, ha! You can't do anything to us, except tell stupid attorney jokes. Big deal. We're crying all the way to the bank."

That shut us up. What could we do? Complain to our Congressman...an attorney? Or our Senator...an attorney?

Thurman's fingers flinched towards his wand again, and the Warrior's face started getting red.

"Calm down, you two," I told them. "Nothing you do to him will change anything."

"Yeah," Wopner said, "and I'd have to sue you."

"Shut up!" I yelled at him. "Or I'll let them hurt you."

He shut up.

"Okay, Wopner, let's have it. What do you want us to tell the telemarketer?"

Ten minutes later, we were in the SUV, heading down the highway. We were subdued.

Knob was the first to break the silence, "Damn, I forgot to ask him about the flies!"

"Huh?" Thurman asked.

"We need to know who's sending them after us. And the killer cloud."

"It's not the attorneys," I told them.

"No?"

"No. It wouldn't make sense. The flies bring the cloud after us, right? And wasn't it the cloud who busted up the attorneys' attack on us?"

"He's got a point," the Warrior said.

"Yeah," Knob admitted.

We were quiet as the miles flew by. The Warrior had pretty much gotten on the highway and driven, no destination in mind. We all felt better as we put miles between us and Judge Wopner.

My mind was spinning with the implications of what we'd

heard. It was so fantastic, but, still, it resonated with truthfulness. And the Judge was right, what could we do about it? And should we bother? Though the legal system had been mucking up human lives forever, he was also right that we needed it. Otherwise, chaos would rule. People could do whatever they wanted to others without fear of punishment.

About the only thing out there powerful enough to fight law and politics was the media. Only through their efforts could the people chip away at the foundations of the huge litigation nest egg built by and for the attorney species.

"So what now?" Thurman asked.

"I think we have to confront the flies or the cloud. Or maybe confront them together," I said.

"Are you crazy?" Knob yelped.

"Yeah, maybe. But if they have anything to do with the person who took Seth's brain, maybe some kind of opportunity will present itself. Unless any of you have a better idea?"

They were quiet.

"Can we think about it?" Knob asked anxiously.

"Of course, I don't want anyone to get hurt. I'd love it if someone could come up with any alternative. But I don't know how much more time we have. How long can Seth live without his brain?"

"He's right," Thurman agreed.

"You've done just fine without yours," Knob chided him.

"When would you want to do this?" the Warrior asked me.

"Tomorrow morning," I said. "Tomorrow we'll call the cloud."

As we drove down the highway, we wondered what the next day would bring.

Chapter Nineteen

"I hate this!" Knob said, his face wrinkled with distaste.

"Aaugh! This is gross!" Thurman agreed. "I'm going to toss my cookies."

"Shut up, and keep an eye out!" I told them.

We were at the park, standing in the open field near a small cove of trees.

A thin brown ring circled the five of us.

"Maybe we should have skipped breakfast," the Warrior said, her face a seasick color.

It had not taken long to find bait for flies. All we had to do was roam the park for fifteen minutes with plastic potty bags in hand. Then we built a ring of stinky crap twenty feet across. Now we stood within the ring, waiting for bluebottle, or greenbottle or whatever flavor of fly might be interested in some nice, fresh piles of doggy doo.

"What are we supposed to do with this stuff when we're done?" Thurman asked, disgust etched on his face.

"I don't know." I honestly hadn't given it a thought.

"Where are they? It doesn't usually take them this long to show up," Knob observed.

"Maybe we should have brought some McDonald's french

fries. We know that attracts them," Thurman said.

"Yeah, they smell better, too," Knob agreed.

"Ugh, I don't even want to think about food," the Warrior groaned.

"I think we ought to haul this stuff over to the Courthouse," Thurman suggested. "Leave it in Judge Wopner's parking space."

"He's already full of shit," Knob said. "He'd never notice."

"We could dump it at my ex's house," the Warrior offered.

"Shhh!" Knob interrupted. He stared intently into the trees.

"What? Do you see something?" I whispered harshly.

"I hear one!" he whispered back.

I believed him. I was actually starting to believe that our local elf-wannabe had extra sensitive hearing and eyesight.

I peered into the trees, my heart pounding. I was dreading the thought of encountering the mighty thumping cloud. Memories of buildings violently blasted into kindling and cars pounded to pancake thinness darkened my thoughts. Still though, I found it almost ridiculous that the arrival of an insect conjured such ponderous thoughts and fear.

"There it is." Knob pointed.

We all peered in the direction he was pointing. It occurred to me that something huge could be sneaking up behind us while we were all waiting in fear and loathing for a tiny bug. Then again, we have the ring of shit to protect us. Except, of course, unless a band of hungry dung beetles chose to descend upon us.

"I see it," Thurman shouted.

"Shhh!" Knob cautioned. "We don't want to spook it."

"Can flies hear?" Thurman wondered.

"I don't know," Knob said. "I guess if they're here to spy on humans, they should be able to."

"I heard that snakes can't hear," Thurman said.

"You're right," Knob said, distracted from watching the fly. "I saw the neatest show on Discovery about snake charmers, and how it's their motion, not the sound that controls the snakes."

"Knob! The fly?" I suggested.

"Oh, yeah." He looked back for the fly. "Where'd he go?"

We all looked around, including on the shit, but couldn't see any sign of a fly.

"What the hell?" Knob asked.

Nobody had an answer to his question.

Usually, a hundred or so pieces of dog crap would have attracted thousands of flies. Instead, there were none. Their absence was startling and eerie.

Whomp!

The ground vibrated slightly.

"I hear it!" Knob shouted.

It was somewhat distant.

WHOMP!

Getting closer.

"Yee-hah!" Thurman yelled.

"What are you so happy about?" Knob screamed at him.

"I don't know!" Thurman screamed back.

WHOMP!

The stand of trees was suddenly splintered by a whirling cloud ball.

"Duck!" Knob hollered.

"Get it, Thurman!" I said quietly. No, not quietly. I bellowed like a walrus in heat. Not really, I whimpered like a scared wimpy man. Yeah, that's the most accurate way to describe the puny little sound that came from my quivering lips.

Thurman whipped out his Harry Potter wand, and brandished it at the cloud.

WHOMP!

The last pulverizing punch whacked into the ground ten feet away from us, splattering dog shit.

"Eeeeuuchhhh!" the Warrior screamed in disgust.

"Gross, man," Knob moaned.

"Arrgggghhh!" I yelled. Mostly because I'd stepped backwards and squished some more dog turds.

The cloud reared back into the sky, and blotted out the sun overhead.

"*Thurman?*"

Thurman's wand waved faster and faster, and I could see colored smoke coming from the tips of it.

Above it, the cloud poised, collecting itself for the final Whomp.

"*Thurman!*"

You see, we believed in Thurman now. We knew that he was an honest to goodness real, live sorcerer. It would be impossible not to, having been whisked out of our universe into a purple fog universe, then brought back here. Unless we'd been mass-hallucinating, we had no choice but to believe.

Now in our desperation to find answers, any answers, we'd decided to risk that our sorcerer could protect us from the power of this unworldly destructive cloud that'd been stalking us.

So we had decided to call the cloud, and rely on Thurman to protect us.

What were we thinking?

"Quick," I yelled, "get your Shields of Stupidity on."

"I can't," Knob screamed. "It only works when we're threatened with female logic."

"It worked on math, too," I hollered.

"Why?"

"I don't know. Maybe it works on anything that has to do with logic."

"We don't have any math around here! What are we going to do?" His eyes were round.

I looked up. The cloud, pulsating with power, was hovering about a quarter mile above us. It hung with a gleeful air, seeming to relish the moment before finally squashing the pesky humans, once and for all.

"Warrior!"

"Yeah?"

"Give us some female logic, quick!"

The cloud started towards us.

"Okay. Always install toilet paper so that the end piece is hanging away from the wall."

"Huh? Why?"

The cloud was picking up momentum. Thurman's wand whirled like a Fourth of July sparkler.

"Because otherwise it hangs against the wall, and it's hard to peel it away from the wall."

"That's stupid," I yelled

"Oh, yeah? No more stupid or inconsiderate than when guys

leave the toilet seat up."

"What's so bad about that?" Of course, living with three guys, our toilet seat is always up. Well, not anymore. It's probably down right now, squashed down, with the rest of our house.

I risked another glance. The cloud was hurtling towards us. "Thurman?" I squeaked.

The Warrior was getting mad. "Because, if somebody has to sit down on the toilet, it's pretty damned rude if the seat is always up."

"So why not simply put the seat down when you have to go?" I suggested, one eye on the cloud ripping at us, the other on the smoke starting to billow from Thurman's wand.

The smell from the shit was getting pungent.

"Because," the Warrior said, grinding the words between gritted teeth, "what if a woman has to go in the middle of the night, and tries to go pee when its dark? She shouldn't have to feel for the lid."

"How's that any different than a guy who has to go in the middle of the night, having to feel around to lift the lid?"

"DAMNITALLANYWAY!" she screamed. "BECAUSE WOMEN ARE SUPPOSED TO BE TREATED LIKE QUEENS BY YOU DAMNED INCONSIDERATE LOUTS. WE'RE SPECIAL! REMEMBER?"

Click. I heard my Shield of Stupidity snap into place.

"Thanks, Warrior," I told her.

"SHUT UP!" she answered.

All of a sudden, I could feel the envelope of pressure from the approaching cloud.

"Watch out!" I yelled.

The smell of the shit was raising, almost in direct inverse proportion to the force hurtling at us from above.

"What the hell is that stink?" Knob shouted.

It was different, yet for some reason, it was kinda familiar.

BBBOOOOOOMMMMMM!

Chapter Twenty

"Buford."
"Huh?"
"Buford."
"What Ford?"
"I said, Buford."
"Phew ford?"
"Bu…ford."
"Oh, 'Buford'?"
"Yes, Buford."
"Oh."

Chapter Twenty-One

"Um?"
"Yes?"
"Uh, what about Buford?"
"I like the name."
I thought about it. Yeah, not so bad.
"Okay, fine with me. I like Buford, too."
"Good."

Chapter Twenty-Two

"Um?"
"Yes?"
"Why?"
"Oh. Sorry. I didn't make that clear, did I? I've decided that I want to be called 'Buford.'"
"Oh." Pause. "Um?"
"Yes?"
"It's not a very, uh, lady-like name, though, is it?"
"Maybe not, but it's a good warrior name."
"Yeah, I guess."
"So, what do you suppose happened?"
"I'm not sure. I haven't opened my eyes yet."
"Me neither. Why haven't you?"
"I dunno. I guess I'm too scared. How about you?"
"Well, I'm not sure, but I think whatever happened somehow got into my mascara, and, like, melted it together. I can't open my eyes right now."
"Oh. I was just kind of hoping…"
"Hoping what?"
"Well, that maybe I wasn't the only scaredy-cat around here."

"No worries, there, mate."
"Knob?"
"Yeah."
"You okay?"
"Yeah."
"Have you opened your eyes, yet?"
"No."
"Scared?"
"Yeah."
"Thurman, you out there?"
"Yeah."
"Are your eyes open?"
"Yeah."
"Are you scared?"
"Um, I don't know. Maybe."
"Oh."
"So, what do you see out there?" Knob asked him.
"Uh, I don't know. It's kind of hard to explain. Maybe you guys ought to open your eyes."
"I was afraid you'd say that," Knob said.
Fearfully, I willed my eyelids to open. Fearfully, they resisted. *C'mon, guys, let's take a look around,* I urged them. *Nope,* they answered.
"Wow!" Knob exclaimed.
There was a ripping sound.
"Ouch," the Warrior said, or should I say, Buford?
"You okay?" Knob asked her.
"Yeah, got my eyelash problem handled," she replied. "I'm okay."
Then I heard her intake of breath. Imagining how this must have affected her bosom, my eyes flew open on their own accord.
"Cool!" was all I could say.

Chapter Twenty-Three

Time Out. There's something you have to know.
You remember, of course, that my name is Guy, right?
I know, you don't hear it much in this adventure, because I'm the one telling the story. So you don't read, "Guy looked up in the sky, and beheld a wonderful sight."

And if you did, you might have pronounced my name wrong, like 'Gee.'

No, not pronounced 'jee' like 'gee whiz,' but with a hard 'g.' Guh...eeee.

But it's not. It's pronounced like the word 'guy.' Which is convenient, because not only am I named Guy, but I am a guy.

I don't think my parents named me this as homage to guy-dom. It had something to do with the fact that Mom considered herself a French nut. Guy is a French name. Fortunately, she wasn't so much the expert that she knew they pronounce it weird.

So she named her new little guy, Guy.
And I think you need to know something about guys.
You probably think you have a pretty good idea what a guy is, don't you?

Someone who takes his shirt off in subzero weather at football games. Someone who strains his neck when the right buns wiggle by. A guy works simultaneously on his golf swing and beer swig, and they like football pools, Doritos, and dogs (both regular and hot). Guys like sports, sports commercials, sports drinks, sports statistics and sports bobble heads. They like ESPN and boxing, and always perk up when the bikini-clad girl walks around the ring between rounds. Guys hate to shop. Guys hate to do crossword puzzles. Guys hate to wait in line, any line. Guys don't get lost, no matter that evidence may suggest otherwise.

Yeah, we all know what guys are.

But I'll bet you don't know everything, so we'll take a little history lesson.

Hey! I see your eyes glazing over. C'mon, unglaze them. This isn't math.

Anyway, it all started back in 1570, when a guy named Guy Fawkes was born. Except he wasn't a guy yet, because back then, guys weren't called guys. It's not that there weren't guys yet. There were. In fact, there have been guys ever since the first cave guy read the first *Pentcave* while taking a dump in the outcave. It's just that they weren't named guys yet.

Until Guy came along.

Not *a* guy.

Guy.

The guy.

One day, one of Guy's buddies got the bright idea of blowing up the English Parliament. Maybe he was French, after all.

Anyway, Guy joined right up, because guys like to blow things up.

And in this case, you get two things at once: big sound and dead politicians, who, as an added bonus, might even be attorneys.

Trouble was, somebody ratted and he got caught. Nobody else, just him. When the King's troops burst into the cellar, there was Guy, sitting on a keg of dynamite, playing Donkey Kong on his Game Boy.

That's another thing about guys. We aren't very smart.

Still, though, when the country found out they missed fireworks and dead politicians, they got upset, and started a whole bunch of bonfires. A year later, they did it again, and had so much fun they decided to do it every year. So every year they have a Guy Fawkes

Day, where they make a big fire and blow stuff up in memory of the very first guy. And they toss in effigies of Guy Fawkes and whomever else they are pissed at for the moment, like George Steinbrenner or the Dixie Chicks. It's just a big old, knock-down, wild-ass party. Kids drag effigies (all of which are named Guy) around town, begging for handouts, asking, "Penny for a Guy?" They use the money for fireworks.

And that's where the nickname 'guy' came from.

So what's it tell you that guys are named for dummies?

And what does it tell you, that, if we knew, we'd think it was cool?

Anyway, back to the story. You needed to know all of this stuff about guys so that you would understand our reaction to what we saw.

"Cool!" I said.

It sure was.

We were still in the park. And there, above our heads, suspended as if by levitation, was the whomping cloud. A roiling black mass of seething anger and fury, suspended ten feet over our head.

"Cool!" Knob said. A guy's vocabulary is oftentimes reduced considerably in times of stress, excitement or lack of thought.

"Cool!" I repeated.

"How're you doing that?" Buford said wonderingly. Buford, not being a guy, was not rendered incapable of cogitative thought by the sight of what we, uh, saw.

"I'm not really sure," our resident sorcerer replied. Purple smoke billowed from his wand and seemed to have enveloped the whomping cloud in a purplish cocoon. The cocoon somehow was keeping the cloud from pounding us into a pile of pancake-people.

Something bonked me on the head.

"Eh, what's this?" It didn't look like bird poop, so I reached down and picked it up. A cigarette butt.

Bonk.

Another one. "A butt," I said.

"Where?" Thurman and Knob said whipping their heads

around in unison.

"Cigarette butt," I clarified.

"Oh," they chimed, disappointed. I guess they'd been hoping... well, they're guys...maybe they just hoped a naked woman had sort of popped up.

Bonk.

"Hey, what's the deal?" I muttered, wiping another butt off my head. "All right," I said angrily, "who's throwing butts?"

In response, a dozen more clonked off my head.

"Dammit, who did that?"

Something buzzed under my nose, and when I twirled to see what it was, more cigarette butts landed all around me, littering the ground at my feet.

"What the hell's going on?"

Suddenly a cloud of ashes enveloped me, and I went into a choking spasm.

"Arrghh!" Knob yelled. "Second hand smoke!"

I stumbled away, blinded and coughing.

"Seth? Wher—" I broke into uncontrollable coughing.

"Got'em, man," I heard from somewhere in the violent smog.

Picking a direction, I staggered in a straight line, hoping that I wouldn't trip over a park bench, or fall into a pond. Then I remembered the poop.

"Watch out for the poop!"

Somebody bumped into me, and I nearly fell.

"Ah, sorry," a voice said.

"Thurman, you okay?"

"Yeah. Look, I have to stay here. Take this."

Something was jammed into my hand. Some kind of rope.

"What is this?"

"Don't worry, he'll get you out of here."

The rope jerked, and I was dragged through the smoke.

"Hey!"

Unable to control it, and unable to let go, I stumbled away, trying to keep my feet.

"Where the..."

Whatever was pulling me was strong. I assumed it was Buford, so I relaxed, and let her pull me to safety.

Blinded, I whacked into something soft and billowly. I reached out, and grabbed a handful of...

"Hey, what do you think you're doing?"

Buford.

"Oops, sorry, I, uh..." Face burning, I let go of her breast.

"Oh, never mind. You couldn't have known," she assured me. "It was a mistake, right?" she asked dangerously.

"Uh, yeah," I fumbled the words out. Still, though, my mind committed the feeling to memory for later enjoyment.

The rope jerked again, and I grabbed her arm as the rope pulled us through the heavy smog.

"Knob, is that you?" I questioned the person on the other side of the rope. For the first time, I noticed that it wasn't actually a rope.

We burst out into the fresh air, and I was able finally to take a deep breath. My eyes burned from the acrid smoke. With some difficulty, I peeled them open, and saw Buford's sooty face, streaked with tears. I probably looked the same. Then I realized that I could see our savior at last.

I looked. Then I blinked. And blinked again.

Chapter Twenty-Four

There was nothing at the end of the rope. But the end wasn't on the ground. It was hovering about a foot and a half above the grass.

"Wheezel?"

Then Knob burst through the smoke, hauling my brother. "Damn, that's rough," he managed to blurt through spasms of coughing.

"Look at that!"

Blinking away the tears, I looked at where Buford was pointing.

A huge, black column of smoke belched from the whomping cloud. The cloud was still being held in stasis by bolts of purple light that came from somewhere inside of the smoky morass. I felt sure that Thurman and his Harry Potter wand were at the other end of the purple lighting bolts.

"That cloud is aiming the smoke at Thurman," Buford said wonderingly.

"It's, like, it's alive, or something," Knob agreed.

"We have to save him," Buford cried.

Suddenly Thurman's disembodied voice came at us from the gloom.

"Ask it what you have to ask."

"He's captured it," Knob exclaimed.

"Hurry," Thurman gasped, grit and smog polluting his words. "I can't hold it for long."

"Cloud!" I said loudly, speaking to somewhere in the middle of the swirling mass.

Nothing.

"CLOUD, LISTEN TO ME!" I yelled.

A blast of air almost knocked me off my feet. "WHAT, SMALL INSIGNIFICANT BEING?"

"It answered you," Buford said incredulously.

"Shhh. Lemme think."

My mind spun rapidly, thoughts and feeling roiling like the cloud itself.

"WHY HAVE YOU BEEN TRYING TO DESTROY US?" I screamed at it.

"YOU ARE NOT WORTHY OF DESTRUCTION. WE MEAN FOR YOU TO DISAPPEAR INTO OBLIVION WHERE YOU BELONG."

For some reason that made me kind of mad.

"OH, YEAH? SO IF WE'RE SO INSIGNIFICANT, THEN WHY ARE YOU WASTING YOUR TIME ON US?"

"TIME IS IRRELEVENT," it thundered.

"OKAY, THEN, MR GREAT AND MIGHTY STINKY AIR, THEN HOW IS IT THAT WE HAVE YOU PRISONER?"

Angry sooty air blasted at me, and I staggered.

"YOU DO NOT CONTROL ME!" The words reverberated in my head.

"OH YEAH, BLOW-HARD?"

"Guy, you're blowing it," Buford muttered, elbowing me aside.

"MR CLOUD," she said, "YOU OVERWHELM US WITH YOUR MIGHTY POWER."

"What are you doing?" I whispered harshly at her.

"Shhh! Just listen."

She turned back to the cloud, which was looking slightly mollified at her flattery.

"MR CLOUD, WE INSIGNIFICANT BEINGS REQUEST

AN AUDIENCE WITH YOU."

The cloud looked pleased, and the column of smoke spewing from its guts reduced somewhat.

"YES, THIS IS APPROPRIATE BEHAVIOR FOR THOSE OF YOUR LESSER STATURE."

"WE FEAR AND RESPECT YOU, MR CLOUD, AND WONDER WITH OUR SMALL BRAINS WHAT IT IS THAT WE HAVE DONE TO DISPLEASE YOU."

She was making me sick with her shameless buttering up.

"YOU SPINED CREATURES HAVE INTRUDED ON ONE WHOSE BENIVOLENCE WE DEEM NECESSARY."

Huh? What was that all about?

"Guys, I'm not sure how much longer I can hold it," Thurman's shaky voice said from the smoke.

Buford quickly asked, "MR CLOUD, OR IF IT IS POSSIBLE THAT YOU ARE A GOD, WE ASK WHO IT IS WHOSE DOMAIN WE HAVE INTRUDED."

That did it.

I yelled at Buford, "It's not a god!"

"Guy, shut up," she whispered harshly.

"Why? I'm not the one full of sh—"

"Guy!" she said, grabbing me by the shirt, and pulling me close. "I know that it's not a god. But we're not going to get any information from it by provoking it."

"Oh."

But it was too late. The cloud must have heard me. Probably because I had been yelling.

FOOMPHH!

A swarm of cigarette butts flooded out of the cloud, accompanied by gusts of smoke. Buzzing like locusts, the butts bounced off us, showering sparks before fluttering to the ground.

"Ow, dammit!" I swore, as one tried branding me. It was a Marlboro. Hastily, I flicked it off of my arm.

"This thing's got more butts than a nudist colony," Knob observed, looking at the cigarettes littering the grass.

"Hey, what are you guys..." Thurman tried to say, before the smog billowed around him. His purple magic was furiously wrestling the pulsating cloud. We watched in horror as the cloud intensified its efforts to break free of Thurman's spell, spitting furious toxic fumes at him.

"Thurman, get out of there!" Buford screamed.

She had her umbrella sword out, and was futilely looking for a way to use it. I doubted that it would do much damage to a cloud.

All of a sudden, there was a flash of purple, and we were gone.

We were back in the purple land.

"That's one strong wand you have there," Knob observed to Thurman, who was standing nearby, looking a little bewildered.

"Thanks," he said dazedly."Holly and phoenix feather, eleven inches, nice and supple, made by Alivan's, master wandmakers."

"Holly?" Knob asked.

"Yes, holly wood."

"Hollywood?"

"No, it's—"

"Why do you keep bringing us here?" I interrupted, indicating the strange, ill-defined, purple world.

He looked at me. "I don't know. Something's drawing us here."

Bits of yellow swirled around us, fluttering like confused butterflies. Knob was trying without success to snag one.

"Eh, what's this?"

Undaunted, he ran thorough the purple fog, leaping and grabbing at them. He looked like an elven Ichobod Crane on hallucinogens. We watched bemusedly for a few moments, and then Buford reached out calmly and trapped one of the cavorting objects. She studied it intensely.

"Hmmm."

"What is it?" I asked.

Amused, she said, "It's a permission slip."

"A permission slip?"

"Yes, listen, 'Please excuse Seth from'—"

"*Seth?*"

"Yes, let me finish. 'Please excuse Seth from gym today, as he has a twisted ankle.'"

"Twisted ankle?"

"Yeah. 'A twisted ankle caused by running down the stairs and tripping over his brother's GI Joe Jeep.'"

"GI Joe Jeep? I used to hav—"

"'Signed,'" she continued, "'Margaret Haber.'"

"That's my mom," I exclaimed. "What's that doing here?"

She grabbed another. Knob was still unsuccessfully leaping and lunging behind her.

"'Dear Ms. Appleton, Seth is home with a fever today. His brother will pick up his homework after school today. Thank you, Margaret Haber.'"

I was stunned.

"I remember delivering that note. Ms. Appleton was his sixth grade teacher."

"Hey, I caught one!" Knob announced gleefully.

He read it silently. "Hey, it's some kind of permission slip."

"Permission slips," I mused. "What would they be doing here?"

"Hey, listen," Knob said. "'Dear Ms. Cregier, Seth Haber has permission to attend the field trip to the museum tomorrow. M. Haber.'"

He looked up. "What a weird coincidence. Whoever this is has the same name as Seth."

"Ms. Cregier. Third grade," I said mechanically.

"I don't think it's any coincidence." Buford frowned.

"Me, neither," I agreed. "But what do you suppose they mean?"

"I always wondered what they did with all those permission slips," Knob remarked.

I looked at my brother, trying to gain inspiration from his blank countenance. *What's going on here, bro?*

"You know," Buford said, after a few minutes of silence, "when we were here before, I remember hearing somebody."

"Yeah, me too," Knob agreed.

I remembered it, too. Just as we were fading out, a voice had called out to us.

"It said, 'Wait. Come back!'" Buford remembered.

"So there's life here, somewhere?" Thurman asked.

"Remember the ladybugs?" Knob reminded him.

"Oh, yeah."

"The air's breathable, after all," Thurman said, sniffing appreciatively.

The air was, in fact, quite nice. No sulphur smells or anything. I remembered reading a science fiction book once about space travel, and the author said that different planets would carry vastly different odors. Like how someone else's house smells different than yours. Different foods, different scents. Sometimes the differences were noticeable, sometimes barely discernable.

I also remembered when we'd go out of town on vacation, and come back a week or so later, our own house would smell strange when we returned. Not bad really, but different. Within an hour, I'd be used to it again.

But this world, whatever it was, had no odor. Or, if anything, it was a clean scent, with better oxygen than we would get in a city.

There was life here. The ladybugs, who were nowhere to be seen now. The unknown voice. And we could breathe.

Where the heck were we?

We were all caught up in our thoughts when Thurman asked, "So, what did we learn from the cloud?"

"Nothing much," Buford said, directing a glower at me.

I lowered my eyes, refusing to meet the glower. This left me staring at certain parts of her anatomy that I'd rather not be caught staring at, so I looked further down. Nicely muscled thighs and calves came into view. Feeling her glower on me again, I averted my eyes altogether, and instead locked in on one of the permission slips and watched it flutter until it disappeared into purple.

"You were cool, man," Knob told Thurman. "Like, you actually caught a cloud. Nobody's ever done that before."

"It wasn't a cloud," I mumbled.

"Huh? What?"

"I said, I don't think it was a cloud."

"What are you talking about?"

"It was smog." I struggled for words, "No, not smog. It was more like cigarette smoke. Like being in a party where everybody's smoking except you."

"Yeah, nasty stuff," Knob agreed.

"I think he's right," Buford agreed. "And there were those butts falling all over us."

"They weren't falling," I said. "That thing was spitting them at us."

"It sure was," Knob said. "Look at the holes in my shirt."

"So what the hell would flies have to do with a cloud of cigarette smoke?" I wondered.

"And why would cigarette smoke try to kill us?" Buford said.

"Do you think it would have answered?" Knob said.

"I don't know. It was pretty arrogant," Buford said. "But Guy messed up any chance we might have had."

"Sorry," I muttered. "I was pissed off."

"So was I," she said. "But sometimes you have to swallow your pride."

"Yeah, easy for you to say," I said under my breath.

She bristled. "No it's not." Then she relaxed somewhat. "I have to admit, I deal with arrogant, misguided pride all the time. That's why I divorced my first husband. If I took issue with every stupid thing my husband or kids said, I'd be yelling all the time. You learn to put up with things."

"I'm not married," I said petulantly.

"Not yet," she agreed. "But believe me, when you are, and you will be some day, you'll learn the art of discretion. Maybe. After a while. A long while," she added, with a smile.

"So, here we are," Knob said, changing the subject. I mentally shot him a message of thanks.

"No food, no water," Thurman agreed.

"We have water," Knob said, grabbing his knapsack.

"Not with the hand wipes again," I moaned.

"Actually, they aren't bad," Thurman said brightly.

"We have to figure out where we are," I said.

"And why we keep coming back here," Thurman added.

"Maybe we should walk around, check the place out," Buford suggested.

"I don't know." I prodded the stuff under my feet. "It's not like we can see what we're walking on. What if we hit a sink hole or something?"

Buford pointed out, "Knob didn't fall through any sink holes when he was running around like a crazy man."

"Yeah," he said, "it's like running on a cushion."

"Or a mat," Thurman added.

"Yeah, a mat, an exercise mat," Knob said.

"Still, it's pretty firm underneath," Buford observed.

"Maybe we can find whoever it was that yelled at us last time we were here," I said.

"I think we're all in agreement," Buford said. "Let's check this place out."

"All right." I felt relieved to have a plan. "So what direction?"

We looked around us at the swirling purple. No one direction looked any different than the other.

"That way." Knob pointed randomly.

"Sounds good to me. Lead on, Unbeliever," Thurman said.

"Me?" I squeaked. "You're the one with the mighty wand."

"I'll lead," Buford declared. She pulled out her umbrella, and strode in the direction Knob indicated.

The terrain proved to be pretty boring, now that the novelty of purple clouds had worn off. The footing, as noticed, was mundane, and we encountered no treachery as we marched through the mist.

"How do we know we aren't going in circles?" Knob said after a time.

"We don't," Buford said bluntly as she strode ahead.

"I wonder if there's an end to it," Thurman wondered wonderfully wonderingly.

"Yeah, and what would we find there?" Knob said.

I looked down at my watch, and noticed that the second hand wasn't moving. "Anybody know what time it is?"

"Yeah, it's, uh... Huh, that's odd, my watch stopped," Knob said.

"Thurman?" I asked, feeling the panic rising.

He looked at his black, studded Goth watch. "It's... Oh, mine's dead, too."

"What's going on with our watches?" Buford asked. We were standing in a semi-circle.

I'd been starting to feel pretty comfortable in this strange place, but with this added proof of weirdness, an icy finger worked its way down my spine. I couldn't help thinking about flocks of ladybugs, and permission slips written years ago by my mother.

"Uh, Thurman?" I asked.

"Yeah?"

"You can get us out of here anytime you want, right?"

"Uh, yeah, I guess so." He didn't seem convinced.

"Why don't you wave it around a little, and make sure it's juice or whatever is still working," I suggested.

"Okay."

He pulled out his Harry Potter wand, holly and phoenix feather, eleven inches, nice and supple, and gave it an experimental wave. A purple spark flashed at its tip.

"It's working," he exclaimed in relief.

"I wonder if there's some reason that your magic is the same color as this place," Knob observed.

"Maybe this place is magic," Buford wondered.

"Like my wand?" Thurman asked.

"Do you think you could conjure anything with that?" I asked Thurman.

"Conjure?"

"Yeah, make something out of nothing. Or transport something here."

"Um, I don't know. I could try."

"Why don't you bring us a pizza, or something?" Knob suggested.

"I'd love some pizza," Buford said, brightening.

"Thurman?" I said to him seriously.

"Yeah?"

"Bisuvios."

"Huh?"

"If you're going to do pizza, make it a Bisuvios deep-dish."

"Oh, okay."

We all watched as our sorcerer's wand carved circles in the air, purple light arcing wildly from its tip. Thurman's lips moved as he concentrated on funneling magic through the little stick. I wondered what song would bring us pizza. He brought us home with "American Pie" last time. I chuckled to myself as it occurred to me that the same song could bring pizza. I wondered if we could get home even quicker next time if he sang John Denver's classic "Take Me Home, Country Road".

We smelled it before we saw it. Rich tomato sauce, four different cheeses, crust inspired by the Greek Gods. Bisuvios Pizza. Manna from heaven.

A purple disturbance marred the air, issuing forth a delicious aroma. The disturbance spun into a flat funnel cloud, and a form began to take shape. Yellow, white, tan and red—all the normal pizza colors—began to take shape before our eyes. My mouth watered.

"You're doing it." Knob sucked in the tantalizing fumes.

"Is it too late to put in an order of Coke?" Buford asked.

Before Thurman could answer, a pizza materialized from the purple gloom, coming into focus as if adjusted by a huge set of binoculars.

"Hey, napkins! Nice touch, Thurman," Knob approved.

I grabbed a wedge of pizza, and lifted it, stringy mozzarella strings clinging to the box.

"Delicious," I mumbled around the joyous concoction.

"Yum," Buford added, her mouth full.

"Smells great," an unknown voice said behind me.

I spun around and froze in horror.

Chapter Twenty-Five

When you think of pizza, you think of Italy. After all, pizza was invented there, right?

Yep.

Or no.

Or yes, and no. Or, yes, but not the way you might think.

An early form of pizza was eaten by people in the Mediterranean (Greeks, Egyptians, Italians, etc.), but you wouldn't have recognized it as pizza. Their pizza, something called *focaccia,* was round and cooked, but the similarity ended there. Instead of gooey cheese, thick tangy sauce and pepperoni, their pizza was topped with oil and spices. Not real pizza, to an American palate. And since the tomato was actually discovered in America, in a way you could say that pizza is an American dish.

Now I don't want to hear any backlash from the Italian community out there, especially by those who say 'dem' and 'doz,' and who might have intimate knowledge of what really happened to Jimmy Hoffa. I'm just trying to add some historical perspective.

When I spun around, I wasn't wondering about the history of pizza. I wasn't mulling that Italians actually thought that tomatoes were poisonous when Spain first introduced them to Europe. I didn't reflect that the first known pizza made with tomato didn't come around until it was introduced in Naples somewhere around 1870.

In fact, what I saw made me forget about pizza altogether.

"What is that?" Knob gasped, pointing a shaky finger.

I was heedless when my pizza plopped onto my shoe.

"Actually, not that," the 'that' said. "I'm a who."

"Like Horton?" Knob suggested.

It laughed. "No, not like Horton, though I love Dr. Seuss stuff."

"You know Dr. Seuss?" I asked in astonishment.

It laughed again, but didn't answer.

Chapter Twenty-Six

You're probably wondering what's going on here.
That's okay, so were we.
Because, standing behind us, was a thingy kind of thing.
A bug.
Or maybe a lobster. Or both. About a foot and a half tall, some kind of mutant combination crustacean-insect. Dark and glistening.

And it was talking.

"Actually, if you don't mind, might I have a piece of that pizza?" it asked.

Then it froze. "Wait! That isn't Bisuvios, is it?"

When we didn't answer, it gleefully slithered up to the box of pizza, reached out a hand, er, claw, or uh, something, and took a piece. Then a tiny little arm popped out of its abdomen, snipped off a piece of cheese, and flipped it expertly into an opening that appeared somewhere about where a neck would have been if it had had a neck.

"Aaahhh. I haven't had a piece of pizza in months," it sighed, delight evident in its voice.

"What, er, who are you?" I asked, watching it with fascination.

It chewed for a moment, wiped what passed for its face with a napkin before answering, "I'm Mark."

"Mark?"

"Well, not exactly Mark. But you can call me that for short."

"Don't you know?" he asked.

That's if he's a he. I'm pretty sure he is. Unless she's of his kind sound like he's of our kind. For the sake of argument, we'll call him a him, unless we learn that he's a her.

"How the heck are we supposed to know who you are?" I said angrily. I was getting tired of his little game.

"Whoa, glum boy here getting a little hostile?" he chided me.

I stepped forward, intending to step on the little bastard.

He saw me coming, and scooted backwards on little lobster feet.

"Guy!" Buford said, grabbing my arm, and holding me back. "We've talked about this. Tone it down."

"But, he—"

"Guy!"

Reluctantly, I backed down to DEFCOM three.

"Okay." I glared sullenly at the critter, mentally measuring how hard I'd have to stomp to flatten him like a pancake. "You're lucky, dude," I growled.

"Guy!"

"Sorry," I uttered, not sorry at all.

"And you call me a berserker," she said, but she was smiling.

Then she turned around, and faced the contentedly munching creature. "Okay, Mark, what kind of creature are you? What are you doing here? Why are we supposed to know who and what you are?"

"Hey, hey, little lady. Not so fast. Not so fast."

"Who are you calling 'little lady'?" she growled.

"Buford," I cautioned. "Don't be like Guy." I prodded my chest, the Irritable One.

"Shuddup," she snapped at me. "And you," she pointed at the creature, "don't you dare dissemble with me."

"Disassemble?" Mark asked.

"Dissemble," Knob said, leafing through the dictionary he'd suddenly whipped out.

"How'd you get that out so quickly?" Thurman asked him.

"Elf-speed," Knob answered. He ran a finger down a page. "Here you go, it means, '...to conceal under a false appearance...'"

"Hey, good word," Thurman approved.

"Yeah, there's something going on with you," Knob accused the creature.

"You dissembler," Thurman added.

We surrounded Mark, drawing him into a circle for our inquisition.

"Wait, wait, wait. I'll tell you everything," Mark cried. "Sheesh, can you blame a guy for wanting to eat first?"

"You aren't a guy," I said darkly.

"Hey, close enough," it protested. "Look, can we eat while I talk?"

The pizza was getting cold. And seeing that we were respecters of pizza etiquette, it was a reasonable request.

We watched the creature chew. After a few moments, when it didn't seem inclined to launch into explanation, we picked up our own pizza slices and ate warily.

I glanced at Seth, watching the husk of my brother's body chew mechanically, keeping the body alive for the hopeful return of its brain. I wondered again how it was that his body continued with functions like eating and breathing without the brain, which controls both voluntary and involuntary functions. Was it something else that had been stolen? The soul? Personality? Or what?

I shrugged mentally. Whatever it was, I vowed that we were going to get it back, and restore Seth to normal. Or what passed for normal in his case.

Mark, or whatever its true name was, finished off its pizza, and wiped almost daintily.

"All right. No good deeds go unpunished. I'll talk. Watcha wanna know?"

The unexpected offer threw us.

"Okay, I'll bite. Who are you, really?" I asked.

"Well, I'll start by giving you my full name. Mark's not my first name. That's what probably threw you. My first name is really

Telly."

A pregnant pause.

"Like, uh, Savalas?" Knob ventured.

"Yeah. Now do you get it?" It asked.

Another pregnant pause.

"Uh, Telly Mark?" Thurman asked.

"Yep. Get it?" he asked expectantly.

"Telly Mark, Telly Mark, Telly Mark," I said, bewildered. "No, can't say that I get it."

"Sheesh, you people are so dense!" the little crustacean/bug grumbled. "Telly Mark It." He emphasized each syllable and ending on a questioning note.

"Telly Mark It?" I asked. I sounded like a parrot, even to myself.

It gave an exasperated sigh. "Okay, you stupid people. Telly Mark It Er. If you don't get it now, you're just too gosh-darned stupid to exist."

"Telly Mark It Er?" Thurman said, sounding the phrase slowly like a newly arrived immigrant.

"Hey, I get it, 'telemarketer,'" Buford said excitedly.

There was a moment of silence. And not for the purpose of prayer.

"You're a *telemarketer*?" My hackles raised, and I felt a growl developing.

"You have a lot of nerve showing up here," Knob said disapprovingly.

"Where's my brother's brain?" I shouted

"Calm down," Telly Mark said to me.

"*Calm down?* You stole my brother's brain, and you want me to *calm down*?"

"Yes, look, I admit, we made a mistake—"

"You're damned right you made a mistake."

"Yeah, you're right. It's too small. Not enough room."

"*What?*"

"Yeah, can't fit all of our stuff in here. We're jammed to the gills. We need a bigger one."

"We're in his brain?"

"In a sense. We're in his brain in much the manner that you

would be when you're on the Internet. Too bad about the limited storage space, though, otherwise it would be ideal, since it was pretty much cleared out when we got here. That, plus the size limitations…"

"*Limitations?* What's wrong with my brother's brain? It should be plenty big enough!"

"Well, it isn't. So we were planning on getting a new one, anyway," Telly said. "Besides, I couldn't stand all the ladybugs. Not only that, but your mother's permission slips are driving me crazy. She's like, crazy or something."

"Don't you dare make fun of my mother!"

He was right, but I didn't want to hear it.

"Still though. I'm pretty proud of what we did, given the limited space."

"It's not limited. My brother's darned-near a genius. His brain is huge."

Where was I getting all of this? Seth has the attention span of a gnat. He struggles just tying his shoes. The only place he's a genius is on PlayStation.

"You guys want to take a look around?" Telly Mark asked, ignoring my outbursts.

"Sure, I'm up for it."

"Shut up, Knob!" I growled.

"Me, too."

"Shut up, Thurman."

"Sounds great."

I didn't tell Buford to shut up.

"We'll get back to your issue in a moment," Telly Mark said to me.

He got up, and skittered towards the surrounding mist. I had halfway expected him to move backwards, like a lobster, but he didn't. The purple cloud parted for him, and we followed where he led. To my surprise, as we walked, shapes emerged from the gloom, taking on form as we got closer.

"Here's our calling area," Telly Mark, said, indicating a maze of cubicles that materialized before us. There was a phone at each cubicle, with a teleprompter screen. The cubicles were deserted, and the teleprompter screens dark.

"As you can see, we're not very busy, right now," Telly Mark said sadly.

"What happened?" Buford said, her voice echoing.

"The lawyers," he said glumly.

"Ah, the lawyers," we chorused.

"But," and he brightened, "we've diversified. And actually, we're still doing quite well."

Chapter Twenty-Seven

A cavernous area materialized out of the gloom. Like the phone center, this area was crowded with computers, but we could see that each was manned. Or womaned. Or somethinged. The creatures at the computers were not human, so I couldn't tell whether they were male or female, or whether their species had the equivalent of male and female.

"You think this place is small?" I said, feeling dwarfed and intimidated by my little brother's brain.

"And here's the Virus Center," Telly Mark said proudly, ignoring my question.

"Virus Center?" Buford said, puzzled.

"Yeah, we make viruses here."

"Like the flu?" Knob asked.

"No. Sheesh, you people. Computer viruses. We make computer viruses here."

"Why would you do that?"

"Are you guys really this obtuse?" Telly Mark said angrily. "Look, right here we make computer viruses. And over there," he pointed where more of the creatures were hunched over computer screens, "is where we make the cures."

"You make viruses and their cures?" I said blankly.

"Duh! How can we sell them the cure if they don't have a virus?"

"So you guys are the ones creating all that mess out there?" Buford breathed.

"Nah. I'd like to take all the credit, but we get a lot of help from computer geeks. We hire them whenever we find a good one. Some of them are pretty good at worms, too."

"Worms?"

"Yeah, you know, computer worms."

"Isn't a worm the same thing as a virus?"

"Nah, not quite. I mean, they're similar, but different. A virus gets into your computer, copies the heck out of itself, and blows everything up that way. A worm acts with intent, always eating or destroying something specific. Small, but significant difference."

"So you guys make them?"

"Sure, we're able to create a pretty big demand for our services." Telly Mark gave an evil satisfied chuckle.

"You are slime," I seethed.

He shrugged. "Hey, what can I say?"

Leading us on, we walked through a twisty tunnel, emerging into another cavern with more computers and more creatures.

"Here's the delivery system," he said, sweeping his claw grandly.

"Delivery system?"

"Yup. Worms and viruses don't do any good if you don't have a way to deliver them."

"So how do you deliver them?" Knob asked.

"I think he's talking about spam," I told him.

"Right you are," Telly Mark said, beaming at his sharp pupil. "We send out everything from penis pills, solicitations for on-line medication, to offers to make gobs of money without ever getting off your fat ass."

"People actually fall for this stuff?" Buford gasped.

"You bet. You humans are incredibly stupid and gullible."

"Are you responsible for the Nigerian scams, too?" Knob asked him.

"Yeah, that's ours. One of our best-sellers, actually."

"What's the Nigerian scam?" Buford wondered.

"Ha, funny stuff. We send emails supposedly from the son of a deposed tyrant or something of an African government. He writes that he's running for his life with millions of dollars of illicit money looted from their government. But while he's running, he manages to get online, locate some schmuck in Kalamazoo or Dayton, and offers to give them a huge cut if they help him get the money out of the country."

"But how would someone from Africa find someone in Kalamazoo?" Buford asked.

"He doesn't. That's the point. There's no one in Africa. It's all a scam."

"Then why send an email to Kalamazoo?"

"That's the where the scam comes in. If someone's stupid enough to answer, we reel them in like a big, fat, stupid fish. We'll tell them that we need them to front us money for duties, or to bribe African officials, whatever. You'll be surprised how many people can come up with money, if they are driven by enough greed."

"Wow. They deserve what they get, then."

"See! We're doing a service here!" Telly Mark said.

"No you aren't," I told him.

"What? Whatja mean?"

"Innocent people get hurt. The people usually targeted end up stealing from their employers or relatives."

"So?"

I snorted, and ignored him.

Nonplussed, he strode ahead. Well, if you can call how he walked a 'stride.'

"Why did you move out of all of your telemarketer offices?" Thurman asked.

"Yeah, that was a tragedy. Actually, it got too hot for us. First, they passed that 'Do Not Call' registry. Then they started exploring ways to track spam down. That was what finally did it. We had to pull our horns in. Anyway," he indicated around us, "this is perfect for tax reasons."

We were still walking, and now entered another winding corridor.

"Here's the Bill Gates Room," he said.

"Bill Gates," Thurman gasped. "He's one of you?"

"No." Telly Mark snorted. "Though he might as well be. I'm fairly sure he's some kind of alien. Anyway, we pattern some of our rip-offs off stuff we pick up from guys like him."

"Like what?" Buford said, wide-eyed.

"You know, he gobbled up any competition to his services, and sold products that only worked if you bought other products of his. He had some pretty slick scams going. Like how all of the computer companies introduce processors that are incrementally faster than the ones previously."

"Huh?"

"Think about it. A few years ago, your fastest processor was maybe 75 MHz. Then they came up with 150 MHz, 250, 300, 500. Every six months they got faster. But only a bit at a time. Nowadays, processing speeds are in the GHz's, but every six months they get just a teeny bit faster. So no matter what you do, there's always something faster out there."

"It's like a carrot," Buford said, shocked. "They just keep the carrot out there."

"You don't think they could have introduced a much faster machine at any time?" Telly Mark said. "Hah. It was better to get faster in small increments, so that the consumer had to keep buying to keep up."

"That's sneaky stuff," Thurman said.

"Yeah, I wish I woulda had a piece of that action," Telly Mark added mournfully.

"Do you have anything to do with the oil companies?" I asked him.

"Oil companies? What makes you ask that?" he said.

"I don't know. Kinda sounds like your speed."

"Huh. No. But you're right that's another one we missed out on."

"What are you talking about?" Buford asked, thoroughly confused.

"This guy here," and Telly Mark nodded in my general direction.

"Guy?" Knob asked.

"Yeah, that's what I said. Anyway, this guy—"

"Guy." Buford interjected.

"What? That's what I said. This guy—"

"Guy!" Buford, Thurman and Knob all chorused.

"That's what I'm saying!" Telly Mark exclaimed, getting frustrated.

"His name is Guy," Buford said, taking pity on him.

"Guy?"

"Yeah."

"Oh. Okay, I get it. Anyway, Guy...?" and he gestured questioningly towards me.

We all nodded.

"All right. I got it. Anyway, Guy guessed what's going on with the oil companies. Am I right?" he asked me.

I nodded.

"You guys ever heard of William Wainright?" he suddenly asked.

None of us had.

"Thought not. He's worth a couple billion dollars. Want to guess where he got the money?"

Nobody knew.

"Patent?" I ventured.

He nodded approvingly. "Score one for the, uh, for Guy!"

"Patent?" Buford asked.

"Yep," Telly Mark said, getting into his story. "Good old William Wainright was a scientist, and he made a wonderful discovery. He discovered an engine that ran on, get this, exhaust fumes and human waste."

"What?" Thurman exclaimed.

"Yeah, they called it the Crap-Mobile. You could just pull up to a Porta-Potty, run out a hose, and gas up."

"Whoa. I never heard about that," Knob said, looking puzzled.

"You wouldn't. As soon as he applied for a patent, he was approached by someone working for a certain industry, money changed hands, and the secret was locked in a vault, perhaps never to see the light of day again."

"That's incredible," Buford said. "How do you know all this?"

Telly Mark gave a smug smile. "We have our ways," he said mysteriously. "But you can believe it."

"How come they don't just destroy the secret?" Knob asked.

"Think about it. Fossil fuels are finite. Someday we actually will run out of oil. Then the threat to oil won't matter. And by then, maybe they'll be ready to introduce some of them, themselves."

"Them?" Buford asked.

"Yeah, 'them,'" Telly said, smirking. "What? You don't think that safe's filled with all kinds of other patents?"

"What? Are you saying that the oil companies buy up every patent that threatens them?" Knob said, shock written on his face with a Sharpie.

"You're surprised? That the oil companies lack morals?" he said, sarcasm lacing his words.

"Remember after 9/11?" I reminded them.

"9/11?" Knob asked.

"Yeah, gas stations were charging up to five bucks a gallon right afterwards?"

"Oh, yeah. Opportunistic bastards. Yeah, I guess I understand."

I suddenly remembered something. "You know. I have something for you," I said to Telly Mark.

"Yeah?"

I dug in my pants pocket, and brought out the note from Judge Wopner. I leaned over and gave it to Telly Mark.

He sliced it easily open with his claw. My eyes widened.

As he read, his lips moving, I looked over at Knob. He looked back. It hadn't escaped him how quickly and easily that claw cut through the envelope.

"Huh. Interesting," Telly Mark mumbled.

"What's it say?" Thurman asked, forgetting his manners.

"Huh? Oh, none of your business," the little crab creature said. "But I assume it wouldn't hurt for you to know. He's saying we can come back."

"Who's saying who can come back?" Knob asked.

"The lawyers. They're done messing with us. They've got a new target now. And, you guys will find their next goal pretty interesting."

"Why, who's next?" I asked.

"The oil companies. They're going after the oil companies next!" He laughed, a weird screeching sound that made my butt cheeks quiver. I peeked, interested to see if Buford's were quivering, too.

"So why would they let you come back? What's that all about?"

"Oh, they don't really care about us," he said. "They just go where the money is. They're simply, purely, completely mercenaries. Except they work for themselves."

"Then why would he want you to come back?" Thurman wondered.

"That? They use us. They need our contacts and expertise. Remember, no one trusts attorneys, so they can't learn the way the rest of us do. They need us to learn the real scuttlebutt about what's going on in the world."

"You guys work together?" I asked, amazed.

"Sure, when we aren't fighting," he said.

"What's going on?" Knob was bewildered.

"World domination, what else?" Telly shrugged.

"World domination? You're trying to take over the world?" Thurman asked.

"Sure."

"What are the attorneys trying to do?" I asked.

"Take over the world."

"They're trying to take over the world?" I said, shocked.

"Yep."

"And you're trying to take over the world?"

"Yep."

"You're both trying to take over the world?"

"Yep."

"And you're on opposite sides?"

"Not exactly."

"Then you're on the same sides?"

"Not exactly."

"Which one is it?"

"Whatever it is at a particular moment."

"That's a strange way to fight," I observed.

"Yeah," he admitted. "That's probably why it's taking so long."

"We're not going to let you!" I declared.

"Oh, yeah?" he said, amused.

"Yeah! We'll stop you!" Knob challenged.

"How do you plan on doing that?" Telly asked, not appearing the least concerned.

"I'll stomp you!" I'd been wanting to stomp him ever since I met him.

"I don't think you'll be able to do that," he said quietly, not budging.

"Oh yeah?" my turn to say.

"Yeah."

"You and what army?" I said sarcastically.

"This one." With a wave of his claw, purple fog slid open like a curtain.

There was an army.

Chapter Twenty-Eight

"Oh." Then Telly Mark started laughing like a bad guy on a *Scooby Doo* cartoon.

"Bwah, ha ha, bwah, ha ha."

"Why do they always laugh like that?" Thurman asked.

"Who?" I asked, distracted by the sight of thousands and thousands of evil creatures who all looked like Telly Mark. They were waving their claws threateningly.

"Bad guys. They always laugh. Are they happy or something?"

"Yeah," Knob agreed. "Why do bad guys always laugh like that?"

"I think it's a mental thing," Buford observed.

"Mental?"

"Bi-polar disease. Actually, more like depression and mood swings. When something goes good for them, they go to extreme happiness."

"But this isn't good," I said.

"For them, it is."

"Yeah, I guess so."

"So when the Joker laughs on *Batman,* it's because there's

something wrong with him mentally?"

"Yep."

"And when the evil guys laugh on *Scooby Doo* it's because they are mentally deranged?"

"Yep."

"So those shows are mocking people with mental disorders?"

"Yep."

"That's sick!"

"Pretty much."

"We gotta get out of here, guys," Knob said.

The army started approaching, clicking their claws and grinning at us with evil lobster expressions.

"Thurman, get us out of here!" I yelled.

"I can't," he said. "Not enough time to whip up a spell."

"Buford? Can you buy us time?"

She immediately whipped out her umbrella. "Let me see what I can do," she growled.

She collected herself, probably imagining all of the stupid things her husband and kids do on a daily basis. I thought about the damage she'd do all these creatures and smiled. Bad guys aren't the only ones who are happy.

The lobster-bugs kept coming.

"Buford!" I was getting concerned.

"Buford!" Knob echoed, in case she hadn't heard me.

"Uh, guys?" her voice was smaller than I would have expected.

"Yeah?"

"Nothing's happening."

"What?"

"Nothing's happening. I'm not changing."

"What do you…I mean, is it not that time of month…?" I faltered. This was a subject guys usually avoided like shopping malls.

"I don't think that's it." To my surprise, she was plainly confused. "I mean, it's toward the end, but there should be a few more days still." She looked down at herself and grimaced. "And I'm still bloated."

Despite the converging lobster-bugs, I took this as an invitation to examine her alleged bloatation. Nope. She didn't look bloated to me, except maybe two particular items that were larger than was usually standard with her particular model of human. I examined them with care, just to be sure.

Telly Mark yelled at us, "Ha, ha, there's no moon here, you dopes!"

How'd he know?

"We have to get out of here," Knob said, gesturing at the army that was marching steadfastly towards us. They looked particularly unfriendly.

"There's only one thing to do," I said.

"What?" Thurman asked.

"Run!"

We wheeled as one, and ran. I snagged Seth's arm and pulled him into the purple fog.

Knob led the way, long legs pumping furiously. We followed the elf through the Virus Center, past the telemarketer cubicles, and into twisting passages. We could hear the sounds of pursuit behind us, clacking sounds reverberating and echoing around us.

"Where to?" Knob panted.

"I don't know," I gasped. "Just keep running."

"Look," Thurman said, skidding to a stop and pointing.

"Are you crazy?" I yelled. "Don't stop!"

"What is it?" Buford said, looking at where he was pointing.

I stopped, too, and saw what he saw. A black opening in the purple. It looked like the face of a cave.

"Let's go," Thurman said. He ducked into the opening and was swallowed by the black gloom.

"Thurman!" I yelled. "Don't go..."

Then he was gone.

Nervously, I looked back, where the sounds of the army were gaining.

"What's going on, guys?" Knob called out. When he had noticed we were no longer following, he had halted a few dozen yards away.

"We have to stick together," Buford declared, and she followed where Thurman had gone, disappearing into the inky darkness.

"C'mon," I yelled to Knob, and I pulled Seth into the

opening...

...where suddenly we burst into the open...

...and I crashed into something soft and...

"Whoa!"

...the sight was amazing...

...something that I never, ever, expected to see in my life...

...I gave serious consideration to running back into the tunnel again...

...so that I could turn around, and come back in here...

...and feel what I felt...

...and see what I saw...

...again...

We stared. Then we stared some more. Then, just for chuckles, we stared some more. I was speechless. Nobody else said anything, so I assume they were speechless, too. The soft object that I had crashed into said nothing.

After a moment, the connections in my brain between speech and thought linked up again, so I said the first thing that came to mind, "Uh, excuse me."

Buford, whose delectable bottom had halted my progress, was still staring and said absently, "No problem."

I turned my attention back to the wonderful, magnificent sight.

"It's the moon," I whispered reverently.

"Yeah," Knob said wistfully.

"It's gorgeous," Buford breathed.

I looked up, and quailed.

"Earth!"

Above, threatening to crush the tiny planet we were on, was the looming shape of Earth. I recognized it because of my vast experience in watching science fiction shows.

"Whoa," Thurman agreed.

"We're...on the...moon?" Knob marveled.

"Yeah," Thurman said.

"Then...I...can't..." Knob fell to his knees, eyes wide in panic.

"Knob!" Buford said, alarmed.

He gasped loudly. "I..." He reached toward her, clutching his throat, and fell over, apparently in convulsions.

"Knob," I said, calmly.

"What?" he blurted, chest heaving from the effort.

"Knob, we can breathe."

"Huh, wha…"

"Yeah, there's atmosphere here."

He stopped choking, and took a hesitant breath. "Hey, we can breathe."

A clatter of crustacean shell arrived behind us.

Then a thought hit me with incredible force, and I wheeled around.

The lobster-bug army froze as one, and braced themselves, perhaps thinking I was getting ready to unleash a weapon of mass destruction on them. A huge fly swatter, a cooking pot, or maybe a fart.

"Hey, this isn't my brother's brain!" I screamed at Telly Mark. The army flinched.

"Yeah, I know," he said. "I lied."

"*You lied?*"

"Hey, what do you expect? I'm a telemarketer." He shrugged, his antennae quivering mockingly. "C'mon you mooks, let's get them!"

The army, realizing that I was unarmed, came running at us again roaring exoskeleton warcries.

I grabbed Seth, and ran after Thurman, Knob and Buford.

The surface of the moon is pretty much what you would expect, except for the grass. There shouldn't be grass on the moon. But there was, and we were running across it, heading for a city ahead of us. At least it looked like a city. Skyscrapers rose three to ten stories in the air. But not like skyscrapers you'd see on Earth. As we got closer, we could see figures walking the streets between buildings that seemed to sprout haphazardly from the surface. There was no rhyme or reason to the placement of the buildings, which, as we got closer, all proved to be cylindrical.

"Round buildings?" gasped Buford, as we ran up and down the uneven surface. There were craters pockmarked throughout the landscape, with grass growing gaily both inside and outside of their surfaces.

As we ran around a particularly deep crater, the placement and shape of the buildings all of a sudden made sense.

I screeched to a halt, and whipped around to face our pursuers.

They also screeched to a halt, and looked at me apprehensively. Maybe I was ready to use that weapon of mass destruction.

I looked up and down their rank and file, looking for Telly Mark.

"It's a disguise," I accused him.

"Huh?"

"This." And I pointed at the city behind me. "Everything's disguised to look like craters."

"Yeah. So?"

"We have a settlement on the moon?" I screamed at him.

"Yeah. So?"

"We settled the moon and terra-formed it!" My mind was spinning with the implications.

"Big deal."

"It *is* a big deal! Why doesn't the world know? What is going on here? Don't you realize how important this is?"

"Yeah, but to us, not to you," he said.

"Wha...? I mean, when did this..." I was stumbling for words.

"You stupid humans," Telly Mark said. "Do you really think that you'd land a man on the moon in 1969, and then ignore it for the next forty years?"

"Huh?"

"Yeah, you had manned missions almost every single year since the first landing in 1969. But they were secret."

"Secret?"

"Yeah, secret."

"But why...I mean, NASA would..."

"Why did NASA pretend they didn't?" he prompted.

"Uh, yeah."

"Because they had to keep a secret."

"A secret?"

"Yeah, what, you deaf or something?"

"What kind of secret?" I asked, stunned.

"Us."

"Us?"

"Us, as in us," he said, gesturing to his bug-lobster army.

"You mean, we…"

"Yup, you discovered life on the moon. Us."

"You?"

"Yes, us."

"But why?"

"Well, all of your big-wigs decided that people might not be able to handle the truth, so they tried to integrate us into your society slowly."

"How's that?"

"We got jobs, started paying taxes, and started intermingling with you humans."

"But I never…"

"No, you wouldn't. But you talked with us almost every day. We're sociable creatures and we really like to talk. It doesn't matter what we talk about, nor does it matter if we're being yelled at or hung up on."

"You mean, you…"

"Yep. Our first contact with most of the human race came on the phone."

"You called trying to sell…?"

"Yeah. That's our strength. We call, we sell, we get hung up on. Doesn't matter, we call back. It's a living." He shrugged. "Besides, the important thing is that we get to talk. We love to talk. We love to ask questions. We love to never take 'no' for an answer. Don't ask me why."

"But that's so…"

"Tenacious?"

"No."

"Persevering?"

"No."

"Valiant?"

"No."

"Then what?"

"Intrusive."

"Huh?"

"No, not just intrusive. Insensitive and infuriatingly insufferable."

"Hey, good use of adjectives," Telly Mark said, approvingly. "Hey, look, I hate to burst this exchange of ideas, but we've got to get on with killing you guys."

"Wait!"

"What?"

"What's all that Roswell stuff? Were you involved there, too?"

"Nah, not at first. The 1947 stuff was all stuff from you humans. Of course, now that it has such a splendid reputation, it makes a great shuttle bus stop. Anytime we want to go to Earth, we pop down to New Mexico, and if anyone sees our ship, it goes down as more unexplained Roswell stuff. And everyone thinks it's really top secret experiments with your Air Force. The confusion helps keep everything camouflaged."

"Oh."

"Are you done with your questions? Because we'd really like to get on with the killing and stuff."

"Oh. Well, I did have one more question."

He looked exasperated. "Okay, one more." Then he waggled his claw at me. "But just one."

"Okay. The question is, 'what's that?'" I pointed behind them.

They all turned to look, and I wheeled around and took off running, pulling Seth behind me.

We quickly caught up with Buford, Thurman and Knob, who had been watching from a discreet distance. We bolted for the closest building.

There was a terrifying roar from behind us as the army realized they had been tricked by the oldest trick in the book. I heard the shuffling of the large body of creatures as they regained their pursuit.

"There's a door," I gasped, as we neared the building. As we got closer, I could see that the texture of the buildings was rock-like, perhaps to fool observers on Earth. I wondered if the grass would show up on powerful telescopes.

"I heard what he said," Buford panted, as we scampered

through craters.

"Yeah," I managed.

Knob, faster than the rest of us, skidded to a stop near the door, and was yanking its handle.

"Do you think everyone's in on this scam?"

"What...do...you...mean?" It was hard to talk when you're running as fast as you can from an army of lobster-bug-creatures-from-the-moon on the moon.

"I mean, scientists, the government, the telephone company."

"I...don't...know," I gasped.

How could she keep her breath? She was running as hard as I was.

"I can't get in! It's some kind of futuristic lock or something!" Knob exclaimed, rattling the doorknob.

We caught up and milled around him.

"Maybe another building," I said, panicked.

"There's no time. Look." Thurman pointed.

We looked and saw that the army had maneuvered so that they were chasing us with their two flanks having outpaced the vanguard of the troops, effectively enclosing us in a pincher-like movement.

"We're trapped!" I yelled.

Knob was yanking at the doorknob, frantically trying to get in. Thurman whipped out his wand, and twirled it in the air, trying to conjure a spell to get us out of here. I could see that he wouldn't have enough time.

"We have to delay them!" I said harshly to Buford, who appeared deeply in thought.

"I feel funny," she said.

"There's nothing funny about this!" I shrieked.

She looked at me. "Not funny, amusing. Funny, like feeling weird."

I looked at the army, which had slowed its approach now that we were surrounded. "I think you're going to feel weirder in a few minutes."

"I...feel..."

"Buford?"

Knob was still rattling the doorknob and Thurman was

murmuring. Electric static charged the air as his spell began to draw energy from the cosmos. I feared his attempts would be futile. Knob started banging on the door.

"I..." Buford said.

"*Buford?*" I was getting scared for her.

"...feel..."

Her body started shaking.

Chapter Twenty-Nine

"**...CRANKY...**"

"Huh?"

"YEAH!" she suddenly shouted, whipping out her umbrella-sword.

"All right!" I yelled enthusiastically. "You're back!"

"YOU AIN'T KIDDING!" she said, turning to meet the army. The army skidded to a complete stop, having witnessed her transformation from a very cute, very buxomy woman, to a swelled up Hulkish type creature with immense veiny boobs that looked more like weapons than something to cuddle up with. There wasn't, in fact, much cuddly about our warrior at the moment.

There was a nasty gleam in her eyes as she contemplated the army. Calculating her first mayhem, she took a step towards them.

In trepidation they took a step backwards.

"I wonder how she managed..." I wondered, wonderingly.

She took another deliberate step at the army, eyeing them maliciously.

They all shuffled another step backwards, fuzzy antennae vibrating fear and apprehension. The sight was amazing. Hundreds of thousands of black, armored creatures, all cowering before one transformed housewife.

"ALL RIGHT, BOYS," she growled, "WHO'S FIRST TO DIE?"

None of them volunteered.

Then she leaped.

Meanwhile, Knob was still struggling with the locked door behind us, and purple stuff swirled around from Thurman's incantations. And me, you ask? I was holding hands with my catatonic brother, unable otherwise to be of help to anyone.

"DIE YOU SCUM-SUCKING WORTHLESS BUGS!"

A clang of metal was followed by a colossal clatter of shells.

"We aren't bugs," one of them yelled at her.

"THEN DIE, YOU SLIMY ARTHROPODS!" she screamed.

"We aren't arthropods, either," the voice countered.

"I DON'T CARE! DIE!"

Still though, there were too many of them. As she scythed through them they reformed behind her, like an amoebae. There was no way she could destroy them all before they got us.

"Thurman," I said shakily, "how you doing, there, buddy?"

Buford sprinted across my vision, cutting down scores of telemarketers, leaving disembodied shells, antennae, and claws twitching in her wake. Her powers were, if anything, more powerful than before. Still though, there was only one of her, and many, many of the creatures. Too many.

As she waded through the army, effortlessly scattering the horde, a group of creatures led by Telly Mark saw their opportunity. Unprotected, Knob, Thurman, Seth and I were defenseless, while Buford was distracted by her efforts.

With Telly Mark at their head, they suddenly broke, surging in our direction. I looked around frantically for a weapon, but there was nothing available. The sound of their exoskeletons clinking and clacking was a horrible sound, and I froze in fear as they rushed at us, claws snapping.

Just before they reached us, I looked at my impassive brother. "Good-bye, Seth. I wish I'd been a better brother. I love you."

"AIEEEEEE!"

Suddenly a blur swept like a tornado before us, tumbling

the bug-lobsters like bowling pins. Buford had looped back, and swinging her sword in wide arcs, was sending the creatures into scattered retreat. Incredibly, several of the creatures leaped at her, over her sword, landing on her back and in her hair. Bellowing like some great beast, she tore at them, even as more eagerly piled on. I was reminded of piranhas attacking an unsuspecting swimmer.

Just then something prodded me from behind. It felt like some Jack-in-the-beanstalk giant poking gently, harnessing its great strength, trying to get my attention without causing injury. I swung around, and saw the purple cloud. Quietly building strength at the tip of Thurman's wand, it was nearing critical mass. All of a sudden something grabbed me and hurled me into space and time.

"Oh, never mind. I got it." Knob said. "All you have to do it lift this…"

Too late. We were gone.

Chapter Thirty

"I don't get it," Knob said calmly.
"Huh?"
"I don't get it. Why do we keep ending up here?"
I opened my eyes and beheld the golden arch.
Thurman was sitting across from me, his wand still aloft. There was no sign of the purple smoke.
"Ow, dammit, dammit!"
Buford jumped up from her seat, frantically pummeling herself.
"Whoa! You got bugs on you," Knob said, leaping up. He pulled ineffectively at a shelled tail that was frantically flipping.
"They're all over her," Thurman exclaimed.
"I hate bugs! Get them off! Get them off!" Buford screamed, backpedaling in fear and confusion. She didn't look anything like a warrior now.
I grabbed one of the bug-lobster creatures. Its shell was smooth and dry, so I was able to grip it tightly. I yanked at it, and Buford screamed in response. One of its claws was twisted in her hair. It had a startled look on its face.
"Damn bug!" I said angrily, and looked for something to hit it with.

"Here, man, use this," Knob said, thrusting something into my hand. A lobster cracker. Not cracker, like what Polly likes, but one of those metal crackers, like you'd use on nuts. Not nuts, like what we, uh, guys have, protect and hold sacred, or like those people who think that they are nuts, but not crazy nuts, more like they are crazy nuts who think that they are nuts, like Brazil nuts or cashews. Bless you! Thank you.

Just kidding, he didn't have a lobster cracker.

"Here, man, use this," Knob said, thrusting something into my hand. It was a claw hammer. Not claw, like what the lobster-bug had at the ends of its arms, but claw, like…oh, never mind.

I was kidding again. He didn't give me a hammer either.

What really happened is that I balled up a fist, and socked the lobster-bug between the eyes.

"Oh, dammit, what'd you do that for?" it spat angrily.

"Let go of her, or I'll stuff your antennae where the sun don't shine," I threatened.

"Oh, yeah?"

"Yeah!"

"Oh, yeah?"

"Yeah!"

"Oh, stop it, you two," Buford said, having recovered her wits. With blinding speed, she grabbed the thing's antennae, and stuffed them where the sun don't shine.

"Ow!" it cried. It was all curled up, trying to pull its sensitive antennae out of its butt without further damage.

"You guys want the same treatment?" she growled at the other lobster-bugs who were hanging on various parts of her anatomy.

"Uh, no." They let go, and dropped to the floor.

They stood there, looking up at us, and we stood there, looking down at them. It looked like a satisfactory stalemate, so I took the opportunity to ask Buford a question that had been bothering me, "So, Buford?"

"Yes?"

"What, uh, happened back there with you?"

"You mean the PMS thing?"

"Uh, yeah." I rushed on, "It seemed like you had trouble, uh, converting for a few moments, but when you turned it on it was like you were stronger than ever."

"Yes, I'm still trying to figure out what happened. All I can guess is that when we went to the moon, the lack of the moon's gravitational pull messed up the hormones."

"Yeah, I was kind of thinking that, too. But then, *wham*, you had it back, in spades."

"I was confused at first, too. Then when I saw Earth hanging over our heads, I figured out that its greater gravitational pull exceeded anything the moon could ever exert."

"Yeah, that makes sense."

We lapsed back into silence, but the silence was almost immediately broken.

"No pets in here."

I looked up. A pimply teenaged boy was looking severely at me.

"Huh?"

"Cancha read?" he asked, his words distorted by a huge gleaming mass of metal in his mouth. I had the irrational urge to whip out a large magnet. He pointed to a sign on the door.

"No shirts, no shoes, no service," I read obediently.

"Not that sign, the other," he said sarcastically.

"No roller-blading."

"No! That one!" He pointed a furious finger.

"No pets. So?"

"Right, that means no pets."

"He's not a pet. He's my brother."

Someone had given Seth some fries, and he was chewing mechanically, dipping them first into ketchup.

"I wasn't talking about him. I was talking about them!"

"Them who?"

"Them," he said, pointing at a dozen lobster-bugs milling uncertainly around my feet. One of them picked a french fry off the floor and ate it.

"Not mine," I said nonchalantly.

"Guy?"

"Yeah?"

"Actually, we might be able to use them," Buford said.

"What do you mean?"

"Yeah, what do you mean?" one of the lobster-bugs echoed.

"Think *ostage-hay*," she said.

"Ostage-ay?" I wondered, confused.

"Ostage-hay," the lobster-bug put in helpfully. "That's pig-Latin for—"

"Oh, shut up," Buford interjected. "Yeah, hostage. We can use them as hostages."

The lobster-bugs started shuffling innocently sideways towards the exit.

"Oh, no you don't," Knob said, moving to block them off.

"You can't use us as hostages," one of them said.

"Oh, yeah? Why not?" I asked.

"Uh, well…"

"Our lives are meaningless," another one put in.

"Meaningless?"

"Yeah, nobody cares about us," another chimed.

"But, if we told Telly Mark that we had you…" I started.

"He'd laugh. We aren't important."

"Yeah, we're worthless," another put in.

"Expendable."

"Nothing," another said.

"Void-creatures," another wailed.

Suddenly they all broke down, and started crying.

"Sheesh," I said, and looked at Buford. She quickly wiped a tear from her eye. "Aw, c'mon, don't tell me you're falling for this hogwash," I said.

Knob choked down a sob.

"Knob, stop it!"

"Poor little things," he said, sniffing loudly.

"Sure, Telly Mark doesn't care," I said hotly. "He doesn't care about anything. I'm sure these guys have mothers…"

"We don't ever know our mothers," one of them said.

"Yeah, they just lay eggs somewhere, and leave us to fend for ourselves."

"Okay, but you have families of your own…" I started.

"No-o-o-o!" one of them cried. "Only one male fertilizes all of our females."

"One male? What do you mean? Like every female has a

whole bunch of males, but only one can fertilize?"

"No. There's only a single male who procreates with every female of our species. The rest of us, we're nothing," it sobbed.

My mouth dropped open. "One male?"

"That's why we're so lonely," it said.

"Lonely?"

"Yes, we have no families, no friends, nobody cares about us."

"Yeah," another put in. "That's why we are telemarketers. We don't mind being hung up on, cussed out, or anything else. We enjoy the abuse, because it's the only real contact we get with families."

"You mean, by interrupting?"

"Yeah, that's why we call during dinnertime and popular television shows. We know there's a good chance a family is there. So we call, and somehow, just talking with you humans..."

"...we feel better. We feel loved. As if, as if...we had...family of our own."

"And now you are taking all of this away from us..."

"...with your new laws...threats of suits..."

"...attorneys..."

"Yeah, attorneys..." they chimed together.

They stood forlornly, tears and sincerity leaking from their beady black eyes

The concept was dazzling. The things I had learned today. Telemarketers are aliens from the moon who take jobs just so they can call us, and establish a contact where somehow they derive emotional satisfaction out of the contact, even if the call is abusive and hostile.

"But, Telly Mark...?" I started.

"Yeah, him," one of them seethed. "He's the one."

"The one?"

"Yeah, the fortunate Procreator," another spat.

"He's your Procreator?"

"Yes," he wailed.

"How long has he been the Procreator?" I asked.

"Oh, I don't know," one said hesitantly.

"I do," another shot. "It's been about thirty years now. That's when we got into telemarketing."

"Was there another before him?" I wondered.

"No. Before him, we had families, like humans."

Really?

"But how did he become this Procreator?" I asked.

"Uh...I'm not sure. Do you know?" one asked another.

"Um...I don't know. I sorta assumed..."

"You guys don't know?" another asked the first two.

"Why? Do you know?" they asked him.

"No. I figured you knew."

"Well, we didn't know," the first one stated.

"Doesn't anybody know?" I asked them.

They looked at one another. They stood there in a small group, having lost all ability to procreate, for a reason they did not know. And now, their pathetic lives were spent interrupting the dinnertime of an alien species, just trying to horn in on their family time.

"So you guys don't have sex?" the pimply-faced McDonald's employee asked. I had forgotten he was here.

"No."

"Me neither," he said.

Big surprise there.

A sound outside drew my attention.

"Do you hear that?" I said, my ears perked like a fruit bat.

"What?" Thurman asked.

"It's back."

"The Whomping Cloud," Knob said, his elf ears twitching.

"I'm tired of this," Thurman yelled. "It's time to deal with that thing, once and for all!"

"What are you going to do?" Buford asked him.

"You'll see," he told her. "Knob?"

"Yeah?"

"You got something to read in there?" He pointed at Knob's knapsack.

"Yeah, sure," Knob said, quickly riffling through his backpack, and pulling out a thin magazine. "Here ya go. There's an excellent article here about how they've discovered that mosquitoes can carry a virus that attacks cancer cells in mice."

"Sounds like a good deal for mice," Thurman said.

"Uh, yeah," Knob said.

"So how's that do us any good?" Thurman added.

A look of confusion passed over Knob's face, but he recovered quickly. "Uh, if you, like, uh, read *Of Mice and Men*, you'll…"

Buford bailed him out. "Mice and humans react the same way to cancer and treatment."

"Oh," Thurman said. "Okay, sounds interesting. Follow me, guys."

He took the magazine, and went outside.

We paused, and then trailed after, wondering what he had in mind. What kind of magic spell would require a magazine article?

The sound of the Whomping Cloud was getting louder. It sounded angry. I think it was still a little upset over how we'd thwarted it the last time we were here.

"Man, look at all the flies," Knob observed.

I hadn't noticed them. Probably because they were all keeping a safe distance away, buzzing around the trash cans lining the parking lot and the dumpster at the back of the restaurant. Knob must have noticed them with his extraordinary elf senses. But now it was obvious how the cloud knew we had returned.

I wondered where Thurman was headed. I looked around. There was a construction site next to the McDonald's. A sign announced that a Subway Restaurant would be opening there in the fall. I also noticed they had replaced the dumpster that had been flattened in our last visit.

It looked like Thurman was going to take us into the construction site. Maybe he needed the room for spells and magic. Plus, no innocent people would be caught up in the upcoming fracas.

He suddenly veered, and headed for a blue Porta-Potty.

"Where are you going?" I asked his back.

"Try to hold the cloud off for a few minutes," he said, and went inside.

"I guess when ya gotta go, ya gotta go," observed Knob.

"Yeah, I guess," I agreed, perplexed by his decision to take a dump before battling an angry cloud.

I scanned the horizon, looking for signs of the Whomping Cloud.

"There it is," Knob exclaimed, pointing off into the distance. He had taken over watching Seth, who was holding his hand like a little toddler.

I looked where he pointed, and there it was. It was bouncing up and down like a manic yo-yo, probably attacking all of the Grand Prixs and McDonald's restaurants in its path. It was definitely headed in our direction. I felt sorry for the McDonald's, but not for the Grand Prixs. Too many of them have tailgated me, cut me off, raced me for merges, and generally committed every driver abuse, with the sole exception of driving too slow. As far as I was concerned, the Whomping Cloud could head on up to Detroit, and take out GM's assembly plant.

"Sir?"

I felt a tiny tug on my pants leg, and looked down. "Huh?"

"What about us?" one of the lobster-bugs asked plaintively. They had followed us out of the building, and were milling about meekly.

"What about you?" I parroted.

"What do you want us to do?"

"Uh, just wait here," I told them.

I watched the cloud approach.

"No, wait," I amended, "why don't you guys get out of the line of fire or something? I don't want you getting hurt."

"You care if we get hurt?" one of them asked incredulously. They all wore shocked expressions on their faces. Not really. They have little shell-like crustacean faces totally incapable of expressing emotions. Still, though, I could tell they were surprised. Probably because they were all making surprised-like exclamations and mewlings.

"Yeah, I guess," I said.

"Wow! Nobody's ever cared about us before," another said.

"We're not leaving! We'll fight with you!" another announced.

"Yeah! We're with you!" they exclaimed.

"Don't make us leave," the first one said, tears glistening in its eyes.

"Yeah! Don't make us leave," they sang.

"All right! All right! Just don't get in the way," I said irritably.

"Yayyyyyy!"

I turned back to the cloud, mulling over what we could do to hold it off until Thurman was done. I couldn't think of anything. Buford couldn't fight it. Knob was useless. I didn't figure there was anything I could do to hurt a cloud. The lobster-bugs, while full of enthusiasm, weren't equipped to take on an out of control force of nature. What could we do? Then a thought occurred to me.

"You know what that is?" I asked, gesturing towards the onrushing cloud.

"The cloud?" one of them answered.

"Yeah."

"Oh, that. It's, or it was, one of our allies."

"Allies?"

"Yeah. The cigarette companies are allies with Telly Mark," it said.

I remembered the cigarette butts that had rained down on our heads during our battle with the cloud.

"So what does a cloud have to do with cigarettes?" I asked.

"It's not a cloud," one of them said.

"At least not a regular cloud," another put in.

"It's smoke," the first one added.

"Smoke?"

"Yeah. Mostly second-hand smoke. They collected it, and gave it life. Now it works for them."

"Works for them?"

"Dirty work. Like rubbing out enemies and stuff like that."

Hmmm. Second-hand smoke, animated and transformed into a weapon. Insidious. Amazing what the cigarette companies come up with.

I thought of something else.

"So, what would your people do if we could somehow get rid of Telly Mark?" I asked.

"Get rid of him? What do you mean?"

"I don't know yet. But if he weren't around, would your

people go back to normal, maybe start making your own families again?"

"Like in the old times?" one asked, eyes shining with wonder.

"Yeah, like in the old times. One female, uh, whatever you are, with one male."

"We could do that?" it asked.

"Why not? What would stop you?"

They paused, thinking it over. I could see that the idea was exciting them.

Finally, one asked, "So how would we go about this?"

"Yeah," another said, "he's very powerful."

"I don't know," I hedged. "Let's see how things work out."

WHOMP!

I jumped, having lost track of the cloud during our conversation. It was within a hundred yards and had just taken out the corner bus stop.

"Knob, you were supposed to have been watching it," I accused him.

"Oh, sorry, I got caught up in what you guys were talking about," he apologized.

I banged on the Porta-Potty. "Hey, Thurman, get out here! Whomping Cloud's here!"

"Hang on," he answered, his voice muffled. "I'm almost ready."

Almost ready?

"Grrrrrrr." Buford was gearing up, whipping up some PMS for the upcoming fight. I knew there was nothing she would be able to do.

WHOMP!

A construction crane disappeared, crunched to a small flat iron hunk of metal.

"Thurman?" I said, totally panicked.

"Okay, I'm ready, lure it over here," he said.

Lure it over? It was coming like a freight train.

"Consider it lured," I said agreeably.

"Let me know when it's in range," came his muffled voice.

In range? Of what?

"Okay," I agreed again.

WHOMPP!

A pile of excavated dirt flattened suddenly. The next one would be right on top of us.

"Uh, Thurman, I think it's in range now." Nervously, I looked for the tell-tale purple smoke of Thurman and Harry Potter-made magic.

"Okay, here I come," he said, and the door of the Porta-Potty swung open.

I looked overhead, and my blood froze. The Whomping Cloud was poised directly over us, black and roiling, immense and ready to pulverize. I knew then that we were going to die.

The door clattered plastically as Thurman stepped out, magnificent in his Goth-black attire. More than ever, he looked like a full-fledged sorcerer. It was incredible how I had become a total believer in his power and ability.

I searched searchingly for the wand of power, and the purple that would obliterate this cloud once and for all. But there was no wand. No purple magic. The only thing in his hand was the crumpled up magazine carrying the news of how mosquitoes might help cure cancer in mice. I hoped that when I was dead, which I had a bad feeling was going to be very, very soon, that the mice would appreciate what mosquitoes had done for them.

A rushing wind sound warned that the Whomping-Second-Hand-Smoke-Cloud had begun its descent, and I looked up in fear and revulsion.

"EEEKKKK!" the lobster-bugs squealed in unison.

"RRRRRRRRRR!" Buford growled ineffectively.

"Peeeyyouuuuu!" Knob groaned.

Peeyouu?

All of a sudden the stench hit me, and I was knocked to the ground. Other bodies thumped into the dirt next to me.

From there, I was in perfect position to see what happened next.

Chapter Thirty-One

A green cloud billowed out of the open Porta-Potty door and streamed upwards at the onrushing Whomping Cloud. The green cloud was odorous, repulsive, guaranteed to take the chrome right off a faucet. And entirely man-made.

Man-stink, the most powerful force in the world, capable of clearing a room in an instant. Thurman had cooked up a bouquet of noxious aroma, intensified it with reading material, and unleashed it unfiltered and untamed. And now it was rushing upwards to fulfill its destiny.

The resulting explosion rattled the molecules in the air, shaking the ground and building, exploding the windows in the restaurant. Sparks shot through the air. Coke cans shot their contents out of a nearby pop machine.

I would have fallen to the ground, but I was already on the ground. So instead, I was shoved really hard into the ground, sinking almost two inches into the topsoil.

We lay on the ground, shaken and stunned by the shock waves.

After a few moments, we finally stirred.

"Hnnggghhh!" I said, clutching my head.

I looked above. The sky was clear. No sign of the Whomping

Cloud.

"That was awesome. What'd you eat to make that?" Knob said admiringly to Thurman.

"Whew, that was, um, interesting," Buford added, delicately waving her hands in front of her nose to dispel the lingering odor.

"Ah, ha!" a voice accused, from behind us.

Painfully, I rolled over to confront our accuser. Telly Mark and his army, black shells glistening in the sun, were lined up in the parking lot.

"Uhhg, how'd you get here?" I croaked.

"That's for me to know, and you to, well, you're never going to know," he sang.

"I'm getting pretty sick of you," I said wearily.

"Too bad. I'm used to it. Anyway, what'd you do to my cloud?"

"Ah, it *is* yours," I accused.

"Yeah, I borrowed it from a buddy at Phillip Morris."

"And the flies?"

"Fly spies, the best out there. Heck, you know your own government has them now? It's like 1984, but worse."

"So what now?" I asked him.

"Easy. You die."

"And my brother's brain?"

"Oh, that I'm going to keep. He's excellent company, you know."

"You know we aren't going to go peacefully," I said conversationally.

"I wouldn't expect you to, after all you've done so far."

"Okay, you going to give us a head start?"

Before he could answer, we were running across the field.

His army roared as they took up the chase.

As I sprinted, I noticed that the dozen bug-lobster creatures we'd brought along were keeping pace with us, and showing no signs of taking hostile action against us. I shrugged inwardly, and concentrated on running.

Then there was a roar ahead of us. I looked up, and to my horror, I saw another army rushing at us.

"That way." I pointed another direction, and we veered towards the only opening available. I wondered if maybe they were funneling us this direction as a trap.

Somebody caught up to me, and ran alongside, breathing easily. Buford, in full PMS splendor, her umbrella sword unsheathed and ready for action.

"Two armies," she said.

"Huh?"

"There are two armies here."

"What are you talking about?" I gasped. The run was more of an effort for me.

"They aren't the same army. They're two separate armies."

I slowed, and squinted in the direction of the second army. All I saw was a mass of humanity charging towards us in an unbroken line. Thousands and thousands in full voiced roar.

"She's right," Knob said. "Hey," he said pointing at the army, "I know that guy!"

"Huh? What are you talking about?" I said in a mixture of fear and irritation.

"That guy! See him? In the black robe?"

Slowing, I followed where he was pointing, and could make out an individual, running with the army, a black cape billowing behind him.

"You know him?" I asked.

"Yeah, Wopner."

"*Judge Wopner?*" I asked incredulously.

"Oh, yeah, I recognize him now," Buford said. Her eyes weren't quite as good as Knob's elven eyes, but they were battle-trained.

Two armies, just to annihilate five people and a few deserters?

"It's the lawyers!" Knob exclaimed.

They were getting closer, and I saw that he was right. A great army of judges, lawyer-politicians, tort lawyers, criminal lawyers, contract lawyers, collection lawyers, estate lawyers, with their minions of paralegals, legal secretaries, law clerks, bailiffs and other hangers on, all assembled into a mighty army of half a million, were flowing through the city like a horde of ravenous locusts.

On the other side, an army of telemarketers, aliens from the moon, numbering a half a million, were pouring over the field in a pincher movement that I saw no way to escape.

"We have to make it to that opening," I gasped, pointing at the only escape path left us. I had no clue what we would do if we succeeded in escaping this trap, but vowed to run and fight and do whatever it would take to live and breathe and do all those things that guys live to do.

"Oh, no!" Knob screamed, skidding to a stop.

I slammed into him, and we tumbled to the ground. A foot thudded into my stomach, and Thurman was hurtled head first over us. Buford easily leaped over, escaping collision, but slid to a halt.

"Look!" Knob said, leaning up, and pointing a shaky finger.

I looked, and despaired when I saw a third army had entered the fray. One bigger than the other two combined. It had appeared in a rush, filling the void between the two armies, moving with a speed and precision brought on only by extended training.

Chapter Thirty-Two

"We're dead," Thurman moaned.

"Thurman, start cranking up your wand," Knob urged, refusing to accept defeat.

"I can't. There's no time," Thurman responded.

"Where would we go, anyway?" Buford said, defeat finally etched in her face. "Lawyers are everywhere. Telemarketers are everywhere. They've beaten us."

Here we were, an elf, a sorcerer, a warrior, a skeptic, a zombie, and twelve alien crustaceans, totally surrounded by millions of angry, screaming foes, all rushing to eradicate us from the world. Who were we to try to fight against such power and fury?

"Guys, and, uh, Guy," Thurman said, having to yell over the thundering noise, "it's been a blast. I can't think of anyone I'd rather have hung around with."

"I hope my kids will be okay." Buford sniffed, all signs of the warrior gone. She looked young and vulnerable.

I stood up, and hugged my unresisting brother, feeling tears well up in my eyes. "Hey, I love you, kid. I just hope somehow you know it."

The ground shook from the force of the approaching armies. I was having trouble keeping my footing as I clung to Seth.

"Guy!" Knob screamed in my ear. I could still barely hear him.

"Yeah!" I yelled back.

"That's a new army!" he said.

"Huh?"

"It's not telemarketers or lawyers."

"So, what is it, the United States Army?"

"No!" Suddenly his eyes got big. "It's something else. Something way different!"

"What are you talking about?" I shouted angrily. Here I was, getting ready to die, and Knob's playing question games.

"Hey, we're saved!" he yelled, and started waving his arms happily, trying to flag down the late-coming army.

"We are!" Buford breathed. "We really are."

And now I could see, and what I saw was the most shocking thing I'd ever seen. No seriously! I'm not kidding. More shocking than my zombie brother, more shocking than seeing the monster at the telephone company, more shocking than meeting telemarketers and learning they are aliens from the moon, more shocking than a hostile cloud of second hand smoke.

Then the army split in two, one half racing towards the approaching lawyer army, and the other heading off the telemarketing army. Both of those armies hesitated, as if to consider the unexpected foes who had suddenly appeared.

Now that they were closer, I saw that indeed there was an army that was mightier than the lawyers, better trained than the telemarketers, more numerous than the U.S. Armed Forces.

Their uniforms were splendid, their hats cocky, and made of paper. They were full of youthful energy, unencumbered by the weight of years of failed expectations, warfare, and appellate court decisions.

They were clothed in brown, red, white, blue, and yellow, and represented all walks of society and humanity: African American, Asian, Caucasian, Indian. I was speechless with awe, as I beheld the army of so many colors and television commercials. The level of teen-aged hormones charged the atmosphere with angst and unreasonableness.

And now something else made sense. It made sense that

we were drawn to this place, that no matter where we went, we returned here. It made sense that the widow of Ray Croc realized what good humans were, and thus donated a billion dollars to the United Way when she died. The founder of McDonald's restaurants, with their charity for sick children, their infusion of part of our social culture, had surely been aghast at what had been happening in our culture.

And then there was the suit. Where the attorneys sued McDonald's because an old lady didn't know that coffee was hot. McDonald's paid out the nose for that. They changed their packaging to warn senile people not to spill hot liquid on themselves. And the attorneys were not done, and tried to sue McDonald's because people got fat from their own lack of control.

And then they started something, an army, if it were. And others joined them. Then more joined, and more. And now they joined in battle.

Tens of thousands of McDonald's employees, tens of thousands of Burger King employees, Pizza Hut employees, Subway, Jack-in-the-Box, Taco Bell, Hardee's, Kentucky Fried Chicken, Popeye's, Wendy's, Arby's, Dairy Queen, Godfather's Pizza, Domino's, Baskin Robbins, Dunkin Donuts, Krispy Kreme, Taco Johns, White Castle, Blimpie, and others whose dietary excesses I did not recognize.

The entire Fast Food Nation had chosen sides in the battle between mankind and those insidious parasites that feed on mankind.

The attack was sudden and furious. I watched in shock as a McDonald's employee ran up to a lawyer, and threw a cup of hot coffee in his face.

"Aaaiieeeee!" the attorney screamed, clutching himself in agony.

An attorney-medic rushed up to him. "Are you scalded?"

"No!" the attorney wailed. "But you have to get it off! Get it off!"

"Why, what's wrong?" the medic asked, rummaging in his medkit.

"It's ordinary coffee, not a latte!" the attorney said, crumpling in agony.

"Inhumane!" the medic groaned. "This is a major violation of the Geneva Convention."

Meanwhile, a brigade of Burger King employees hauled up huge vats of bubbling french fry grease, and poured it on some lobster-bug telemarketers.

"Aaaaieeeeee!"

The smell of boiled lobster filled the battlefield. My mouth watered, and I wondered if they might be edible.

Some attorneys tried to mount an offensive, and charged towards a group of pimply faced grill cooks. The cooks whipped out caulk-guns, and shot streams of Big Mac sauce on the ground in front of the attorneys. The lawyers hit the sauce, and spun out of control, briefcase and legal papers flying.

I heard a popping sound, and kid's toys rained down on the lobster-bugs, clattering as they hit their shells. Then there was the ghastly sound of choking, as the toys lodged in the lobster-bugs' throats from the pieces not meant to be handled by telemarketers or children under three.

Biggie-sized fries, Big Gulps and Whoppers fell from the skies, shot from catapults, crushing masses of lawyers and lobster-bugs.

The carnage was shocking, repulsive and decidedly one-sided. Broken and battered attorneys and bug-lobsters littered the field. Ambulances poured into the field, followed closely by reinforcements, attorneys whose specialties were ambulance chasing. But is was for naught as the attorneys were simply overwhelmed.

In the middle, an island of ourselves, we were untouched, even as the melee continued unabated.

"C'mon," I said, pulling Buford's arm.

"What?"

"We have to find Telly Mark," I said, pulling her into the battle. Bug-lobster shells crunched, and I had to place my feet carefully to avoid slipping in torts, which had spilled all over the battlefield.

"Why? He'll get his finally," she said with grim satisfaction.

"We have to get Seth's brain back! This might be our last chance."

"Oh, jeez, I forgot!" She took the lead, beginning the transformation to unstoppable berserker as she stepped into the carnage. We would quite likely need these powers to work our way through the tumult.

I followed, hauling Seth behind me. Knob and Thurman took up rear guard. Thus arrayed, we wormed our way through the combatants. Strangely, no one tried to stop our passage, or engage us in battle. The sight of our formidable warrior probably played a huge factor in this. Because of this, the biggest problem was working our way over and through fallen soldiers from one army or another.

"Hey, no pets, remember?"

Alarmed, I looked at the voice. It was the pimply-faced McDonald's employee. "Just kidding, man," he said, flashing his braces. He turned around just in time to smack an attorney on the head with a spatula.

"There he is!" Knob said, pointing at a group of the bug-creatures that had rallied around one of their leaders.

He was right, it was Telly Mark! He was surrounded by a horde of bug-lobsters, who were valiantly fending off the attacks of a contingent of Wendy's employees. A freckle-faced girl with red hair and pig tails led the Wendy's charge.

We stopped short, trying to figure out how to get through the combatants.

"Hey, Telly Mark, we demand the right to procreate," a voice called out behind us.

Surprised, I turned around. It was one of the bug-lobsters who had joined our group. I hadn't noticed that they had stayed with us.

Telly Mark heard his name, and turned towards us. Surprisingly, he looked happy to see us.

"Hey, stupid humans," he called out, in greeting. "Glad you could make it."

"I want my brother's brain back!" I yelled over the crowd.

"What?"

"I said, I want my brother's brain back!" I hollered.

"What? I can't hear you."

The sound of the fighting was drowning out my voice.

Frustrated, I tried to push my way closer. But the struggling bodies were packed together, and I couldn't close the gap.

"LOOK OUT," a rough voice said, and pushed me none too gently to the side.

Buford reached into the pack, arbitrarily grabbing collars and claws. She tossed them, and whatever they were connected to, over her shoulder, and moved into the space she had created. We crowded in behind her as she worked her way through the combatants.

In this manner, we reached the small hill on which Telly Mark had rallied his troops.

"Hey, there," he said cheerfully, when he saw us charge up. "Care to join the party?"

"Your party is over," I said brusquely.

"What are you talking about? We're just getting warmed up," Telly Mark told me.

"I want Seth's brain back, now!"

"No way. I need it to keep me company."

"Huh? What do you mean, company?"

"I'm lonely!"

"Lonely? You are the single Procreator for your entire species," I said hotly.

"Oh, that? That's different. I'm addicted to humans. And ever since the government made it impossible to call your elderly, I just can't live without human companionship."

"There are other ways to get companionship," I yelled at him, "without hi-jacking someone's brain!"

"I don't care!" he said. "I'm keeping it. It's mine! And if I die," he glared at me, "I'm taking the brain with me."

He fished a small container out of a hidden pouch on his abdomen, and shook it threateningly in his larger claw. I knew that that claw could easily crush the container, and with it, any hopes of my ever seeing my brother recovered.

The fighting around us was quelled. They had all noticed the drama taking place on the little hill. Attorneys, restaurant employees and aliens all paused, temporarily suspending hostilities. All except for one White Castle trainee, who was industrially stuffing hamburgers in a paralegal's ears.

A lone chicken McNugget flew by, dripping honey-mustard sauce.

"Hey, that looks good," Knob said. "I'm starved."

"What do we do?" Buford whispered. "If we attack, he'll destroy Seth."

"I don't know." My brain was churning.

"Thurman, you got any spells that would help?" Knob asked.

"Um, I don't know, maybe *wingardiam leviosa*."

"You can do that one?" Knob asked.

"Yeah, I think so. I watched the movies pretty carefully."

"Cool. Hey, if we get out of this, think you could use that to help me dunk a basketball? I've always wanted to do that."

"Sure, I guess."

"How's a levitating spell going to help us here?" I whispered.

"I'll levitate the container out of his claw. Then you guys jump him, and keep him out of the way while I levitate it over here."

I thought about it. It might work.

"Okay, do it!" I said.

He stepped forward, waving his Harry Potter wand. Purple sparks danced around its tip.

"Whoa, cool," a bug-lobster exclaimed.

"Pretty," a Burger King french fry girl cooed.

"It's like Harry Potter," a court reporter added. Being a guy, I did not fail to notice that she had very nice legs.

Thurman puffed up, and stood tall, clad in black Goth, his arms commanding the power of the cosmos, and concentrated in a way I hadn't seen since the time we played *Invasion of the Space Reptiles* on PlayStation.

The end of the wand disappeared in swirling plum, and sooner than I expected, a jet of purple ectoplasm shot out. It neatly snared the container, and with a pickpocket's dexterity, snitched it out of the surprised Telly Mark's claws. It had happened so quickly, he had no chance to crush and destroy Seth's brain.

"Ya-hoo!" I yelled, and leaped over the lobster-bugs, hands outstretched to grab Telly Mark and squeeze the life out of him. Buford and Knob were right with me, roaring battle cries.

Together, we flew at the surprised creature, but Telly Mark

recovered swiftly. Just as we were about to land and crush him, the back of his shell flipped up, like a huge beetle. With a loud buzzing sound, he lifted from the ground.

Buford, Knob and I collided and landed in a tangled mess.

I rolled, and watched in horror as the telemarketer buzzed towards the container floating lazily towards Thurman. He was going to win the race.

"*He can fly?*" I cried.

"Oh, yeah, now I remember," said one of the lobster-bug creatures. "That's why he's the Great Procreator. We were trying to breed this into our species."

"So that's why flies were your allies?" I asked, beginning to understand.

"Aha!" Telly Mark had caught up to the container. He scooped it out of the purple magic, and triumphantly held his trophy aloft.

"And now, because of you, I will destroy this forever!"

"Don't!" I screamed. "Keep it, if you must. But don't kill him!"

"Too late!" he cried, triumphantly. "I'll get another."

And he began to squeeze.

"Noooo!" I cried.

CRUNCH!

Bits and pieces of flotsam and jetsam fell to the ground.

Thurman dropped his wand, and suddenly lunged.

Chapter Thirty-Three

"You want to sue him?" a voice asked me.

"Huh?" I was dazed.

"I asked if you want to sue him."

I turned around. Judge Wopner.

"Uh, no, I guess not. What good would it do me?"

"Hey, you never know. Maybe he has an estate or something, and we could go after that."

"No. I really don't."

"I'd do it contingency," he said, a note of pleading in his voice.

"I can't. There are too many lawsuits in this world anyway. I'm not going to add to the mess."

"Okay, your loss," he said, and strode away, his robe billowing behind him like Superman's cape.

"Get him to drink it," Knob said.

"Here, bro." I held the container to Seth's lips, and he drank mechanically.

I held my breath, waiting to see what would happen.

"What happened back there?" Buford asked, watching.

"Told you he was real," Thurman declared. He leaned over, and patted the air a foot above the ground.

"How'd he jump that high in the air?" Knob asked.

Thurman gave him a severe look. "Jeez, you guys just don't get it. He's a ghost dog. He didn't jump. He flew!"

"Oh," Knob said.

"Well, anyway, you made a great catch."

"Thanks," Thurman said, mollified.

"What catch?" Buford asked.

"The container," Knob said. "When Weezel bit Telly Mark, he dropped the container and Thurman caught it before it hit the ground."

"Oh."

"Man, there's not much left of him," Knob said, gesturing at the broken pieces of shell, crab-like legs and antennae, which was all that was left of Telly Mark.

"Hey, where am I?" a voice croaked.

Seth!

Epilogue

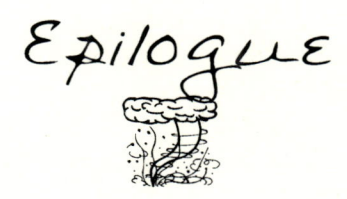

I kind of miss the telephone's ringing. It's usually quiet, and nowadays Mom discovered that it is entirely possible to reach me using Bell's invention. Especially since it had finally been restored to its original purpose.

After an initial period of excessive fondness, I pretty much treat Seth like a little brother again, which I think is a relief to both of us. Too much gushiness just doesn't feel right. But I sure think differently about him, and somehow there's a whole different relationship between us than ever before.

After the Quest, our company pretty much broke up. We don't see much of Buford, the Warrior, who has her own family matters to tend to. I think about her with a warm smile whenever I see that there's a big sale at the department store. Knob and I are still roommates, but Thurman moved into his own apartment. He's dating the redheaded manager from Wendy's, and felt he needed more space. Every once in a while I see a purple glow coming from his neighborhood, and know that he's keeping his newfound skills intact.

Knob and I live in the same place, which had been rebuilt by insurance companies. As good as new, though we haven't been able to build up a decent mess on the floor, yet. We don't remember buying insurance, but we must have, and it was a good thing that we had. Seth, who visits frequently, has pretty much claimed the basement as his home away from home, and says he'll move there when he's old enough.

These thoughts were going through my mind one afternoon as I sat on the back stoop, sipping an Amstel Light. A fly buzzed by, and I raked it with a suspicious look.

"Hey, man." The screen door opened, and Knob stepped out, munching a Cardiac Arrest sandwich. I could see green pepper, tuna, and something that I hoped wasn't beef tongue.

"Hey," I acknowledged.

He folded himself against the wall, and I handed him a beer.

We watched the graveyard together, thinking about the world and those that seek to rule it.

The sun reached towards the horizon, pulling itself towards evening.

A mosquito bumped against the wall. Recognizing that it was female, I restrained myself from squishing it. Knob's eyes followed it protectively. He had retired his elf ears, but had not lost the increased hearing and sight he had gained in our adventure.

Then a commotion from the front of the house got our attention. Someone was banging on the door.

Without great alarm, we went inside and walked to the door.

Before we could get there, purple smoke billowed, the locks clicked audibly and the door crashed open. A black clad figure burst into the room.

"Guys!" Thurman cried. "Pack up! We have to go!"

"Huh?"

"They're here! C'mon, hurry! There's not much time!"

"What are you talking about?"

He turned shining eyes at me. "What else? A Quest!"

"A Quest?" I groaned.

"A Quest?" Knob said excitedly. "All right!"

He ran upstairs.

"What's going on, Thurman?"

"I don't have time to explain, Unbeliever, but get your stuff." He grabbed me, and pushed me into my room. He hurriedly started jamming junk into my travel bag.

Seth pounded upstairs. "I'm coming, too!"
"Hey, where are my ears?"
Minutes later, we were gone.

Patricia Storms
illustration • design • creative abundance

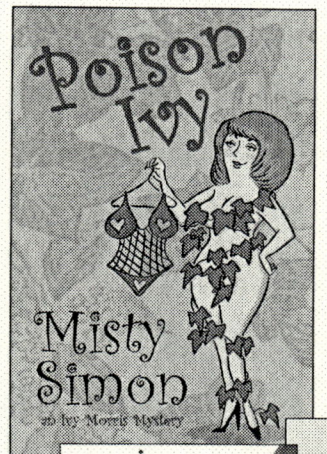

Patricia Storms is a freelance illustrator, designer and cartoonist. She is also a successful book cover designer. She loves books, and it shows in the quality of her work. To see more of her creative abundance, explore her web site at:

www.stormsillustration.com

Printed in the United States
47209LVS00006B/25-36